THE JOLLIEST TERM ON RECORD

ANGELA BRAZIL

THE JOLLIEST TERM ON RECORD

I

The New School

"KATRINE!" said Gwethyn, in her most impressive manner, "have you noticed anything peculiar going on in this house the last two or three days?"

"Why, no," replied Katrine abstractedly, taking a fresh squeeze of cobalt blue, and mixing it carefully with the rose madder and the yellow ochre already on her palette. "Nothing at all unusual. Gwethyn, be careful! You nearly sat down on my brigand, and his head's still wet!"

"Peccavi! I didn't see he was there," apologized Gwethyn, rescuing the canvas in question, and placing it in a position of greater safety on the mantelpiece. "Considering you've got absolutely every single chair littered with books, paints, and turpentine bottles, there really doesn't seem a spot left to sit upon," she continued in an injured tone.

"Except the table," returned Katrine, hastily moving a box of pastels and a pile of loose drawings to make room. "Please don't disturb my things. I've been sorting them out, and I don't want to get them mixed up again. Squat here, if you're tired, and leave the bottles alone."

"I am tired. I'm nearly dead. I bicycled all the way to Lindley Park and back with Mona Taylor on the step. She would make me take her! And she's no light weight, the young Jumbo!"

"Poor martyr! would you like a drink of turpentine to revive you? Sorry the chocs are finished."

"Don't mock me! Mona's a decent kid, but she really was the limit to-day. I'll see myself at Jericho before I let her climb on my step again. But Kattie, to go back to what I was saying before you interrupted me—haven't you noticed there's a something, a most decided something in the wind?"

"Your imagination, my dear child, is one of your brightest talents. You're particularly clever at noticing what isn't there."

"And you're as blind as a bat! Can't you see for yourself that Father and Mother have got some secret they're keeping from us? Why are we having our summer dresses made in April? Why are all our underclothes being overhauled and counted? Why did two new trunks arrive yesterday, with K. H. M. and G. C. M. painted on them in red letters? Why did Father just begin to say something last night, and Mother shut him up in a hurry, and he look conscience-stricken, and murmur: 'I'd forgotten they don't know yet'? Girl alive! if you're blind I'm not. There's something exciting on foot. I'm wild to find out what. Why doesn't Mother tell us? It's too bad."

"She's just going to now," said a voice from the door, and a small, bright-eyed little lady walked in, laughing. "You shan't be kept in the dark any longer, poor injured creatures! I'll make a clean breast of it at last."

"Mumsie!" cried both girls, jumping up, and sweeping away the books and painting materials that encumbered the one arm-chair. "Sit here, you darling! It isn't turpentiny, really! Here's the cushion. Are you comfy now? Well, do please begin and tell. We're all in a dither to know."

"Brace your nerves then, chicks! First and foremost, Father has been asked in a hurry to go out to the Scientific Conference at Sydney, and give the lectures on Geology in place of Professor Baillie, who has been taken ill, and can't keep his engagement. He has accepted, and must start by the 28th. He wants me to go with him. We shall probably be away for three months."

"And leave us!" Gwethyn's voice was reproachful. "Are we to be two sort of half orphans for three whole months? Oh, Mumsie!"

"It can't be helped," replied Mrs. Marsden, stroking the brown head apologetically. "What a Mummie's baby you are still! Remember, it's a great honour for Father to be asked to take the Geology chair at the

3

Conference. He's ever so pleased about it. And of course I must go too, because — — "

The girls smiled simultaneously, and with complete understanding.

"If you weren't there to remind him, Mumsie, Daddie'd forget which days his lectures were on!" twinkled Katrine. "Yes, and I verily believe he'd put his coat on inside out, or wear two hats, or do something horrible, if he were thinking very hard of the Pleistocene period. He'd be utterly lost without you. No, you couldn't let him go alone!"

"It's not to be thought of," agreed Mrs. Marsden hastily.

"Pack Kattie and me inside your trunk," urged Gwethyn's beseeching voice. "I'd like to see Australia."

"Too expensive a business for four. No, we've made other plans for you. Get up, Baby! You're too heavy to nurse. Go and sit somewhere else — yes, on the table, if you like. Well, Father and I have talked the matter thoroughly over, and we've decided to send you both for a term to a boarding-school we know of in Redlandshire."

"To school!" shrieked Katrine. "But, Mumsie, I left school last Christmas! Why, I've almost turned my hair up! I can't go back and be a kid again — it's quite impossible!"

"No one wants you to do that. I have made special arrangements for you with Mrs. Franklin. You are to join some of the classes, and spend the rest of your time studying painting. Mrs. Franklin's sister, Miss Aubrey, is a very good artist, and will take you out sketching. Isn't that a cheering prospect? You've wanted so much to have lessons in landscape."

"Not so bad — but I'm suffering still from shock!" returned Katrine. "School's school, anyhow you like to put it. And when I thought I'd left for good!"

"And where do I come in?" wailed a melancholy voice from the table. "You're Katrine, and I'm only Gwethyn. I'm too mi-ser-able for words,

4

Mumsie, you've betrayed us shamefully. I didn't think it of you. Or Daddie either. Do please change your minds!"

"No; for once we're hard-hearted parents," laughed Mrs. Marsden. "I wrote last night and arranged definitely and finally for you to go to Aireyholme on the 21st."

"I suppose I can take Tony with me?" asked Gwethyn anxiously, quitting her seat on the table to catch up a small Pekinese spaniel and press a kiss on his snub nose. "He'd break his little heart with fretting, bless him, if I left him behind. Wouldn't you, Tootitums?"

"I'm afraid that's impossible. We must board Tony out while we're away. I dare say Mrs. Wilson at the market gardens would look after him, or Mary might take him home with her. Now, Gwethyn, don't make a fuss, for I can't help it. I'm doing the best I can for everybody. You don't realize what a business it is to start for Australia at such a short notice, and have to shut up one's house, and dispose of one's family, all in three weeks' time. I'm nearly distracted with making so many arrangements."

"Poor darling little Mumsie!" said Katrine, squatting down by the arm-chair, and cuddling her mother's hand. "You'll be glad when it's over and you're safe on board ship. Which way do people sail for Australia? I don't know any geography."

"We go through the Suez Canal — —"

"Oh, Mumsie! Hereward!" interrupted both the girls eagerly.

Mrs. Marsden's eyes were shining.

"I'm not counting on seeing him," she protested. "It's wildly improbable he'd get leave, and we only have a few hours, I believe, at Port Said. Still, of course, there's always just the possibility."

"Now I understand why you're so keen to go to Australia," said Gwethyn. "You darling humbug! You'd have made Daddie accept a lectureship on the top of Chimborazo, or at the North Pole, if there were a chance of seeing Hereward for ten seconds on the way. Confess you would!"

"I suppose I'm as weak-minded as most mothers who have an only son in the army," said Mrs. Marsden, rising from her basket-chair. "One can't keep one's bairns babies for ever. They grow up only too fast, and fly from the nest. Well, I've told you the great secret, so I'll leave you to digest it at your leisure, chicks. Aireyholme is a delightful school. I'm sure you'll enjoy being there. Perhaps you're going to have the time of your lives!"

Left alone, the two girls were not slow in discussing the wonderful news. The room where they were sitting was a large attic, which had been converted into a studio. The drab walls were covered with sketches in oils, water-colours, pencil or chalk; a couple of easels, paint-boxes, palettes, drawing-paper, and canvases, and a litter of small articles — india-rubbers, mediums, pastels, and stumps — gave a very artistic general effect, and suggested plenty of work on the part of the owners. Both the sisters were fond of painting, and Katrine, at any rate, spent much of her spare time here. With her blue eyes, regular features, clear pale complexion, and plentiful red-gold hair, Katrine looked artistic to her finger-tips. She was just seventeen, and, owing to her extreme predilection for painting, had persuaded her parents to take her from the High School, and let her attend the School of Art, where she could devote all her energies to her pet subject. On the strength of this promotion she regarded herself as almost, if not quite, grown up — a view that was certainly not shared by her mother, and was perhaps a determining influence in Mrs. Marsden's decision to send her to a boarding-school.

Gwethyn, two years younger, was a bright, merry, jolly, independent damsel, with twinkling hazel eyes and ripply brown hair, a pair of beguiling dimples at the corners of her mouth, and a nose which, as Tennyson kindly expresses it, was inclined to be tip-tilted. Unromantic Gwethyn did not care a toss about "High Art", though in her way she was rather clever at painting, and inclined to follow Katrine's lead. She liked drawing animals, or niggers, or copying funny pictures from comic papers; and sometimes, I fear, she was guilty of caricaturing the mistresses at school, to the immense edification of the rest of the form. While Katrine painted fairies, Gwethyn would be drawing grinning gargoyles or goblins, with a spirited dash about the lines, and much humour in the expression of the faces. Sometimes these artistic efforts, produced at inopportune moments in school, got her into trouble, but wrath from head-quarters had little permanent effect upon Gwethyn. Her irrepressible spirits bobbed cheerily up again when the scoldings were over, and her eyes, instead of being filled with penitential tears, would be twinkling with suppressed fun.

Just now she was sitting on the table in the studio, hugging Tony, and trying to adjust her mental vision to the new prospect which opened before her.

"It's hard luck to have to leave the 'High' when I'd really a chance for the tennis championship," she mourned. "I suppose they'll play tennis at this new school? I hope to goodness they won't be very prim. I guess I'll wake them up a little if they are. Katrine, do you hear? I'm going to have high jinks somehow."

"Jink if you like!" returned Katrine dolefully. "It's all very well for you — you're only changing schools. But I'd left! And I'd quite made up my mind to turn up my hair this term. Of course I'll like the landscape-painting. I can do lots of things for the sketching club while I'm away, but—it's certainly a venture! Perhaps an adventure!"

"It'll be a surprise packet, at any rate," laughed Gwethyn. "We don't know the place, or the people we're going to meet, or anything at all about it. Kattie, I felt serious a minute ago, but the sight of your lugubrious face makes me cackle. I want to sketch you for a gargoyle—a melancholy one this time. That's better! Now you're laughing! Look here, we'll have some fun out of this business, somehow. I'm going to enjoy myself, and if you don't play up and follow suit, you're no sister of mine."

7

A fortnight later, the two girls were waving goodbye from the window of a train that steamed slowly out of Hartfield station. Even Gwethyn looked a trifle serious as a railway arch hid the last glimpse of Mumsie standing on the platform, and Katrine conveniently got something in her eye, which required the vigorous application of her pocket-handkerchief. They cheered up, however, when the city was passed, and suburban villas began to give place to fields and hawthorn hedges. After all, novelty was delightful, and for town-bred girls three months of country life, even at school, held out attractions. It was a four hours' journey to Carford, where they changed. The express was late, and, somewhat to their dismay, they found they had missed the local train, and would have to wait three hours for the next. As it was only eight miles to Heathwell, the village where the school was situated, they decided to ride there on their bicycles, leaving their luggage to follow by rail. The prospect of a cycling jaunt seemed far pleasanter than waiting at an uninteresting junction; it would be fun to explore the country, and they would probably arrive at school earlier by carrying out this plan.

Through the sweet, fresh-scented lanes, therefore, they started, where the young leaves were lovely with the tender green of late April, and the banks gay with celandine stars and white stitchwort, and the thrushes and blackbirds were chanting rival choruses in the hedgerow, and the larks were rising up from the fields with their little brown throats bubbling over with the message of spring. On and on, mile after mile of softly undulating country, where red-roofed farms lay among orchards full of blossom, and a river wandered between banks of osiers and pollard willows, and the sleek white-faced cattle grazed in meadows flowery as gardens. It seemed a fitting way to Eden; but the girls had not quite anticipated the little Paradise that burst upon their view when a bend of the road brought them suddenly into the heart of Heathwell. Surely they must have left the present century, and by some strange jugglery of fate have turned back the clock, and found themselves transported to mediæval times. The broad village street ran from the old market hall at one end to the ancient church at the other, flanked on either side by black-and-white houses so quaint in design, and so picturesque in effect, that they might have stepped from a painting of the seventeenth century. The cobble-stoned cause-way, the irregular flights of steps, the creepers climbing to the very chimneys, the latticed windows, the swinging inn-sign with its heraldic dragon, all combined to make up a scene which was typically representative of Merrie England.

"Are we awake, or are we in an Elizabethan dream?" asked Katrine, dismounting from her bicycle to stand and survey the prospect.

"I don't know. I feel as if I were on the stage of a Shakespearian play. A crowd of peasants with May garlands ought to come running out of that archway and perform a morris dance, then the principal characters should walk on by the side wings."

"It's too fascinating for words. I wonder where Aireyholme is?"

"We shall have to ask our way. Ought one to say: 'Prithee, good knave, canst inform me?' or 'Hold, gentle swain, I have need of thy counsel'?"

"We shall start with a reputation for lunacy, if you do!"

The school proved to be not very far away from the village. Aireyholme, as it was aptly called, was a large, comfortable, rather old-fashioned house that stood on a small hill overlooking the river. Orchards, in the glory of their spring bloom, made a pink background for the white chimneys and the grey-slated roof; a smooth tennis lawn with four courts faced the front, and in a field adjoining the river were some hockey goals.

"Not so utterly benighted!" commented Gwethyn, as she and Katrine wheeled their bicycles up the drive. "There's more room for games here than we had at the 'High'. I'm glad I bought that new racket. Wonder what their play's like? I say, these are ripping courts!"

To judge by the soft thud of balls behind the bushes, and the cries that registered the scoring, several sets of tennis were in progress, and as the girls turned the corner of the shrubbery, and came out on to the carriage sweep before the front door, they had an excellent view of the lawn. Their sudden appearance, however, stopped the games. The players had evidently been expecting them, and, running up, greeted them in characteristic schoolgirl fashion.

"Hello! Are you Katrine and Gwethyn Marsden?"

"So you've turned up at last!"

"Did you miss your train?"

"Miss Spencer was in an awful state of mind when you weren't at the station. She went to meet you."

"Have you biked all the way from Carford?"

"Yes, and we're tired, and as hungry as hunters," returned Katrine. "Our luggage is coming by the 5.30. We missed the 2.15, so we thought we'd rather ride on than wait. Where can we put our bikes?"

"I'll show you," said a tall girl, who seemed to assume the lead. "At least, Jess and Novie can put them away for you now, and I'll take you straight to Mrs. Franklin. She'll be most fearfully relieved to see you; she gets herself into such stews over anybody who doesn't arrive on the nail. I'm Viola Webster. I'll introduce the others afterwards. You'll soon get to know us all, I expect. There are thirty-six here this term, counting yourselves. Did you bring rackets? Oh, good! We're awfully keen on tennis. So are you? Dorrie Vernon will be glad to hear that. She's our games secretary. I wonder if Mrs. Franklin is in the study, or in the drawing-room? Perhaps you'd better wait here while I find her. Oh, there she is after all, coming down the stairs!"

The new world into which Katrine and Gwethyn were speedily introduced, was a very different affair from the High School which they had previously attended. The smaller number of pupils, and the fact that it was a boarding-school, made the girls on far more intimate terms with one another than is possible in a large day-school. Mrs. Franklin, the Principal, was a woman of strong character. She had been a lecturer at college before her marriage, and after her husband's death had begun her work at Aireyholme in order to find some outlet for her energies. Her two sons were both at the front, one in the Territorials, and the other as a naval chaplain. Her only daughter, Ermengarde, had lately been married to a clergyman. Tall, massive, perhaps even a trifle masculine in appearance, Mrs. Franklin hid a really kind heart under a rather uncompromising and masterful manner. She was a clever manager, an admirable housekeeper, and ruled her little kingdom well and wisely. Both in features and personality she resembled an ancient Roman matron, and among the girls she was often known as "the mother of the Gracchi".

Mrs. Franklin's sister, Miss Aubrey, who lived at the school, was an artist of considerable talent. She superintended the art teaching, and gave the rest of her time to landscape-painting, in both oil and water colours. It was largely the fact that Katrine might have sketching lessons from Miss Aubrey which had influenced Mr. and Mrs. Marsden in their choice of Aireyholme. The art department was a very important feature of that school. Any talent shown among the pupils was carefully fostered. The general atmosphere of the place was artistic; the girls were familiar with reproductions of pictures from famous galleries, they took in The Art Magazine and The Studio, they revelled in illustrated catalogues of the Salon or the Royal Academy, and dabbled in many mediums—oil, water colour, pastel, crayon, and tempera. The big studio was perhaps the pet room of the house; it was Liberty Hall, where anybody might pursue her favourite project, and though some of the attempts were certainly rather crude, they were all helpful in training eye and hand to work together.

Of the other mistresses, Miss Spencer was bookish, and Miss Andrews athletic. The former was rather cold and dignified, an excellent and painstaking, though not very inspiring teacher. She spoke slowly and precisely, and there was a smack of college about her, a scholastic officialism of manner that raised a barrier of reserve between herself and her pupils, difficult to cross. Very different was Miss Andrews, whose hearty, breezy ways were more those of a monitress than of a mistress. She laughed and joked with the girls almost like one of themselves, though she could assert her authority emphatically when she wished. Needless to say she was highly popular, and although she had only been a year at Aireyholme, she was already regarded as an indispensable feature of the establishment. Into this busy and highly organized little community Katrine and Gwethyn, as new-comers, must shake themselves down.

CHAPTER II

A Scrape

KATRINE and Gwethyn had been given a bedroom over the porch, a dear little room with roses and jasmine clustering round the windows, and with an excellent view of the tennis lawn. They arranged their possessions there after tea, and when their photos, books, work-baskets, and writing-cases had found suitable niches the place began to have quite a home-like appearance.

"It's not so bad, considering it's school," commented Gwethyn; "I believe I'm going to like one or two of those girls."

"I don't know whether I'm going to like Mrs. Franklin," objected Katrine. "She's inclined to boss as if one were a kid. I hope Mother made her quite understand that I'm past seventeen, and not an 'ordinary schoolgirl'."

"You're younger than Viola Webster, though, or that other girl—what's her name?—Dorrie Vernon," returned Gwethyn. "What have you got there? Oh, Katrine! A box of hairpins! Now you promised Mumsie you wouldn't turn up your hair!"

"I was only just going to try it sometimes, for fun. When a girl is as tall as I am, it's ridiculous to see her with a plait flapping down her back. I'm sure I look older than either Viola or Dorrie. Most people would take me for eighteen." Katrine was staring anxiously at herself in the glass. "I'm not going to be treated here like a junior. They needn't begin it."

"Oh, you'll settle them all right, I dare say!" answered Gwethyn abstractedly. She was calculating the capacities of the top drawer, and, moreover, she was accustomed to these outbursts on the part of her sister.

Katrine put the hairpins, not on the dressing-table, but in a handy spot of her right-hand drawer, where she could easily get at them. It was absurd of Gwethyn to make such a fuss, so she reflected. A girl of only fifteen cannot possibly enter into the feelings of one who is nearly grown up.

She preserved a rather distant manner at supper. It would not be dignified to unbend all at once to strangers. Gwethyn, always too hail-fellow-well-met with everybody, was talking to her next neighbour, and evidently eliciting much information; an unrestrained chuckle on her part caused Mrs. Franklin to cast a glance of surprise at that particular portion of the table. By bedtime both the new-comers were feeling serious; they would not for the world have confessed to home-sickness, but Katrine observed that she hoped vessels bound for Australia never blundered into German mines, and Gwethyn said she had seen in one of the papers that there was an outbreak of enteric among the troops in Egypt, and she wondered if it were in Hereward's regiment; neither of which remarks was calculated to raise their spirits.

The beds had spring mattresses, and were quite as comfortable as those at home. By all ordinary natural laws the girls, tired with their journey, ought to have slept the slumbers of the just immediately their heads touched their pillows. Instead of doing anything so sensible, they lay talking until they were both so excited and so thoroughly wideawake that sleep refused to be wooed. Hour after hour they tossed and turned, counting imaginary sheep jumping over gates, repeating pieces of poetry, and trying the hundred-and-one expedients that are supposed to be infallible brain lullers, but all with no effect. Outside, owls were hooting a continual dismal concert of "twoo-hoo-hoo!"

"I like owls from a natural history point of view," groaned Katrine, "and I've no doubt they're only telling one another about fat mice and sparrows; but I wish they'd be quiet and not talk! They're far more disturbing than trams and taxis."

"Talk of the peace of the country! I should like to know where it is!" agreed Gwethyn, turning her pillow for the fourteenth time. "There's a cock crowing now, and a dog barking!"

"It's impossible to sleep a wink," declared Katrine, jumping out of bed in desperation, and drawing aside the window curtain. "I believe it's getting light."

There was a stirring of dawn in the air. All the world seemed wrapped in a transparent grey veil, just thin enough for objects to loom dimly through the dusk. She could see the heavy outlines of the trees at the farther side of the lawn. A thrush was already giving a preliminary note, and sparrows were beginning to twitter under the eaves.

"What's the use of stopping in bed when one can't sleep?" exclaimed Katrine. "Let us dress, find our machines, and go for a spin."

"What! Go out now?"

"Why not? People are supposed to get up early in the country."

"All right! If you're game, I am."

The two girls had not been accustomed to much discipline at home, and their notions of school rules were rudimentary. The idea of getting up so early and going out to explore struck them both as delightfully enterprising and adventurous. They made a hurried toilet, crept cautiously downstairs, and found the passage at the back of the house, where their bicycles had been temporarily placed the night before. It was an easy matter to unbolt a side door, and make their way through the garden and down the drive. Before the day was much older, they were riding along the quiet dim road in that calm silence that precedes the dawn. The air was most fresh and exhilarating. As their machines sped through the grey morning mist, they felt almost as if they were on aeroplanes, rushing among the clouds. At first all was dark and vague and mysterious, but every minute the light was growing stronger, and presently they could distinguish the gossamer, hung like a tangled magic web upon the hedges, in dainty shimmering masses, as if the pixies had been spinning and weaving in the night, and had not yet had time to carry off the result of their labours.

"It's just like a fairy tale," said Gwethyn. "Do you remember the boy who sat on the fox's tail, and they went on and on till his hair whistled in the wind? Those rabbits ought to stop and talk, and tell us about Brer Terrapin and the Tar Baby. I'm sure Uncle Remus is squatting at the foot of that tree. We shall meet the goose-girl presently, I expect."

"What a baby you are! But it is lovely, I agree with you. Oh, Gwethyn, look at the sky over there! That's a fairy tale, if you like. Let's stop and watch it."

It was indeed a glorious sight. The colour, which at first had been pearly-grey, had changed to transparent opal; then, blushing with a warmer hue, grew slowly to pink, amber, and violet. Great streamers of rosy orange began to stretch like ethereal fingers upwards from the horizon. The fields were in shadow, and a quiet stillness reigned, as if the world paused, waiting in hope and expectancy for that fresh and ever wonderful vision, the miracle of the returning dawn. Then the great shimmering, glowing sun lifted himself up from among the mists in the meadows, gaining in brilliance with every foot he ascended till the light burst out, a flood of brightness, and all the landscape was radiant. At that, Mother Earth seemed to bestir herself. With the new day came the fresh pulse of life, and the reawakening of myriads of nature's children. The first lark went soaring into the purply-blue overhead; the chaffinches began to tweet in the elms; a white butterfly fluttered over the hedge; and a marvellous busy throng of insect life seemed suddenly astir and ahum. It was a different world from that of an hour before—a living, breathing, working, rejoicing world; the shadows and the mystery had fled, and left it as fair as if just created.

"It was worth getting up for this!" said Katrine. "I've never seen such a transformation scene in my life. I wish I could paint it. But what colours could one use? Nothing but stained glass could give that glowing, glorious, pinky violet!"

"I haven't the least idea where we are, or how far away from the school," said Gwethyn. "We rode along quite 'on spec.', and we may have come two miles or five, for anything I know. Yes, it has been lovely, and I see you're still wrapt in a sort of rapturous dream, and up among rosy clouds, but I've come down to earth, and I'm most unromantically hungry. It seems years since we had supper last night. I wonder if we couldn't find a farm, and buy some milk."

"Rose madder mixed with violet lake, and a touch of aureolin and Italian pink might do it!" murmured Katrine.

"No, it wouldn't! They'd want current coin of the realm. Have you any pennies left in your coat pocket?"

"You mundane creature! I was talking of the sunrise, and not of mere milk. Yes, I have five pennies and a halfpenny, which ought to buy enough to take a bath in."

"I don't want a bath, only a glassful. But it's a case of 'first catch your farm'. I don't see the very ghost of a chimney anywhere, nothing but fields and trees."

"Better go on till we find one, then," said Katrine, mounting her machine again.

They rode at least half a mile without passing any human habitation; then at last the welcome sight of a gate and barns greeted them.

"It looks like the back of a farm," decided Gwethyn. "Let us leave our bikes here, and explore."

Up a short lane, and across a stack-yard, they penetrated into an orchard. Here, under a maze of pink blossom, a girl of perhaps twelve or thirteen, with a carriage whip in one hand and a bowl in the other, was throwing grain to a large flock of poultry—ducks, geese, and hens—that were collected round her.

"The goose-girl, by all that's wonderful! I told you it was a fairy-tale morning!" whispered Gwethyn. "Now for it! I'll go and demand milk. How ought one to greet a goose-girl?"

She stepped forward, but at that moment a large collie dog that had been lying unnoticed at the foot of an apple tree, sprang up suddenly, and faced her snarling.

"Good dog! Poor old fellow! Come here, then!" said Gwethyn in a wheedling voice, hoping to propitiate it, for she was fond of dogs.

Instead of being pacified by her blandishments, however, it showed its teeth savagely, and darting behind her, seized her by the skirt. Gwethyn was not strong-minded. She shrieked as if she were being murdered.

"Help! Help!" yelled Katrine distractedly.

The goose-girl was already calling off the dog, and with a well-directed lash of her long whip sent him howling away. She walked leisurely up to the visitors.

"You're more frightened than hurt," she remarked, with a half-contemptuous glance at Gwethyn. "What do you want here?"

"We came to ask if we could buy some milk," stammered Katrine. "I suppose this is a farm?"

"No, it isn't a farm, and we don't sell milk."

The girl's tone was ungracious; her appearance also was the reverse of attractive. Her sharp features and sallow complexion had an unwholesome look, her hair was lank and lustreless, and the bright, dark eyes did not hold a pleasant expression. She wore a blue gingham overall pinafore that hid her dress.

"Where are you from? And what are you doing here so early?" she continued, gazing curiously at Katrine and Gwethyn.

"We've bicycled from Aireyholme— —" began Gwethyn.

"You're never the new girls? Oh, I say! Who gave you leave to go out? Nobody? Well, I shouldn't care to be you when you get back, that's all! Mrs. Franklin will have something to say!"

"Do you know her, then?" gasped Gwethyn.

"Know her? I should think I do—just a little! If you'll take my advice, you'll ride back as quick as you can. Ta-ta! I must go and feed my chickens now. Oh, you will catch it!"

She walked away, chuckling to herself as if she rather enjoyed the prospect of their discomfiture; as she turned into the garden she looked round, and laughed outright.

"What an odious girl! Who is she?" exclaimed Katrine indignantly. "She never apologized for her hateful dog catching hold of you. What does she mean by laughing at us? I should like to teach her manners."

"Perhaps we'd better be riding back," said Gwethyn uneasily. "They said breakfast was at eight o'clock. I haven't an idea what the time is. I wish we'd brought our watches."

They had cycled farther than they imagined, and in retracing their road they took a wrong turning, consequently going several miles out of their way. They were beginning to be rather tired by the time they reached Aireyholme. The excitement and romance of the spring dawn had faded. Life seemed quite ordinary and prosaic with the sun high in the heavens. Perhaps they both felt a little doubtful of their reception, though neither was prepared to admit it. As they wheeled their machines past the lower schoolroom window, where the girls were at early morning preparation, a dozen excited heads bobbed up to look at them. They took the bicycles through the side door, and left them in the passage. In the hall they met Coralie Nelson, going to practice, with a pile of music in her hand.

"Hello! Is it you?" she exclaimed. "So you've turned up again, after all! There's been a pretty hullabaloo, I can tell you! Were you trying to run away?"

"Of course not," declared Katrine airily. "We were only taking a little run on our bikes before breakfast. It was delicious riding so early."

19

"Was it, indeed! Well, you are the limit for coolness, I must say! You'd better go and explain to Mrs. Franklin. She's in the study, and particularly anxious to have the pleasure of seeing you. Hope you'll have a pleasant interview!"

"Hope we shall, thanks!" returned Katrine, bluffing the matter off as well as she could. "I can't see what there is to make such a fuss about! We're not late for breakfast, I suppose?"

"Oh dear me, no! You're in excellent time!" Coralie's tone was sarcastic. "Punctuality is considered a great virtue at Aireyholme. Perhaps you may be congratulated upon it! I won't prophesy! On the whole I wouldn't change into your shoes, though!"

"We don't want you to," retorted Gwethyn.

The two girls tapped at the study door, and entered with well-assumed nonchalance. Katrine, in particular, was determined to show her superiority to the conventions which might hedge in ordinary pupils. A girl of seventeen, who had left school last Christmas, must not allow herself to be treated as the rest of the rank and file. At the sight of the Principal's calm, determined face, however, her courage began to slip away. Somehow she did not feel quite so grown-up as she had expected. Mrs. Franklin had not kept school for fifteen years for nothing. Her keen, grey eyes could quell the most unruly spirit.

"Katrine and Gwethyn Marsden, what is the meaning of this?" she began peremptorily. "Who gave you leave of absence before breakfast?"

"We saw no reason to ask," replied Katrine. "We couldn't sleep, so we thought we'd get up early, and take a spin on our machines."

"Please to understand for the future that such escapades are strictly forbidden. There are certain free hours during the day, and there are definite school bounds, which one of the monitresses will explain to you later on. No girl is allowed to exceed these limits without special permission."

"But I thought Mother said I wasn't to be in the ordinary school," urged Katrine.

"Your mother has placed you in my charge," frowned Mrs. Franklin, "and my decision upon every question must be final. While you are at Aireyholme you will follow our usual rules. I make exceptions for nobody. Don't let me have to remind you of this again."

The Principal's manner was authoritative; her large presence and handsome Roman features seemed to give extra weight to her words. She was evidently not accustomed to argue with her pupils. Katrine, with those steely blue eyes fixed upon her, had the wisdom to desist from further excuses. She left the room outwardly submissive, though inwardly raging. At seventeen to be treated like a kindergarten infant, indeed! Katrine's dignity was severely wounded. "I don't believe I'm going to like this place," she remarked to Gwethyn as they went upstairs.

The rest of the morning until dinner-time seemed a confused whirl to the Marsdens. Last night they had been let alone, but now they were initiated into the many and manifold ways of the school. They were placed respectively in the Sixth and Fifth Form; desks and lockers were apportioned to them; they were given new books, and allotted certain times for practising on the piano. At the eleven-o'clock interval they made the more intimate acquaintance of at least half of their school-fellows.

"Did you get into a scrape with Mother Franklin?" asked Coralie. "The idea of your going gallivanting off on your own this morning! By the by, your bikes have been put in the shed with the others. It's locked up at night. We get special exeats sometimes to go long rides, so don't look so doleful. Shall I tell you who some of the girls are? You know Viola Webster, our captain, and Dorrie Vernon, our tennis champion? That fair one, talking to them, is Diana Bennett. They're our monitresses. Those inseparables are Jill Barton and Ivy Parkins. The one with two pig-tails is Rose Randall; and those round-faced kids are Belgian refugees—Yvonne and Mélanie de Boeck. They're supposed to be improving our French, but as a matter of fact they talk English—of a sort—most of the time. That's Laura Browne playing tennis left-handed. I warn you that she's sure to take you up hotly for a day or two, while you're new, but she'll drop you again afterwards. Anyone else you'd like to ask about? I'll act school directory!"

Coralie rattled on in a half good-natured, half quizzical fashion, giving brief biographical sketches of her companions, introducing some, and indicating others. Most of the girls were collected round the tennis lawn watching the sets. A group of juniors seated on a bench attracted Katrine's attention. Standing near them, though somewhat apart, was one whose thin angular figure and sharp pale face seemed familiar; even without the blue overall pinafore it was easy enough to recognize her. Katrine nudged Gwethyn, and both simultaneously exclaimed: "The goose-girl!"

"Who is that dreadful child?" asked Katrine. "We met her while we were out this morning, and she wasn't civil. Her face is just the colour of a fungus!"

Coralie laughed.

"Oh! that's Githa Hamilton. She's not exactly celebrated for her sweet temper."

"So I should imagine. What was she doing out of bounds before seven o'clock?"

"She's not a boarder. She lives with an uncle and aunt, and comes to school on her bicycle. She's the only day-girl we have. I'd hate to be a day-girl— you're out of everything."

"I shouldn't think such an extraordinary little toadstool would be in anything, even if she were a boarder," commented Gwethyn, who had not forgiven the savage assault of the collie, and the contemptuous "You're more frightened than hurt!" of its mistress.

"You're about right there. Githa's no particular favourite, even in her own form."

22

"If I'd straight lank hair like that, I'd friz it every night," declared Gwethyn emphatically. "She's the plainest girl in the school! That's my opinion of her!"

CHAPTER III

Shaking Down

IF Katrine and Gwethyn had taken a dislike to the "Toadstool", as they nicknamed Githa Hamilton, that elfish damsel seemed ready to return the sentiment with interest. She divined their weak points with horrible intuition, and her sharp little tongue was always armed with caustic remarks. She would stand watching them like a malign imp when they played tennis, sneering if they made bad strokes, and rejoicing over their opponents' scores with ostentatious triumph. At Katrine's airs of dignity she scoffed openly, and she would call in question Gwethyn's really quite harmless little exaggerations with ruthless punctiliousness. The new-comers tried to preserve an airy calm, and treat this offensive junior as beneath their notice; but she was a determined enemy, returning constantly to the assault, and the skirmishes continued.

A complete contrast to Githa's spirit of opposition was the behaviour of Laura Browne. As Coralie had predicted, she took up the new girls hotly. She walked with them or sat next to them on every possible occasion, asked for their autographs, obtained snapshots of them with her Brownie camera, and gushed over their home photos and private possessions.

"It's so nice to have someone at the school with whom I really feel I can become friends," she assured Gwethyn. "The moment I saw you both, I fell in love with you. I believe strongly in first impressions—don't you? Something seems to tell me there's to be a link between our lives. How romantic to have a brother at the front! I think his portrait in uniform is simply perfect. I shall ask you to lend it to me sometimes, when you can spare it. It does one good to look at a hero like that. I wish my brothers were old enough to join. They're at the mischievous age at present. I envy you your luck."

And Laura sighed dramatically. Katrine, mindful of Coralie's hint, received these advances with caution, but Gwethyn, who was not a very discriminating little person, felt rather flattered. After all, it is highly pleasant to be openly admired, your friendship courted, your wishes consulted, and your opinions treated with deference. In the first flush of her enthusiasm she readily drew a sketch in Laura's album, embroidered a handkerchief for her, and proffered peppermint creams as long as the box lasted. She submitted peaceably to lend penknife, scissors, pencils, or any other unconsidered trifles, and when she was obliged to ask for them back, her new friend was so ready with apologies for their non-return that she felt almost ashamed of having mentioned the matter.

Between Githa's evident dislike and Laura's fawning sycophancy was a wide gap. These two had openly declared themselves "for" or "against"; the solid block of the school stood aloof. During their first week, at least, the new girls must be on approval before they settled into the places which they would eventually occupy. Their sayings and doings were closely noted, but public opinion reserved itself. The monitresses were kind, but slightly cool. They did not altogether like Katrine's attitude. She had given them to understand that she had come to Aireyholme as an art student, and not as a pupil, and they resented the assumption of superiority implied.

"We're all art students here," Diana Bennett had replied stiffly.

"But you're not taking special private lessons from Miss Aubrey?" asked Katrine, feeling that she scored by this point.

"Viola and Dorrie and I are going in for the matric., so we haven't much time for painting. It's a jolly grind getting up all our subjects, I can tell you!"

In the privacy of their own study, the three monitresses discussed the matter at some length.

"I rather like them both," said Dorrie. "Katrine's quite an interesting sort of girl, only she has at present far too high an idea of her own importance."

"She's inclined to be a little patronizing," commented Viola. "Of course that won't do. I'm Captain here, and she'll have quite to realize that. We can't let a girl come into the school at seventeen and begin to boss the whole show."

"Rather not! There ought to be a rule to admit no one over fifteen."

"Thirteen would be better."

"Well, at any rate when they're juniors, and have time to get used to Aireyholme ways. I've been here six years, and if anyone knows the school traditions, I ought to. No, Miss Katrine Marsden mustn't be allowed to give herself airs. That I've quite made up my mind about."

"What do you think of Gwethyn?"

"She's a harum-scarum, but I like her the better of the two."

"She's inseparables with Laura Browne."

"Well, you know Laura! She goes for every new girl, and toadies till she's got all she can, or grows tired of it. Gwethyn will find her out in course of time, I suppose."

"The real gist of the matter," said Dorrie, wrinkling her brows anxiously, "is whether I'm to put them in the tennis list. They play uncommonly well."

"Oh, it wouldn't be fair to let new girls represent the school!"

"You think so? On the other hand, the school must win by hook or by crook."

"Well, I don't think it would do to make either of them a champion, putting them above the heads of those who have been here for years."

"It's a difficult question, certainly."

"Difficult? Not at all; I think it's conclusive!" snapped Viola rather sharply. "Those who are trained in Aireyholme methods are best fitted to represent Aireyholme. There can't be two opinions about it."

There was certainly some occasion for the rather jealous attitude which the monitresses were inclined to adopt towards Katrine. By the arrangement which her mother had made with Mrs. Franklin, she was really more in the position of the old-fashioned "parlour boarder" than of an ordinary pupil. She had been placed in the Sixth Form, but took less than half the classes, the rest of her time being devoted to art lessons. While others were drudging away at Latin translation, or racking their brains over mathematical problems, she was seated in the studio, blissfully painting flowers; or, greater luck still, sallying forth with paint-box and easel to sketch from nature. As the studio was the favourite haunt of most of the seniors, these special privileges were the envy of the school. Nan Bethell and Gladwin Riley, in particular, hitherto the Aireyholme art stars, felt their noses much put out of joint, and were injured that their mothers had not made a like arrangement on their behalf. They went so far as to petition Mrs. Franklin for a similar exemption from certain lessons in favour of painting. But the Principal was adamant; the Sixth was her own particular form, she was jealous of its reputation, and by no means disposed to excuse members, whom she had been coaching for months, the credit which they ought to gain for the school in the examination lists. Though art was a pet hobby at Aireyholme, it must not be allowed to usurp the chief place, to the detriment of Mrs. Franklin's own subjects.

In the meantime Katrine, quite unaware of these difficulties, wore her picturesque painting apron for several hours daily, and revelled both in her work and in the companionship of her new teacher. Miss Aubrey was the greatest possible contrast to her sister, Mrs. Franklin. Instead of being tall,imposing, and masterful, she was small, slight, and gentle in manner. "A ducky little thing", most of the girls called her, and Katrine endorsed the general opinion. Miss Aubrey certainly would not have made a good head of the establishment; she was absent-minded, dreamy, and made no attempt to uphold discipline; but in her own department she was delightful. The pupils talked with impunity in her classes, but they nevertheless worked with an enthusiasm that many a stricter teacher might have failed to inspire. There was an artistic atmosphere about Miss Aubrey; she always seemed slightly in the clouds, as if she were busier observing the general picturesque effect of life than its particular details. In appearance she was pleasing, with soft grey eyes and smooth brown hair. It was the fashion at the school to call her pretty. The girls set her down as

27

many years younger than Mrs. Franklin. The studio was, of course, her special domain at Aireyholme; she worked much there herself, and quite a collection of her pictures adorned the walls. The crisp, bold style of painting aroused Katrine's admiration, and made her long to try her skill at landscape-sketching. Miss Aubrey had kept her at a study of flowers until she could judge her capabilities; but at the end of the first week the mistress declared her ready for more advanced work.

"I am going into the village this morning to finish a picture of my own," she announced. "You and your sister may come with me, and I will start you both at a pretty little subject."

Gwethyn, whose time-table had been left to the entire discretion of Mrs. Franklin, was highly elated to find that she was to share some of Katrine's art privileges. She had never expected such luck, and rejoiced accordingly. The fact was that Miss Aubrey wished to continue her own sketch, and to settle Katrine at an easier subject a hundred yards farther down the street. She thought it might be unpleasant for the girl to sit alone, and that the sisters would be company for each other. She would be near enough to keep an eye on them, and to come and correct their drawings from time to time. Much encumbered, therefore, with camp-stools, easels, boards, paint-boxes, and other impedimenta, but feeling almost equal to full-blown artists, the Marsdens, to the wild envy of their less fortunate school-fellows, sallied forth with Miss Aubrey down to the village. Their teacher had chosen a very picturesque little bit for their first attempt—a charming black-and-white cottage, with an uneven red-tiled roof and an irregular, tumble-down chimney. She superintended them while they opened their camp-stools and fixed their easels, then showed them where the principal lines in their sketches ought to be placed.

"You mustn't mind if people come and stare at you a little," she remarked cheerfully. "It's what all artists have to put up with. You'll get used to it. Now I'm going to my own subject. I shall come back very soon to see how you're getting on."

With great satisfaction the girls began blocking in their cottage, feeling almost like professional artists as they marked roof, angles, and points of perspective with the aid of a plumb-line.

"What a lovely little village it is!" exulted Katrine. "And so delightfully peaceful and quiet. There's nobody about."

"Yes, it's heavenly! One couldn't sit out sketching in the street at home," agreed Gwethyn enthusiastically.

Alas! their bliss was shortlived. They had scarcely been five minutes at work when they were espied by half a dozen children, who ran up promptly and joyfully to stare at their proceedings. The group of spectators seemed to consider them an attraction, for they rushed off to spread the gleeful news among their fellows, with the result that in a few moments half the youth of the neighbourhood were swarming round Katrine and Gwethyn like flies round a honey-pot. Evidently the inhabitants of the village regarded artists as a free show; not only did the small fry flock round the girls' easels, but a certain proportion of grown-ups, who apparently had nothing better to do, strolled up and made an outside ring to the increasing and interested audience.

"Do they imagine we're the vanguard of a circus, or that it's an ingenious form of advertisement?" whispered Gwethyn. "I believe they expect me to write 'Sanger's Menagerie is Coming' in big letters on my drawing-board, or perhaps 'Buy Purple Pills'!"

"I should feel more inclined to write 'Don't come within ten yards!'" groaned Katrine. "I wish they'd go away! They make me so nervous. It's horrible to feel your every stroke is being watched. I've put in my chimney quite crooked. Are they troubling Miss Aubrey, I wonder?"

Gwethyn stood up to command a full view of the street. Yes, Miss Aubrey was also surrounded by a small crowd, but she took no notice of the spectators, and was painting away as if oblivious of their presence.

"She doesn't seem to mind," commented Gwethyn. "I wish I'd her nerve."

29

"They seem to find us as attractive as a dancing bear," groaned Katrine. "That fat old man in the blue flannel shirt is gazing at us with the most insinuating smile. Don't look at him. Oh, why did you? You've encouraged him so much, he's coming to speak to us."

The wearer of the blue shirt appeared to think he was doing a kind action in patronizing the strangers; his smile broadened, he forced his way forward among the pushing children, and opened the conversation with a preliminary cough.

"Be you a-drawin' that old house across there?" he began consequentially. "Why, it be full o' cracks and stains, and 'ave wanted pullin' down these ten year or more!"

"It's beautiful!" replied Katrine briefly.

"Beautiful! With the tiles all cracked and the wall bulgin'? Now if you was wantin' a house to draw, you should 'a done mine. It's a new red brick, with bow windows and a slated roof, and there's a row o' nice tidy iron railings round the garden, too. You must come and take a look at it."

"We like the old cottages better, thank you," said Gwethyn, as politely as she could. "Would you please mind moving a little to the left? You're standing just exactly in my light."

"He's a picturesque figure," whispered Katrine, as their new acquaintance heaved himself heavily from the kerb-stone; then she added aloud: "I wonder if you'd mind standing still a minute or two, and letting me put you into my picture? Yes, just there, please."

"You wants to take I?" he guffawed. "Well, I never did! Best let me go home and tidy up a bit first."

"No, no! I like you as you are. Don't move! Only keep still for three minutes," implored Katrine, sketching with frantic haste.

"I don't know what my missis would say at I being took in my corduroys," remonstrated the model, who appeared half bashful and half flattered at the honour thrust upon him. "I'd change to my Sunday clothes if ye'd wait a bit, missie! Well, it be queer taste, for sure! I'd 'a thought a suit o' broadcloth would 'a looked a sight better in a picture."

"See the lady! She's a-puttin' in Abel Barnes!" gasped the children, crowding yet nearer, and almost upsetting the pair of easels in their excitement. "There's his head! There be his arm! Oh, and his legs too! It be just like him—so it be!"

"Keep back and let the ladies alone!" commanded Abel in a stentorian voice. "Where are your manners got to? If you've finished, missie, you'll maybe not object to my takin' a look. Well, for sure, there I be to the life!"

"Wherever that picture goes in all the world, Abel Barnes will go with it!" piped a small awestruck voice in the background.

"Yes, she'll take me away with her," replied Abel, in a tone that implied some gratification—perhaps a touch of vanity lingered under the blue flannel shirt. "If I'd but a-been in my Sunday clothes!" he continued regretfully. "Still, you've only to say the word, and I'll put 'em on for you any day you've a mind to take I again, and you could draw the missis too, and the house, if you like. I were goin' to give the railings a fresh coat o' paint anyways, so I may as well do it afore you begins."

Finding that Katrine would not commit herself to any rash promises, he finally strolled away, possibly to buy a tin of paint, or to review his Sunday garments in anticipation of the hoped-for portrait. The children, filled with envy at his distinction, were all eager to volunteer as models, and began posing in the road in various stiff and photographic attitudes.

"Put in I! Put in I!" implored each and all.

"I shan't put in anybody if you don't behave yourselves," replied Katrine severely. "How can I see anything when you're standing exactly in front of me? Go away at once, and leave us quiet!"

To remove themselves from the vicinity of the interesting strangers was, however, not at all in the children's calculations. They only backed, and formed a close ring again round the exasperated girls, breathing heavily, and keeping up a chorus of whispered comments. Katrine and Gwethyn sighed ruefully, but judged it better to follow Miss Aubrey's example and take no notice, hoping that their tormentors might presently tire, and run off to play marbles or hop-scotch. The cottage proved by no means an easy subject to sketch; it needed very careful spacing and drawing before they could secure a correct outline. It would have been hard enough if they had been alone and undisturbed, but to be obliged to work in full view of a frank and critical audience was particularly trying. Every time they rubbed anything out, a small voice would cry:

"Missed again! She can't do it!"

"I never realized before how often I used my india-rubber," murmured poor Gwethyn. "They seem to think I'm making a series of very bad shots."

"I wonder if I dare begin my sky, or if I ought to show the drawing to Miss Aubrey first," said Katrine. "I believe I shall venture. How I wish a motor-car would come along and scatter these wretched infants, or that their mothers would call them in for a meal!"

There was no such luck. The sight of the mixing of cobalt blue and Naples yellow on Katrine's palette only caused the children to press yet closer.

"Oh, look! This lady be doing it in colours!" they shouted. "She be cleverer than the other lady."

"Katrine, we must get rid of them!" exclaimed the outraged Gwethyn; then, turning to the crowd of shock heads behind, she inquired frowningly: "How is it you're not in school?"

"It's a holiday to-day!" came in prompt chorus.

"There's the Board of Guardians' meeting at the schoolhouse," explained an urchin, poking a chubby face in such close proximity to Katrine's paint-box that in self-defence she gave him a dab of blue on his freckled nose.

"It be luck for us when they have their meetings," volunteered another gleefully.

"But not for us," groaned Gwethyn. "Katrine, I wonder if the Church Catechism would rout them. I declare I'll try! It's my last weapon!"

Vain hope, alas! If Gwethyn had expected to thin the throng by acting catechist, she was much mistaken. The children had been well grounded at Sunday school, and so far from quailing at the questions were anxious to air their knowledge, and show off before visitors.

"Ask I! I can say it all from 'N. or M.' to 'charity with all men'!" piped a too willing voice. "Be you a-going to give I sweets for saying it?" inquired another, with an eye to business.

"Katrine, I shall have to beat a retreat," murmured Gwethyn. "It's impossible to paint a stroke with this sticky little crew buzzing round like flies. I don't like being a public character. I've had enough notoriety this morning to last for the rest of my life. Now then, you young rascal, if you lay a finger on that paint-box I shall call on the schoolmaster and ask him to spank you!"

At this juncture, much to the girls' relief, Miss Aubrey came to criticize their sketches. She pointed out the mistakes in their drawings, and waited while they corrected them.

"It's no use beginning the painting to-day," she remarked in a low tone. "The children are too great a nuisance. I did not know about the Board of Guardians' meeting, or I would not have brought you this morning. We must come another time, when these small folk are safely in school, and wecan work undisturbed. I'm afraid you must have found them very troublesome."

"The ten plagues of Egypt weren't in it!" replied Gwethyn, joyfully closing her paint-box, and beginning to pack up her traps. "You had a crowd, too."

"Oh! I'm more accustomed to it, though I admit I'd rather dispense with an audience. If you want to be an artist, you have to learn to put up with this kind of thing. Never mind! I promise our next subject shall be in an absolutely retired spot, where no one can find us out."

CHAPTER IV

The School Mascot

ALTHOUGH Katrine had come to Aireyholme primarily to study art, she did not escape scot-free with respect to other lessons. Mrs. Franklin was a martinet where work was concerned. She often remarked that she did not approve of young people wasting their time, and she certainly endeavoured to put her principles into practice. She taught the Sixth Form herself. Some of the girls were preparing for their matriculation, and received special private coaching from a professor who came twice a week from Carford; but all, whether they were going in for the examination or not, were taking the same general course. Katrine had pursued her studies at Hartfield High School with very languid interest, and had joyfully abandoned them in favour of the Art School. She was not at all enthusiastic at being obliged to continue her ordinary education, and, indeed, considered the classes in the light of a grievance. It was humiliating to find herself behind the rest of the form in mathematics, to stumble in the French translation, and make bad shots at botany; particularly so before Viola Webster, who listened to her mistakes and halting recitations with a superior smile, or an amused glance at Diana Bennett.

"If we had had you at Aireyholme the last year or two, you would have reached a much higher standard by now," said Mrs. Franklin. "You must do your best to make up for lost time. An extra half-hour's preparation every day would do you no harm. You might get up a little earlier in the mornings."

Katrine, whose object was not so much to repair the gaps left in her education by the Hartfield High School as to amble through the present term with the least possible exertion of her brains, received the suggestion coldly, and forbore to act upon it.

"It's all very well for the matric. girls to get up at six and swat, but you won't find me trying it on!" she assured Gwethyn in private. "What does it matter whether I can work a rubbishy problem, or patter off a page of

French poetry? I've got to take the classes, worse luck, but all the Mrs. Franklins in the world shan't make me grind."

Between Katrine and the Principal there existed a kind of armed neutrality. Mrs. Franklin persisted in regarding her as an ordinary pupil, while Katrine considered that she had come to school on a totally different footing. Neither would yield an inch. Mrs. Franklin was masterful, but Katrine was gently stubborn. It is impossible to make a girl work who is determined to idle. At art Katrine was prepared to slave, and she had already begun to worship Miss Aubrey, but as a member of the Sixth Form she was the champion slacker. The Principal by turns tried severity, cajoling, and sarcasm.

"A most talented essay!" she remarked one day, handing back an untidy manuscript. "One might regard it as a study in tautology. The word 'very' occurs seven times in a single page. It is scarcely usual for a girl of seventeen to make twelve mistakes in spelling."

"I never could spell," answered Katrine serenely.

"Then it's time you learnt. Your writing also is sprawling and careless, and you have no idea of punctuation. I wish you could have seen the neat, beautifully expressed essays that Ermengarde used to write. They were models of composition and tidiness."

A suppressed smile passed round the form. The subject of Ermengarde was a perennial joke among the girls. Mrs. Franklin did not approve of holding up present pupils as patterns, for fear of fostering their vanity, so she generally quoted her daughter as an epitome of all the virtues. It was common knowledge in the school that Ermengarde's achievements had acquired an after-reputation which at the time they certainly did not justify. So far from being a shining ornament of Aircyholme, she had generally lagged in the wake of her form. She had bitterly disappointed her mother by barely scraping through her matriculation, and failing to win a scholarship for college. Poor Ermengarde had no gift for study; she was not particularly talented in any direction, and, shirking the various careers which Mrs. Franklin urged upon her, had taken fate into her own hands by marrying a curate, albeit he was impecunious, and "not at all clever, thank goodness!", as she confided to her intimate friends. When matrimony had debarred Ermengarde from any possibility of a college degree, her mother took it for granted that she would have obtained honours if she had only tried for them, and always spoke of her with regretful admiration as one who had laid aside the laurels of the muses for the duster of domesticity. "Saint Ermengarde", so the girls called her in mockery, lived therefore as a kind of school tradition, and she would have been very much surprised, indeed, had she known the extent to which her modest efforts had been magnified.

Gwethyn, who had been placed in the Fifth Form, found her level more quickly than did Katrine in the Sixth. Her high spirits and harum-scarum ways commended her to most of her new companions. She had a racy method of speech and a humorous habit of exaggeration that were rather amusing. Fresh from V.B. at the Hartfield High School, she fell easily into the work of the form, and if she did not particularly distinguish herself, gave no special trouble. The spirited sketch which she made of Miss Spencer, pince-nez on nose and book in hand, was considered "to the life", and she was good-natured enough to make no less than five copies of it, at the earnest request of Prissie Yorke, Susie Parker, Rose Randall, Beatrix Bates, and Dona Matthews. Her drawings of imps and goblins, with which she speedily decorated the fly-leaves of her new text-books, were immensely admired. General feeling inclined to the opinion that while Katrine gave herself airs, Gwethyn was the right sort, and might be adopted, with due caution, into the heart of the form. It would, of course, be unwise to make too much fuss of her in the beginning; every new girl must gothrough her novitiate of snubbing, but such a jolly, happy-go-lucky specimen as this would not be long in settling into Aireyholme ways.

The new-comers had arrived on 21st April: they had therefore been a little more than a week at the school when the 1st of May ushered in the summer. May Day was kept with great ceremony at Heathwell. The old festival, abandoned for more than a hundred years, had been revived lately in the village, largely at the instance of Miss Aubrey, whose artistic spirit revelled in such picturesque scenes. She had persuaded Mr. Boswell, the local squire, to place a may-pole on a small green near the market hall, and she had herself taught the children of the Council school a number of charming folk dances. The schoolmaster and the vicar both approved of the movement, and gave every facility and encouragement, and the children themselves were highly enthusiastic. This year it was proposed to have a more than usually elaborate performance, and to take a collection in the streets in aid of the Prince of Wales's Fund. May Day fortunately fell on a Saturday, so, as the festival had been well advertised, it was hoped that visitors would come over from Carford and other places in the neighbourhood. Though the actual pageant was to be given by the Council school children, the girls at Aireyholme rendered very valuable help. They made some of the dresses, plaited garlands, stitched knots of coloured ribbons, and last, but not least, were responsible for the collecting. Fifteen of the seniors, wearing Union Jack badges on their hats, and broad bands of tricolour ribbon tied under one arm and across the shoulder, were set apart for the task, each carrying a wooden box labelled: "Prince of Wales's Fund".

The festivities were to begin at three o'clock, to fit in with the times of the local railway trains. The morning was a busy whirl of preparation. Miss Aubrey, with the monitresses as special helpers, flitted backwards and forwards between Aireyholme and the village, making last arrangements and putting finishing touches. Katrine and Gwethyn had never before had the opportunity of witnessing such a spectacle, so they were full of excitement at the prospect. At half-past two, Mrs. Franklin, mistresses, and girls sallied forth to the scene of action, and secured an admirable position on the steps of the market hall, whence they could have a good view of the proceedings.

It was a balmy, sunny day, and the lovely weather, combined with the quaint programme, had tempted many visitors from various places in the district. The trains arrived full, and Heathwell for once was overflowing. Not only had people made use of the railway, but many had come on bicycles, and motor-cars added to the crush. The local shops, and even the cottages, had taken advantage of the occasion to sell lemonade and ginger beer, and had hung out home-written signs announcing their willingness to provide teas and store cycles. The village was en fête, and the general atmosphere was one of jollity and enjoyment.

The children were waiting in the school play-ground, under the superintendence of their teachers and Miss Aubrey. Precisely as the church clock struck three, the procession started. It was led by the band of the local corps of boy scouts, the drummer very proud indeed in the possession of the orthodox leopard skin, which had been presented only the week before by a local magnate. After the scouts came a number of children, dressed in Kate Greenaway costumes, and carrying May knots—sticks surmounted with wreaths of flowers and green leaves. A band of little ones, representing fairies, heralded the approach of the May Queen, who drove in great state in a tiny carriage drawn by a very small Shetland pony, led by a page resplendent in ribbons and buckles. The carriage was so covered with flowers that it well resembled the car of Friga, the spring goddess of Scandinavian mythology, who gave her name to Friday. No deity, classic or Teutonic, could have been prettier than the flaxen-haired little maiden, who sat up stiffly, trying with great dignity to support her regal honours. Her courtiers walked behind her, and after came a band of morris dancers, jingling their bells as they went. The pageant paraded down the High Street, made a circuit round the market hall, and drew up round the may-pole on the strip of green. A platform had been erected here, with a throne for the Queen, so her little majesty was duly handed out of her carriage, and installed in the post of honour. Amid ringing cheers the crown was placed on her curly head, and the sceptre delivered to her, while small courtiers bowed with a very excellent imitation of mediæval grace.

"What an absolute darling the Queen is!" remarked Gwethyn, who, with Katrine, was an ecstatic spectator.

"It's little Mary Gartley," replied Coralie Nelson. "They're the best-looking family in the village — six children, and all have those lovely flaxen curls. I never saw such beautiful hair. Look at that tiny wee chap who's standing just by the pony. That's Hugh Gartley. Isn't he an absolute cherub? We've had him for a model at the studio. We call him 'The School Mascot', because he's brought us such luck. Miss Aubrey's picture of him has got into the Academy, and Gladwin Riley's sketch won first prize in a magazine competition, and Hilda Smart's photo of him also took a prize in a paper. He scored three successes for Aireyholme. He's the sweetest little rascal. Even Mrs. Franklin can't resist patting him on the head, and giving him biscuits."

"He's an absolute angel!" agreed the Marsdens enthusiastically.

When the coronation of the May Queen was duly accomplished, the sports began. A band of dainty damsels, holding coloured ribbons, plaited and unplaited the may-pole, much to the admiration of the crowd, who encored the performance. The fairies gave a pretty exhibition, waving garlands of flowers as they trod their fantastic measure; the morris dancers capered their best, and the Boy Scouts' band did its utmost in providing the music. It was a very charming scene; so quaint amid the old-world setting of the picturesque village that the spectators clapped and cheered with heartiest approval. The little actors, excited by the applause, began to go beyond control, and to run about helter-skelter, waving their garlands and shouting "hurrah!" The crowd also was breaking up. A train was nearly due, and some of the visitors made a rush for the station. A char-à-banc with threehorses started from the "Bell and Dragon". At that identical moment little Hugh Gartley, seeing some attraction on the opposite pavement, threw discipline to the winds and dashed suddenly across the road, in front of the very wheels of the passing char-à-banc. Katrine happened to be watching him. With a leap and a run she was down the steps of the market hall and in the street. Before the child, or anyone else, realized his danger, she had snatched him from the front of the horses, and had dragged him on to the pavement. The driver pulled up in considerable alarm.

"It's not my fault," he protested. "Kids shouldn't bolt across like that."

Finding there was no harm done, he drove on. The incident was over so quickly that it was hardly noticed by the general public. Little Hugh Gartley, much scared, clung crying to Katrine's hand. She took him in her arms and comforted him with chocolates. He made friends readily, and instead of rejoining the May dancers, insisted upon staying with her for the rest of the performance. Katrine was fond of children, and enjoyed petting the pretty little fellow. She kept him by her until the procession passed on its return to the schoolhouse, then she made him slip in amongst the other masqueraders.

The fifteen collectors had been busy all the afternoon handing round their boxes, and anticipated quite a good harvest.

"I shouldn't be surprised if we'd taken seven or eight pounds; many people put in silver," said Diana Bennett. "It will be grand when the boxes are opened."

"You missed the excitement near the market hall," volunteered Coralie. "Katrine Marsden rescued Hugh Gartley from being run over. She snatched him back just in the nick of time."

"Oh, it was nothing!" protested Katrine.

"Indeed it was splendid presence of mind! He might have been killed if you hadn't dashed down so promptly and snatched him."

Katrine's action in saving the school mascot was soon noised abroad among the girls, and brought her a quite unexpected spell of popularity, chiefly with the juniors and the Fifth Form, however. The Sixth, led by the monitresses, still hung back, jealous of their privileges, and unwilling to tolerate one who persisted in considering herself a "parlour boarder", and, as they expressed it, "putting on side!" It was really mostly Katrine's own fault: her previous acquaintance with school life ought to have taught her wisdom; but seventeen is a crude age, and not given to profiting by past experience. Some of the pin-pricks she sustained were well deserved.

On the evening of May Day, being a Saturday as well as a special festival, the monitresses decided to give a cocoa party in their study, and invite the rest of the form.

"We got eight pounds, fifteen and twopence halfpenny in the collecting boxes this afternoon," announced Viola, "and we ought to drink the health of the Prince of Wales's Fund in cocoa. We'll have a little rag-time fun, too, just among ourselves."

"All serene!" agreed Diana. "This child's always ready for sport. What about biscuits?"

"We may send out for what we like. I interviewed the Great Panjandrum, and she was affability itself."

"Good! Cocoanut fingers for me. And perhaps a few Savoys."

"Right-o! Make your list. Tomlinson is to go and fetch them."

"We shall have to borrow cups from the kitchen," said Dorrie, who had been investigating inside the cupboard. "Since that last smash we're rather low down in our china—only four cups left intact."

"Go and ask the cook for five more, then."

"Five? That'll only make nine."

"Quite enough."

"Aren't you going to invite Katrine Marsden?"

Viola pulled a long face.

"Is it necessary? She doesn't consider herself one of the Sixth."

"But she is, really. It seems rather marked to leave her out."

"Oh, well!" rather icily. "Ask her if you like, of course. I'm sure I don't want to keep her out of things if she cares to join in."

Dorrie accordingly ran up to the studio, where Katrine was sitting putting a few finishing touches to the study of tulips upon which she had been engaged during the last week.

"We're having a cocoa party at eight in our study. Awfully pleased to see you. Just our own form," announced Dorrie heartily.

"Thanks very much," returned Katrine casually, "but I really don't think I shall have time to come. I want to finish these tulips."

"Isn't it getting too dark for painting?"

"Oh, no! The light's good for some time yet, and Miss Aubrey's probably coming upstairs to go on with her still-life study. I love sitting with her. She's most inspiring."

"Comme vous voulez, mademoiselle!" answered Dorrie, retiring in high dudgeon to report to her fellow-monitresses. They were most indignant at the slight.

"Cheek!"

"Turns up her nose at our invitation, does she?"

"She can please herself, I'm sure."

"She's no loss, at any rate."

"Look here!" said Dorrie. "I've got an idea. We'll pay her out for this. She's counting on Miss Aubrey going to sit with her in the studio, and having a delightful tête à tête. Let's ask Miss Aubrey to our cocoa party."

"Splendiferous!"

"Girl alive, you're a genius! Go instanter!"

Dorrie hurried off to deliver her second invitation. It was more graciously received than the first.

"Oh! I'm only too flattered! I shall be delighted to turn up. May I bring a contribution to the feast?" beamed Miss Aubrey.

"Done Katrine Marsden for once!" chuckled Dorrie, communicating the good tidings in the study. "She'll be fearfully sick when she finds her idol has deserted her for us."

"I sincerely hope she will."

At eight o'clock an extremely jolly party assembled in the little room underneath the studio, all prepared to abandon themselves to enjoyment, to crack jokes, sing catches, ask riddles, or indulge in anything that savoured of fun. There were not chairs for all, but nobody minded sitting on the floor. Viola's spirit-lamp was on the table, and the kettle steamed cheerily; tins of cocoa and condensed milk and packets of biscuits were spread forth with the row of cups and saucers. Miss Aubrey, throned in a basket-chair, with girls quarrelling for the privilege of sitting near her, held a kind of impromptu court.

"It's been a ripping May Day. Everybody was saying how well you'd engineered the whole thing," Viola assured her. "The folk dances were just too sweet! Those Americans who came in that big car were in raptures. They dropped half a sovereign into my box. They said the May Queen was the prettiest child they'd ever seen."

"Mary Gartley is only second to Hugh," replied Miss Aubrey. "I hear the little chap nearly got run over this afternoon, and Katrine Marsden rescued him. Where is Katrine, by the by?"

For a moment an awkward silence reigned.

"She's in the studio. We invited her, but she wouldn't come," volunteered Dorrie at last.

"Oh!" said Miss Aubrey, with a gleam of comprehension.

Upstairs, Katrine was painting away rather half-heartedly. She wondered why her beloved art-mistress did not arrive. It would be delightful to have her all to herself, without those schoolgirls. The door burst open, and Gwethyn came rushing tumultuously in.

"Kattie! The Fifth are giving a Mad Hatter's party! We're going to have the most screaming fun! They've asked you, so do come, quick!"

"Oh, I don't care about it, child! I'm waiting here for Miss Aubrey."

"Miss Aubrey? Why, she's gone to the Sixth Form party! I saw her walking into their study with a box of chocolates and a bag of something in her hand. They're at it hard!"

A glimpse of Katrine's face at that moment might have soothed the injured feelings of the monitresses. From below rose unmistakable sounds of mirth to confirm Gwethyn's words.

"Aren't you coming? Do hurry up!" urged Gwethyn impatiently.

But to join in the festivities of the Fifth Form after declining those of the Sixth was too great a come-down for Katrine's dignity.

"Run along, Baby! I don't care for nonsense parties. I'd rather stay and paint," she replied, with an air of sang-froid that was perhaps slightly overdone.

"Tantrums? Well, you're a jolly silly, that's all I can say; for we're going to have ripping fun!" chirruped Gwethyn, shutting the door with a slam.

CHAPTER V

Lilac Grange

SO far Gwethyn's impression of Aireyholme had been largely tinged by the prevailing presence of Laura Browne. Laura took her up the very evening she arrived, and had since gushed over her without intermission, monopolizing her almost entirely. It was Laura who explained the school rules, and offered advice on the subject of preparation or practising; Laura who walked with her round the garden, introduced her to the library, and showed her the Senior museum. The temperature of the friendship might be described — on Laura's side at any rate — as white-hot. She took complete possession of Gwethyn, driving off the other girls gently but firmly.

"I'll tell her all about the lessons!" she would declare, waving Rose or Susie away. "Come with me, dearest! Of course I know our work's nothing to you, after your other school, but any help that I can give you, you're more than welcome to. It's so refreshing to have a girl like you here, after these others. Oh, anyone could see the difference! I fell in love with you at first sight. Look at Rose Randall, now; it would be impossible to be friends with her. I couldn't do it. And Beatrix and Marian are unspeakable. No, darling, until you came, I hadn't a chum in the whole school."

As the rest of the form held slightly aloof, Gwethyn found herself flung into the arms of Laura Browne. She had not Katrine's reserve, and would rather be friends with anybody than nobody. She did not altogether care for Laura's fawning manners, but as the intimacy was forced upon her, she accepted it. For ten days they had been dubbed "the lovers", and were constantly in each other's company.

"I hear you've brought your violin, sweetest," said Laura at recreation one morning, as the pair stood watching a set of tennis. "How is it you didn't tell me? I'm dying to hear you play it."

"Oh, I'm only a beginner! I brought it just in case I found time to practise a little. I'm not taking lessons on it here."

"But you will play for me?"

"If you like; but it won't be a treat. I break about a dozen strings every time I tune it."

"A violin has four strings, so you must snip them with a pair of scissors, I should think, if you break twelve each time you tune up," remarked a sarcastic voice from behind.

Gwethyn turned round, and met the scornful eyes of Githa Hamilton.

"That horrid child! Why can't she let me alone?" she whispered to Laura. "She's the image of a toadstool, with her khaki complexion and lank hair."

But Githa's sharp ears overheard.

"Thanks for the compliment! Khaki's a nice patriotic colour. I like my hair straight—I haven't the least desire to friz it out or curl it. If you're going to break a dozen strings tuning your fiddle to-day, perhaps you'll save me the pieces; they make splendid lashes for whips."

"To drive geese with?" retorted Gwethyn.

"Exactly. How clever of you to guess! There are a great many geese in this neighbourhood. I come in contact with them every day."

"Don't mind the snarly little thing!" said Laura, walking Gwethyn away. "Now tell me when I'm to hear your violin. Shall we say a quarter-past two this afternoon in the practising-room? I'll play your piano accompaniment."

"And I'll be there for the surplus strings!" piped Githa, following behind.

"Githa Hamilton, take yourself off!" commanded Laura, routing the enemy at last.

Gwethyn had not opened her violin-case since coming to Aireyholme. She had taken lessons for about a year, and her mother had urged her to try and find time to practise, so that she should not forget all she had learned; but so far there had been so many other things to occupy her, that the violin had been entirely thrust on one side. True to her promise to Laura, she brought it out of its retirement this afternoon, and going to the music-room began to tune it by the piano. Not a string snapped in the process, and the instrument was soon in order. Gwethyn laid it down on the table, and waited. Surely Laura could not be long. She had made the appointment for 2.15, and had expressed herself at dinner as impatient for the time to arrive. The minutes rolled by, however, and no Laura appeared. Presently a smooth dark head peeped round the door.

"Any strings on hand?" inquired Githa, with an elfish grin. "I've come for that odd dozen you've got to spare!"

"I didn't break any," returned Gwethyn shortly.

"Bad news for me! Well, now, I suppose you're at the trysting-place, waiting for the beloved?"

"Laura'll be turning up soon," grunted Gwethyn.

"Sorry to break your heart instead of your strings! I'm afraid she won't turn up. It's a case of 'he cometh not, she said'. The fair one is false and fickle, and loves another! If you're going to have hysterics, or faint, please give me warning. Poor lone heart!"

"What nonsense you're talking! What do you mean?" asked Gwethyn, laughing in spite of herself.

"It's the sad and solemn truth. Laura Browne, regardless of her appointment with you, is now walking round the kitchen-garden arm-in-arm with another love, and gazing admiringly into her eyes. Your image is wiped from her memory; you are a broken idol, a faded flower, a past episode, a thing of yesterday!"

"For goodness' sake, stop ragging!"

"Well, if you prefer it in plain prose, you're superseded by Phyllis Lowman. She's Mrs. Franklin's niece, and comes occasionally to spend a few days here. She arrived just after dinner. We're not keen on her in the school, but Laura truckles to her to curry favour with Mother Franklin. During her

47

visit the pair will be inseparable, and your poor plaintive nose will be absolutely out of joint."

"I don't believe you!" flared Gwethyn.

"Oh, all right! Go and see for yourself! It isn't I who exaggerate!" and with a malicious little laugh the Toadstool beat a retreat.

There were a few minutes left before afternoon school, so Gwethyn, tired of waiting, took a run round the garden. Alas! Githa had spoken the truth. Wandering amongst the gooseberry bushes she met her missing friend, in company with a stranger. They were linked arm-in-arm, and their heads were pressed closely together. As they passed Gwethyn, Laura's eyes showed not a trace even of recognition, much less apology or regret.

"I've been simply vegetating till you came here again, Phyllis darling! I'm living to-day! You sweetest!"

The words, in Laura's most honied tones, were wafted back as the pair walked towards the house. Gwethyn looked after them and stamped.

"So that's Laura Browne and her fine friendship! Well, I've done with her from to-day. She won't catch me having anything more to say to her. I really think this is the limit! I couldn't have believed it of her if I hadn't seen it. The utter sneak!"

Phyllis Lowman spent three days at Aireyholme, during which period Laura was her slave and bond-servant. When she returned home, the latter turned her attention again to her first love. But Gwethyn would have none of her, and received her advances in so cavalier a fashion that she gave up the futile attempt at reconciliation. The other members of the Fifth enjoyed the little comedy. It was what they had expected.

"Gwethyn was bound to be 'Laura-ridden' at first," laughed Susie Parker. "It's the inevitable. Laura's new friendships have to run their course like measles. This has only been a short business, and now we may consider Gwethyn disinfected!"

No longer monopolized by Laura, Gwethyn began to make friends with other girls, and was soon a favourite in the Fifth. Her love of fun, and readiness to give and take, commended her to the form, and on her side she much preferred to be ordinary chums with her comrades, than to be offered a slavish and rather ridiculous worship, such as Laura had tendered.

Since their very trying experiences in the High Street, the Marsdens had begged Miss Aubrey to allow them to abandon that particular subject, and begin another sketch in some more retired place, where spectators would not come to look over their shoulders. Miss Aubrey herself disliked working in the midst of a crowd, so she readily agreed, and at their next painting lesson announced that she had found the very spot to suit them. Nan Bethell, Gladwin Riley, and Coralie Nelson were to join the class that afternoon. Viola, Dorrie, and Diana were also extremely anxious to go, but Mrs. Franklin would not spare her best matriculation students, and sternly set them to work at mathematics instead, much to their disgust. Tita Gray, Hilda Smart, and Ellaline Dickens, the remaining members of the Sixth, were detained by music lessons with a master who came over weekly from Carford. Only five fortunate ones sallied forth, therefore, with Miss Aubrey. The subject which their teacher had chosen was not far off, though rather out of the way. Standing back from the village, at the end of a long lane, was a rambling old house known as "The Grange". It lay low, in a somewhat damp spot close to the river, faced north, and had no particular view. Owing, no doubt, to these drawbacks, and to its inconvenient situation, it had been unlet for several years, and as the owner did not seem inclined to spend money on repairs, its dilapidated condition held out little promise of a new tenant. To anyone anxious for seclusion no more suitable retreat could be found: the long leafy lane which led to its rusty iron gate, the thickness of its surrounding plantation, the tall shrubs in the garden, which almost touched the windows, all seemed so many barriers to discourage the public, and to keep the lonely dwelling apart from the outside world. To the girls it looked mysterious, and it was with almost a creepy feeling that they opened the creaking gate, and made their way through the tangled garden. Everything seemed as overgrown and as quiet as in the palace of the Sleeping Beauty; not a face to be seen at the windows, nor a footstep to be heard in the grounds; the flower-beds were a mass of rank weeds, the paths were covered with grass, and the lawn was a hayfield. In the prime of their beauty, however, were the lilac bushes; they had thriven with neglect, and were covered with masses of exquisite blossom, scenting the whole air, and making the garden a purple Paradise.

"The place ought to be called 'Lilac Grange'!" said Katrine admiringly. "It's a perfect show at present. Are we to paint them?"

"I'm afraid they would prove rather difficult. I have an easier subject for you round at the back," said Miss Aubrey, leading the way to the rear of the house, where a timbered dovecote stood in the old paved courtyard. With its black beams and carved doorway, it seemed of much greater antiquity than the Grange itself, which had probably been rebuilt on the site of an older structure. Miss Aubrey found a favourable view where the afternoon sunshine cast warm shadows upon the lichen-stained plaster, and she at once set her pupils to work, to catch the effect before the light changed.

"What a harbour of refuge this is!" declared Gwethyn, haunted by memories of the High Street. "There isn't a single child to come and disturb us. I call this absolute bliss."

"And a ripping subject!" agreed Katrine.

For a long time the girls worked away quietly, passing an occasional remark, but too busy to talk. At last the Marsdens, who drew more quickly than their comrades, had reached a stage at which it was impossible to continue without advice. Miss Aubrey was sketching the lilac round the corner, so leaving their easels they went in search of her. Not sorry to stretch their limbs for a few minutes, they decided first to take a run round the garden. It would be fun to explore, and Katrine would get rid of the pins and needles in her foot. Under the lanky laurel bushes and overgrown rose arches, along a swampy little path by the river, through a broken green-house, and back across a nettle-covered terrace. Not a soul to be seen about the whole place. It was peaceful as a palace of dreams.

Stop! What was that rustling among the leaves? There was a movement under the lilac bushes, and a slight figure stepped out into the sunshine.

"Githa Hamilton! Whatever are you doing here?" exclaimed the girls.

The pale little Toadstool looked more surprised than pleased at the meeting.

"I may return the compliment, and ask what you are doing here?" she parried.

"We're sketching with Miss Aubrey."

"And I'm—amusing myself! My time's my own after school is over."

She spoke aggressively, almost belligerently. To judge from her appearance, no one would have imagined that she had been amusing herself. The redness of her eyes suggested crying.

"I'm going home now for tea," she snapped. "I left my bicycle by the gate."

When Katrine's and Gwethyn's drawings had been duly corrected by their teacher, and they had settled down again for the final half-hour's work, they mentioned this meeting with Githa to Coralie, who was sitting close by.

"What was the queer child doing?" asked Katrine. "I thought she seemed rather caught. She glared at us as if she wished us at Timbuctoo."

"Oh! was Githa here? Well, you see, it used to be her old home. Her grandfather owned the Grange. She and her brother were orphans, and lived with him; then, when he died, they had to go to an uncle, and the house was to let. Everybody thinks they were treated very hardly. Old Mr. Ledbury had promised to provide for them (they were his daughter's children), but when the will was read there was no mention of them. No one could understand how it was that he had left them without a penny. He had always seemed so fond of them. Their uncle, Mr. Wilfred Ledbury, who inherited everything, took them to live with him, rather on sufferance. The boy is at a boarding-school, but I don't think Githa has a particularly nice time at The Gables."

"What an atrocious shame!" exploded Gwethyn.

"Oh! don't misunderstand me. They're not exactly unkind to her. She's sent to school at Aireyholme, and she's always quite nicely dressed; she has her bicycle, and she may keep her pets in the stable. Only her uncle just ignores her, and her aunt isn't sympathetic, or interested in her. With being a day-girl she's out of all the fun we boarders get. I fancy she's most fearfully lonely."

"Oh! the poor little Toadstool! If I'd only known that, I wouldn't have been so rude to her. I was a brute!" (Gwethyn's self-reproach was really genuine.) "I'll be nice to her now. I will indeed!"

"Don't start pitying her, for goodness' sake! It's the one thing Githa can't stand. She's as proud as Lucifer, and if she suspects you're the least atom sorry for her, it makes her as hard as nails. She never lets us know she's not happy; she always makes out she's better off than we are, going home every day. But I'm sure she's miserable."

"Yes, you can see that in her face," agreed Katrine.

Impulsive Gwethyn, having learnt Githa's story, was anxious to atone for several lively passages of arms, and to make friends. But the conquest of the Toadstool was harder than she expected. Githa's proud little heart resented anything savouring of patronage, and she repelled all advances. No hedgehog could have been more prickly. She refused to play tennis, declined the loan of books, and even said "No, thank you," to proffered chocolates. Instead of appearing grateful for the notice of a girl in a higher form, she seemed to stiffen herself into an attitude of haughty reserve. Finding all attempts at kindness useless, Gwethyn simply let her alone, taking no notice whatever of her, and just ignoring pointed remarks and sarcasms, instead of returning them with compound interest as formerly. Baffled by this new attitude, the Toadstool, after trying her most aggravating sallies, and failing to draw any sparks, relapsed into neutrality. Her dark eyes often followed Gwethyn with an inscrutable gaze, but she steadfastly avoided speaking to her.

Gwethyn did not greatly concern herself, for she had found three most congenial chums. Rose Randall, Beatrix Bates, and Dona Matthews were kindred spirits where fun was concerned, and in their society she spent all her spare time. As for Katrine, she was not likely to trouble about a Fourth Form girl. She just realized Githa as a plain and very objectionable junior, but never gave a thought to her or her affairs. At present Katrine's mind was devoted to art, and had no corner to spare for minor interests. Under Miss Aubrey's tuition she was making strides, and was beginning to put on her colours in a far more professional manner. She really had a decided talent for painting, as well as a love for it, and she had come prepared to work. Her teacher, glad to find such enthusiasm, gave her every encouragement. She took her out sketching daily, allowed her to watch while she herself painted, and took infinite trouble to set her in the way of real art progress. Katrine's easel had never before had so much exercise. She planted it in a variety of situations, at the instance of Miss Aubrey, whose trained eye could at once pick out suitable subjects for the brush. Heathwell was a very Paradise for artists, with its deep lanes, its hedges a tangle of honeysuckle, wild rose, and white briony, its quiet timbered farmsteads set in the midst of lush meadows, its flowery gardens, and its slow-flowing river with reedy, willowy banks. Those were halcyon days to Katrine, whether she sat in the sunshine among the pinks and pansies of a cottage garden, sketching the subtle varied stones of a weather-worn gable against the rich brown of a thatched roof, the bees humming in and out of the flowers, and the pigeons cooing gently in the dovecote close by; or whether Miss Aubrey took her to the shelter of thick woods, where the warm light, shimmering through the leaves, cast flickering shadows on the soft grass below. There were glorious mornings when Nature seemed to have washed her children's faces, and turned the world out in clean clothes; golden noons when all was a-quiver in a haze of heat, and the sky a blue dome from horizon to zenith; and still, quiet evenings, when the elms were a blot of purple-grey against a pale yellow afterglow, and the uncut hayfield such a soft, delicate, blurred mass of indefinite colour that she gave up the vain effort to depict it, and simply sat to gaze and wonder and enjoy. Down by the river the calm pools would catch the carmine of the sky, till one could fancy that one of the ten plagues had returned to earth, and that the waters were turned into blood. Each leaf of the willows seemed to reflect a shade of warmer hue, till all was bathed in a glow of ruddy light, and looking over the gently quivering reed tops to the splendour across the horizon, one could almost see angels between the cloud bars.

Miss Aubrey, who had lived many years at Heathwell, had a score of rustic acquaintances. The cottage folk often sat to her as models. Their quaint ways and ingenuous remarks opened out a new phase of the world to Katrine. She became immensely interested in the villagers, from Abel Barnes, who still urged the claims of his bow-windowed red-brick villa as a subject for her brush, to bonny little Hugh Gartley, whose cherubic beauty she vainly tried to transfer to canvas.

She found the Gartleys a fascinating family. There were so many of them, and they were all so fair and flaxen-haired, with such ready smiles and winning manners. How they contrived to fit into their very small cottage Katrine could never imagine. She had spoken once or twice to the mother, a good-natured, untidy, slatternly young woman, whose income never seemed to run to soap; but she avoided the father, an idle ne'er-do-weel with a reputation for poaching.

"It is very difficult to help the Gartleys," said Miss Aubrey. "The children are most attractive, but it is simply encouraging pauperism to give to them while Bob Gartley stays at home drinking and refusing to work. I hope you haven't given them any money?"

"Only a few pennies to Hugh and Mary—they looked so pretty," admitted Katrine guiltily.

CHAPTER VI

An Awkward Predicament

FOR some days Katrine had been convinced that there was another artist in the neighbourhood. She had caught a glimpse of an easel fixed in a field, she had found a tube of paint lying in the road, and had noticed upon a paling the scrapings of a palette. She had not yet, however, been vouchsafed a sight of the stranger, against whom she had conceived a violent prejudice. She had come to regard Heathwell as the private sketching property of herself and Miss Aubrey, and regarded the new-comer in the light of a poacher on their art preserves. He or she—she did not even know the sex of the intruder—might very well have chosen some other village, in her opinion, instead of fixing upon this particular Paradise. All the same, she was inquisitive, and would have liked very much to see the unknown artist's work. One afternoon Miss Aubrey took the Marsdens to a little subject in a meadow on the road to the river. She watched them begin to draw in a picturesque railing and hawthorn stump, then went herself to another position in the field. Left alone, the girls worked for some time in silence, Katrine with whole-hearted absorption, and Gwethyn in a more dilettante fashion. The latter did not care to stick at things too long. She soon grew tired, and threw down her brush.

"Ugh! It makes me stiff to sit so still. I'm going to walk round the pasture. Do come, Katrine! Oh, how you swat! You might take two minutes' rest. We're just above the road here, and I believe somebody's sitting down below. I can smell tobacco. I'm going to investigate."

Gwethyn came back in a few moments with her eyes dancing.

"It's an artist!" she whispered. "He's painting in the road exactly below us. I can see his picture through the hedge. Come and look!"

Such exciting information broke the spell of Katrine's work. She put down her palette at once, and followed Gwethyn. It was impossible to resist taking a peep at the interesting stranger's sketch.

"You must promise not even to breathe. I should be most annoyed if he happened to see us," she declared.

"All right! I'll be mum as a mouse, and walk as softly as a pussy-cat. I'll undertake it won't be my fault if he divines our existence."

Very gently the two girls crept along the edge of the pasture, trying not to rustle the grass, and heroically refraining from conversation.

"Here we are!" signalled Gwethyn at last, pausing at a thin place in the hedge, which might have been made on purpose for a peep-hole. Through a frame of sycamore leaves they could peer into the road exactly at the spot where the rival easel was pitched. The artist's back was towards them; theycould see nothing but his tweed suit, his grey hair under a brown hat, and the skilful right hand which kept dabbing subtle combinations of half-tones upon his canvas. He seemed utterly unconscious of their presence, and worked away in sublime ignorance that two pairs of eyes were following every stroke of his brush. He was no amateur, that was plain. The girls were sufficient judges of painting to recognize that though the sketch was still at an elementary stage he had made a masterly beginning. Katrine watched quite fascinated, trying to decide what colours he was using, and in what proportion he had mixed them. If she could only see his palette, she might perhaps discover the secret of that particularly warm shadow he was in the act of placing under the near tree. She craned her head a little forward through the hedge. Gwethyn, equally anxious to see everything possible, pressed closely behind her. Whether it was the heat of the sun, or whether a sycamore leaf tickled the end of her nose, I cannot tell. The cause is immaterial, but the awful and tangible result was that Katrine—Katrine, who prided herself upon prunes and prism—burst without warning into a violent and uncontrollable sneeze! Naturally the artist turned at the unwonted sound, to catch an astonishing vision of two dismayed faces peeping like dryads from the greenery behind him.

Katrine dashed off like a thief detected red-handed, but she had hardly gone a yard when Gwethyn seized her by the arm.

56

"Katrine! Stop! There's no need to run in that silly way. Can't you see it's Mr. Freeman?"

"What's the matter, girls?" asked Miss Aubrey, who had walked up to correct their drawings.

Katrine felt caught on both sides, but there seemed nothing for it but to pass off the affair as well as she could.

"We've met an old friend of my father's," she explained. "I suppose we may say 'How do you do?' to him over the hedge?"

If the girls were surprised to see Mr. Freeman, he was equally astonished to find them at Heathwell.

"Didn't know you were at school here. It's a grand part of the world for sketching. Never saw so many paintable bits in my life. My diggings are in the village. Yes, come down and look at my picture, if you like."

Mr. Freeman had often been a guest at the Marsdens'. The girls knew him well. He had criticized Katrine's earliest art efforts, and had painted a portrait of Gwethyn when she was about seven years old. He seemed to have grasped the humour of the present situation, for he gazed up the bank with twinkling eyes. Katrine hastily introduced Miss Aubrey over the top of the hedge, not a very dignified method of presenting a friend, but the only one available. Fortunately Miss Aubrey was not Mrs. Franklin! An invitation to make a nearer acquaintance with the picture was irresistible. Katrine took her teacher by the arm, and pulled her gently in the direction of the gate. She offered no objection.

"I was most extremely glad for Mr. Freeman to meet Miss Aubrey," Katrine confided to Gwethyn afterwards. "Two such good artists positivelyought to know each other. They've each got a picture in the Academy, and—isn't it funny?—in the very same room—numbers 402 and 437!"

"They seemed to find plenty to talk about," returned Gwethyn. "I hope Mr. Freeman really will look us up at school."

Not only did their artist friend take an early opportunity of calling on them at Aireyholme, but he asked Miss Aubrey to bring them to see his sketches in the little studio he had rigged up in the village. It was a treat to be shown his charming interpretations of Heathwell and its inhabitants. He had already requisitioned some of the Gartley children as models, and was in ecstasies over their picturesque appearance. His study of the High Street at sunset was a poem on canvas.

"This beats every other place I've ever stayed at for painting," he announced. "Now I've found this studio, I shall stop here for the summer. There's any amount to be done."

"You'll certainly find plenty of subjects round about," agreed Miss Aubrey.

"I wonder if the painting is altogether the whole of the attraction," mused Gwethyn, who in some respects was wise beyond her years.

Miss Aubrey was an immense favourite at Aireyholme, but among all the girls she had no stancher and more whole-hearted admirer than Githa Hamilton. Githa was not demonstrative—she never said much; but whenever possible she haunted her idol like a drab little shadow, watching her with adoring eyes, and hanging upon her words. Miss Aubrey had a very shrewd suspicion that Githa was lonely at home and left out at school. Realizing her peculiar disposition, she made no great fuss over her, but every now and then managed unobtrusively to include the girl in some special expedition or particular treat. At an early date in June she arranged to take a few members of the painting class on a Saturday excursion to Chiplow, where a fine old abbey would provide a capital subject for an afternoon's sketching.

Chiplow was on a different line of railway from Carford, therefore the Heathwell local trains were of little use in getting there. The quickest route was to bicycle to Chorlton Lacy, a station on the South Midland line, seven miles away, whence they could book excursion tickets to Chiplow. Only girls possessing bicycles were available for the jaunt, and as for one reason or another several of these were obliged to be excluded, Miss Aubrey invited Githa to accompany them and make up the dozen required for the issue of the special cheap holiday bookings. The poor little Toadstool turned up radiant with delight, and looking really almost pretty in her khaki-coloured cycle costume, scarlet tie, and poppy-trimmed Panama. A Union Jack fluttered from her newly-polished machine, and in the basket which hung from the handle-bars she had a store of home-made toffee as well as her sketch-book.

In first-rate spirits the party set off along the road, riding in style through the village, with much ringing of bells to scare away children. They free-wheeled for nearly a mile downhill, and then had a splendid level stretch of road beside the river bank.

"We're getting along capitally," said Miss Aubrey. "At this rate we shall be at the station half an hour too soon."

"Unless we meet with some excitement!" ventured Gwethyn hopefully.

If Gwethyn craved for excitement, she was soon to find it. They had not gone half a mile farther before their way was barred by an enormous bull, which, to judge by a gap in the hedge, must have broken out of a neighbouring field. There it stood, in a dip of the road, right in their path, tossing its great head, pawing the ground, and bellowing lustily. The cyclists jumped off their machines, decidedly scared by the apparition that faced them.

"Oh, but doesn't it look a splendid subject?" gasped Katrine, whose artistic instincts were uppermost even at such a crisis. "If we could only draw it!"

"Don't be idiotic!" cried Nan Bethell. "It would be like taking a snapshot of a lion when it's rushing at you with open jaws!"

"I'm sure Rosa Bonheur or Lucy Kemp-Welch would have sketched it."

"Then they'd have been impaled, one on each horn, and serve them right for tempting Providence. Look at the dust the creature's raising in the road!"

All the party were in consternation. Miss Aubrey, who felt the responsibility of her charge, and moreover had a natural fear of bulls, for once almost lost her presence of mind.

"What are we to do? It would be madness to try and ride past it. I suppose we shall have to turn back home," she fluttered.

"Can't we call for help? Halloo!" shouted some of the girls.

"There's nobody about."

"I see a hat in that field!"

"It's only a scarecrow!"

Then Githa, who had been standing silently by her bicycle, suddenly assumed direction of the situation.

"Stop shouting! You'll excite the bull!" she commanded. "Now let us stack our machines in the ditch, and climb over this fence into the field. Come along, quick! This way!"

It seemed such excellent advice that even Miss Aubrey obeyed quite meekly. Leaving their bicycles below, they all scrambled hastily up the bank and over some hurdles into a field.

"We're safe, but we shall lose our train!" lamented Gladwin Riley.

"Not a bit of it! We'll turn up in time at the station, you'll see!" replied Githa. "Just leave it to me!"

She broke a stick from the hedge, picked up several large stones, and then ran along the meadow for some distance and climbed another fence. All at once the girls realized her intention. She was descending into the road in the rear of the bull.

"Stop her! Stop her!" shrieked Miss Aubrey.

By that time, however, Githa was half-way down the bank. Before the bull had time to realize her presence and turn round, she began a vigorous onslaught with stones upon his hind quarters, shouting at the pitch of her lungs. Her sudden attack had exactly the effect she hoped. The bull, enraged by the noise and the stones, rushed blindly forward along the road, passing the bicycles without notice, and stampeding in the direction of Heathwell.

"Someone will stop him before he gets into the village," murmured Miss Aubrey at the top of the bank.

The brave little Toadstool received an ovation as the rest of the party climbed down from the post of vantage. She took her honours ungraciously.

"What's the use of making a fuss? Anyone with two grains of sense would have thought of it. For goodness' sake, let me get on my machine! We haven't overmuch time, and we don't want to miss our train standing palavering."

"How just exactly like Githa Hamilton!" commented Hilda Smart, as the girls resumed their interrupted ride.

After all, they arrived at the station with five minutes to spare, just long enough to book their excursion tickets and to leave their bicycles in the left-luggage office. They were fortunate enough to find an empty carriage, and crammed themselves in somehow; it was rather a tight fit for a dozen, but it felt so much jollier to be all together. Chiplow was an hour's journey away; a few of the party had been there before, but to most it was a new experience. The abbey was one of the show places of the county, and the old town had a historic reputation. There was plenty to be seen in the streets alone: the houses were of the sixteenth century, and very picturesque — many of them with carved wooden pillars, and with dates and coats-of-arms over the doorways. Miss Aubrey took her charges into the church, a dim, ancient edifice with a leper window, a sounding-board over the pulpit, and, almost hidden away in the transept, a "ducking-stool for scolds". The girls looked at the curious old instrument of punishment with great curiosity; and Githa, who had brought her camera, took a time exposure of it.

"Poor old souls!" said Katrine. "It was too bad to souse them in the pond just because they waxed too eloquent. I've no doubt the husbands deserved it. If everybody who talks too much nowadays were treated to the cold-water cure, we should be a taciturn set."

"It might be a wholesome warning in some cases," laughed Miss Aubrey. "It's really very trying when people babble on all about nothing, and insist upon one's listening to them."

After lunch at a café in the town, the party adjourned to the abbey, a most romantic ruin, standing among woods by the side of a river. The monks of old must have been true artists to choose such unrivalled sites on which to rear their glorious architecture. It was an exquisite jewel in a perfect setting, and Miss Aubrey was soon in ecstasies over delicate pieces of tracery and perpendicular windows. She set her class to work on an arched gateway overhung by a graceful silver-birch tree. It was not a particularly easy subject, and most of them did not accomplish more than the drawing, though Katrine and Nan managed to put on a little colour during the last half-hour. Everyone was very loath to leave when Miss Aubrey at last declared it was time to close the sketch-books. Their train was due at six, and they must have tea before starting, so it was impossible to linger any longer.

Katrine had bought a guide-book at the abbey, and studied it over the tea-table at the café. She was dismayed to find how many objects of interest in the town they had missed.

"I should like to see the old house where Mary Queen of Scots stayed," she exclaimed. "It's only just down the street here. Miss Aubrey, Gwethyn and I have finished tea; may we go and look at it? We'll be ever so quick."

"You can if you like, but don't miss the train. If you turn up Cliff Street, exactly opposite the hospital, it will bring you straight to the station, and save your walking back here. Six o'clock, remember!"

"Oh, thank you! There's heaps of time. Come, Gwethyn!"

The Marsdens marched off with their guide-book, and easily found the old house in question, which was now used as an Alms Hospital for superannuated and disabled soldiers. They so dutifully curtailed their inspection of it, that Katrine declared they might safely go and look at the ruins of the city gate, which, according to her guide, must be quite close by. Whether the book was unreliable, or whether Katrine, in her haste, missed the right turning, is uncertain, but after wandering vainly round several streets the girls found themselves down by the bank of the river.

"You said we had plenty of time, but you didn't look at your watch," panted Gwethyn. "If that clock over there is right, we shall never catch ourtrain. Oh, you are a genius to-day! A prince of path-finders!"

Katrine came to a sudden halt. Gwethyn's remarks were unpalatable, but strictly true. There were exactly ten minutes to spare. To go back to the station would require at least twenty.

"It's the only train available by our excursion tickets," wailed Gwethyn. "I believe there's a later one about nine or ten o'clock, but they'll make us pay the difference between cheap bookings and ordinary fare."

"I can see the glass roof of the station across the river, and there's a bridge in front of us. It's probably a short cut, and will save half the distance," announced Katrine hopefully. "Come along! Perhaps we can just do it!"

The girls scurried forward in frantic haste. What convenient things bridges were! Why, of course, there was the railway quite close on the other side. They tore across the creaking planks in triumph, feeling that every step brought them nearer to the station. But alas! for the vanity of human wishes! The farther side of the bridge was closed by a turnstile, and a fiend in human form was basely and mercenarily demanding the one thing in the world which at present they could not muster—a penny toll! It seemed absurd to be in the depths of destitution, but it was the fact. They had given the money for the day's excursion to Miss Aubrey, who acted as paymaster for the whole party, and the few pence they had kept they had spent on the guide-book and some chocolates. To be at one's last penny is a proverbial expression, but Katrine and Gwethyn had never before realized the dire extremity of being absolutely without a single specimen of that useful coin of the realm. They rummaged in their pockets, hoping against hope that some stray copper might have slipped into an obscure corner, and have been overlooked. Gwethyn even felt the bottom of her coat, in case a threepenny-bit could have strayed between the material and the lining. In the meantime the keeper of the bridge stood with outstretched hand, awaiting his dues, casting an impatient eye back into his toll-house, where his tea was rapidly cooling upon the table.

"We find we haven't any money with us," faltered Katrine at last. "Would you please let us through without, and we'd send you stamps to-morrow?"

"Couldn't do it," responded the man surlily. "This bridge is a cash concern, and I never give credit."

"But we want to catch a train," pleaded Gwethyn, "and there isn't time to go back through the town."

"Our tickets are only available by this train, and our friends are waiting for us at the station," added Katrine.

"I've heard tales like this before! Don't you try to come over me! You either pays your pennies, or you won't go through this gate!"

"If we left something as a pledge?" cried Katrine in despair. "Here's my paint-box, or my coat, or—yes, even my watch!"

"You must let us pass!" declared Gwethyn tragically.

"Must, indeed! I'm put here in charge of the bridge, and a pretty thing it would be if I was to let everyone through scot-free! I've my orders, and I'll do my duty," said the toll-keeper officiously, waving away the articles which Katrine was vainly trying to press upon him.

The poor girls were waxing hysterical. The precious moments were hurrying by, and already a suggestive whistle in the distance gave ominous warning of the approaching train. To be left behind in Chiplow was a prospect too appalling even to contemplate. They had serious thoughts of either attempting to push past the official, or to make a dash and climb the railings, both of which proceedings would be equally undignified and illegal.

At this desperate and critical moment a little figure suddenly rushed up from behind—a gasping, panting figure, with hair flying in wild elf locks, and pale cheeks scarlet for once.

"Open the gate quick!" it commanded. "Threepence? Here you are! Come on! We'll just do it!"

There was no time even to greet their deliverer. The three girls simply tore along the road that led to the station, with their eyes fixed on the signal, which was already down. The Toadstool was swift of foot, and had indomitable pluck, or, winded already, she could never have managed that last wild spurt.

"Caught it by the skin of our teeth!" exclaimed Katrine a minute and a half later, as, nearly exhausted, the girls were hustled into a compartment by the distracted Miss Aubrey, just the moment before the train started. "Oh, dear! I've never had such a scramble in all my life! I'm half dead!"

"Githa Hamilton, you're an absolute trump!" whispered Gwethyn, when she recovered sufficient breath for speech. "That horrid man wouldn't let us through. We should have had to stop in Chiplow. It was good of you to come after us!"

"No, it wasn't!" snapped the Toadstool rather gaspily. "I did it to please Miss Aubrey; I didn't care twopence about you two. She was getting anxious, so I said I'd follow you and round you up somehow. A precious job I had, asking people if they'd seen two girls in Panama hats! Whatever induced you to go down by the river? You pair of sillies! It would have just served you jolly well right if you'd been left in Chiplow after all!"

CHAPTER VII

The Mad Hatters

IF Katrine was determined that her career at Aireyholme should be "Art before all", Gwethyn's school motto might be described as "Fun at any price". Her high spirits were continually at effervescing point, and she was fast acquiring the reputation of "champion ragger" of the Fifth. There were rollicking times in the form, jokes and chaff to an even greater extent than had obtained before her advent. Half a dozen of the girls had always been lively, but now, under Gwethyn's sway, their escapades earned them the title of the "Mad Hatters". The influence spread downwards and infected the juniors. Eight members of the Fourth formed themselves into a league dubbed "The March Hares", and by the wildness of their pranks sought to outdo their seniors. There was a rivalry of jokes between them, and whichever scored the most points for the time held the palm. Needless to say, their efforts were scarcely appreciated at head-quarters. Things considered intensely diverting by the form were viewed very differently by mistresses and monitresses, and both Hatters and Hares were liable to find themselves in trouble.

I have mentioned that Katrine and Gwethyn slept in a little room over the porch. The door was in the middle of a long passage leading to other bedrooms, occupied by the Fourth and Fifth. The Aireyholme dormitory discipline was tolerably strict, and usually the girls were a well-conducted crew.

One morning some unlucky star caused Gwethyn to open her eyes before the usual 6.30 bell, and aroused in her a spirit of mischief. Taking her pillow, she stole along the passage to No. 9, and awoke Marian, Susie, and Megan.

"Come along!" she proclaimed. "Let's find Dona and Beatrix, and go and rout up the March Hares. There's time for a little artillery practice before the bell rings. Bolsters are heavy ammunition, and pillows light. You can take your choice! Anyone refusing to do battle will be proclaimed coward.

All the fallen will be buried with the honours of war. Get up, you soft Sybarites!"

Finding their bedclothes on the floor, and severe tickling the penalty of a love for slumber, the occupants of the various dormitories on the landing turned out and followed their leader.

"Hares versus Hatters!" commanded Gwethyn. "You may duck and dodge, but anyone fairly hit is to be considered fallen. The bedrooms are trenches. Remember, mum's the word, though!"

The battle began, and waged fiercely. The missiles flew hither and thither. Some of the girls were good shots, but others had the proverbial feminine incapacity for a true aim. There were wildly thrilling encounters, frantic chasings, and wholesale routs. In their excitement the combatants completely forgot the necessity for silence; they chuckled, groaned, hooted, and even squealed. Small wonder that, long before the fight was fought to a finish, an avenging deity in a dressing-gown appeared upon the scene and proclaimed a compulsory peace.

"Girls! Whatever are you doing?" demanded Viola. "You ought to be thoroughly ashamed of yourselves. Go back to your rooms at once! You know this kind of thing is not allowed."

The delinquents seized their missiles and beat a hurried retreat, while Viola, who was wise in her generation, sounded the bell as a signal for the rest of the school to rise and dress.

"They'll get into mischief again if I leave them larking about in their rooms, and it won't do anybody any harm to be up a quarter of an hour earlier for once," she decided. "But I'll see they put in the extra time at preparation. The young wretches!"

The head girl was as good as her word. She kept a stern eye on the sinners directly they appeared downstairs.

"The morning's a good time to work," she announced grimly. "If you're fond of early rising, I'll call you all every day at six, and arrange for prep. at half-past instead of at seven. No doubt you'd benefit by it."

The jokers, who had not calculated upon an increased allowance of school hours, sought their desks glumly. But there was a further trial in store for them. When they were seated at breakfast, Mrs. Franklin took her place at the table with an air of long-suffering and injured patience.

"Girls!" she began, in a martyred voice, "I have been most hurt, most pained, at what occurred this morning. Anything more thoughtless and inconsiderate I could not have imagined. I had passed a bad night, and I was snatching a short sleep, when I was awakened by an uproar that is without all precedent. When Ermengarde was here, such a thing never occurred. There was a different spirit abroad in the school. Every girl, even the youngest junior, was careful for my comfort, and would not have dreamed of disturbing me. I fear now an entirely selfish feeling prevails in the Fifth and Fourth Forms. I am grieved to see it. Our traditions at Aireyholme have been very high. I beg the standard may never be lowered."

No names were mentioned, but Hares and Hatters were conscious that the eyes of the rest of the school were fixed upon them with scornful reproach. They ate their breakfast in a state of dejection.

"I never dreamed Mrs. Franklin would take it that way!" mourned Rose afterwards to her fellow-delinquents.

"Diana Bennett says we are a set of brutes," sighed Beatrix ruefully. She admired Diana, and winced under her scorn.

"The others were wild at getting extra prep. this morning. They're ready to take it out of us," remarked Susie.

"Look here," said Gwethyn, "I think the best way to settle the whole business will be to go and apologize to Mrs. Franklin. Say we didn't know she had a headache, and we're sorry. That ought to square things."

"Right-o! Then Diana may stop nagging."

At the eleven-o'clock interval a dozen girls reported themselves at the Principal's study, and with Rose as spokeswoman, tendered an embarrassed apology. Mrs. Franklin was not inclined to treat the matter too lightly; she considered herself justly offended; but after listening with due gravity, she solemnly and majestically forgave them.

"I suppose I cannot expect all to be as naturally thoughtful and kind-hearted as Ermengarde," she added, "but I try to stand in the place of a mother to you here, and I hope to meet with some response."

I am afraid Mrs. Franklin would have been grieved again if she had heard the laughter that ensued when the girls were out of ear-shot of the study. They were really sorry to have hurt her feelings, but the mention of the impeccable Ermengarde was always a subject for mirth.

"I have it on absolute authority that Ermengarde once made another girl an apple-pie bed!" tittered Susie. "It was Nell Stokes who told me. She was at Aireyholme then, and slept in the same dormitory."

"What happened?"

"History doesn't relate. I should say Saint Ermie got disciplined and did penance. She wasn't canonized then!"

Although Mrs. Franklin was apt to be a little pompous and over stately, she was very good to the pupils on the whole, and they thoroughly respected her. They sympathized deeply with her anxiety for news from the war, where her two sons were serving their country. Many of the girls had brothers or cousins in the Army, and each morning an enthusiastic crowd collected to hear the items which Mrs. Franklin read out to them. They were not allowed to look at the daily papers for themselves, as Mrs. Franklin considered many of the details unsuitable for their perusal; but she gave them a carefully-edited summary of the course of events, with special particulars, if possible, of regiments in which they were interested. The occasional letters received by girls from relatives at the front were subjects for great rejoicing. They compared notes keenly over the experiences related. Katrine and Gwethyn scored considerably, for their brother Hereward was a fairly regular correspondent, and gave vivid accounts of his campaigning. It was at Gwethyn's suggestion that the school held what they called a "Heroes' Exhibition". Every girl with a relative engaged in the war was requested to lend his photograph, any chance snapshots she might have of him, any newspaper cuttings narrating his achievements, and any of his regimental buttons, if she were lucky enough to possess them. These contributions were arranged on a table with an appropriate background of flags and sprigs of laurel. A penny each was charged for admission, and catalogues of the exhibits were sold at one halfpenny. As all the girls, the mistresses, and three of the servants patronized the show, the sum of five shillings and twopence halfpenny was cleared, and put in the Belgian Relief Fund Box. Gwethyn had wished to add a competition with votes for the handsomest hero, but Mrs. Franklin sternly vetoed the idea.

"It would have been ever such fun, and the girls would have loved it!" Gwethyn assured her chums in private, "but of course I see the reason. Mrs. Franklin's sons may be very estimable, but they're both plain, and of course Hereward's photo would have won the most votes; he's by far the best-looking!"

"You utter goose! That wasn't the reason," snubbed Rose Randall. "Besides which, if it comes to a question of looks, your brother isn't in the running with my cousin Everard."

Gwethyn's fertile brain was continually at work. In spite of the madness of some of her propositions, she was really an acquisition to the Fifth. She could always be counted upon for new suggestions, and on wet days she would invent games, get up charades, or engineer impromptu entertainments with the ingenuity of a variety manager. One afternoon the heavy rain prevented the girls from taking their usual outdoor exercise between dinner and school. Very disconsolately they hung about, grumbling at the downpour. Only the Sixth Form were privileged to use the studio on such occasions; the younger ones, flung on their own resources, killed time as best they could. The Fourth suffered more particularly, as it was their afternoon for the tennis courts, and they had had bad luck lately in the matter of weather on their special tennis days.

"I declare, I'm sorry for those poor kids!" said Gwethyn. "This is the third Wednesday their sets have been stopped. They are standing in the corridor, looking like a funeral. Can't we liven them up somehow?"

"All serene! Let's ask them into our form room and play games," agreed Rose. "Where are the rest of us? Jill, go and hunt up Susie and Beatrix. It's far more fun when there are plenty. I say, you kiddies there, come along and have some jinks! Pass the word on."

The juniors responded promptly to the invitation. They flocked into the Fifth room, and settled themselves anywhere, on desks or floor.

"What's the game?" they asked hopefully.

"It's quite a new one," explained Gwethyn, who had had a hasty private conference with some of her chums. "It's called 'The Oracle of Fortune'. I'm to be blindfolded so that I can't see the least peep; then you're all to march round me in a circle. When I tap with this stick, you stop, and I point at somebody who comes forward."

"Oh, I know! French blind-man's-buff. That's nothing new!" exclaimed Madge Carter.

"No, it's not French blind-man's-buff," returned Gwethyn, so crushingly that Madge was sorry she had spoken. "I don't feel your faces while you giggle—it's something quite different. I tell your characters. If they're correct, you walk on. If I make a mistake, you may take my place as oracle."

"Who's to judge if they're right?"

"The general opinion!" frowned Gwethyn.

"But suppose— —"

"Oh, suppress that dormouse!" exclaimed some of the March Hares. "Where is there a big handkerchief to bind your eyes? You mustn't have the least little teeny weeny scrap of a peep-hole left. We'll take care of that."

Bandaged to the entire satisfaction of all spectators, Gwethyn took her place in the centre of the room, and the girls commenced to circle round her. At a rap from her stick they halted. She pointed blindly to an unknown figure, who stepped silently forward.

"List to the Oracle!" proclaimed Gwethyn dramatically. "Sweet temper, kindness, and modesty here go hand in hand. Pass on, gentle maiden, thou art worthy!"

Bertha Grant, a small and inoffensive junior, retired into the ring amid the applause of the audience, and the march continued. At the next halt Myrtle Goodwin, a particularly turbulent and mischievous member of the Fourth, responded to the rap.

"Whom have we here?" murmured the Oracle. "Alas! my inner sense tells me this is imp, not angel. Go and amend thy misdeeds. I feel the darkness of thy shadow."

Again a round of clapping certified to the correctness of the character given. The girls began to think the game rather fun. Laura Browne happened to be the next chosen.

"Fair on the surface, but false below," was the verdict. "The professed friend of everybody, but the chum of nobody. Full of promises, but shy of performance."

"She can see! She must be able to see!" shouted the girls, much struck by the aptness of the remarks.

"No, I can't. Not one hair-breadth. Look at my bandages for yourselves," declared Gwethyn emphatically (though she murmured "Done you, Laura Browne!" under her breath). "Does anybody imagine I can see through two silk handkerchiefs? I haven't Röntgen-ray eyes!"

72

The real fact was that Gwethyn and Rose had arranged beforehand a code of signals. The characters were to be of three classes—good, moderate, and bad. When the march stopped and a girl stepped forward, Rose was to give her confederate the required information by means of a cough, a tap on the floor, or a laugh. For certain of the girls, special signals of identification had been arranged. Laura was one of these, and as luck would have it, the lot had fallen to her early in the game.

"Go on and try me again," commanded Gwethyn. "Anyone who likes may consult the gipsy."

At the next halt Rose signalled as usual, and the Oracle responded.

"Whom have we here? A junior remarkable for her charm of disposition, a girl with many friends, a favourite in her form——"

Here Gwethyn was interrupted by an outburst of giggles.

"Wrong for once!"

"This doesn't fit!"

"The Oracle's not working!"

Gwethyn tore off the silk handkerchiefs that bandaged her eyes. She saw at once what had happened. Amid the noise of the tramping she had misinterpreted Rose's signal "junior bad" for "junior good". Instead of addressing one of the pattern members of the Fourth, she had been eulogizing Githa Hamilton. The poor little Toadstool stood with a very curious expression in her dark eyes. Keen delight was just fading into bitter disappointment. She looked round the circle of tittering girls. Not one endorsed the good character, or had a kind word to say for her—all were clamouring against the falseness of this description. Her face hardened. Gwethyn perceived it in a flash. "Does she really care what they think of her?" she speculated. Gwethyn's instinct was always to fight on behalf of the losing side, and at this moment Githa seemed to stand alone against the whole room. Moreover, the Oracle was not disposed to own up that she had made a mistake. She stuck, therefore, to her guns.

"If Githa's not a favourite, she ought to be. It's your own lack of appreciation. Where are your eyes? She's a jewel, if you'd the sense to see it. There, I'm sick of the whole business. If anybody likes to take my place, I'll resign. Or shall we play something else instead?"

Perhaps the girls thought the game was growing rather too personal. Nobody offered to act gipsy, and someone hurriedly suggested "Clumps". In less than a minute the crowd had divided into two close circles, and the catechism of "animal", "vegetable", or "mineral" began briskly.

Githa took no open notice of Gwethyn's unexpected championship, but from that afternoon her attitude changed. Instead of continually snapping, or exercising her wit in sharp little remarks, she was unusually quiet. She would watch Gwethyn without speaking, and often followed her about the school, though always at a short distance and with no apparent intention.

It was at this crisis that Gwethyn one morning received bad news. Tony, her Pekinese spaniel, and the idol of her heart, had been put out to board when the Marsdens left home. His foster-mistress, a respectable working woman, wrote occasionally to record his progress. Hitherto her letters hadbeen satisfactory, but to-day her report was serious. Katrine found Gwethyn weeping violently in the sanctum of their bedroom.

"What's the matter?" she asked in some anxiety.

"Matter! Oh! whatever am I to do? Read this."

"DEAR MISS MARSDEN,

"I did not answer your inquiries before about the poor little dog, hoping he might pick up a bit, but indeed he frets like to break his heart. The children next door worries him, and he won't eat, and he has gone that thin it is pitiful to see him. I do my best, but he does not like being here. He is getting just a bag of bones, and my husband says it is nothing but home-sickness. Will you please tell me what I am to do about him?

"Your obedient servant,

MARY CARTER."

"The darling! The poor darling! Breaking his little heart for his missis!" sobbed Gwethyn. "I knew he'd never be happy at the Carters' cottage. A bag of bones! Oh, my Tony! Katrine, have you got a penny stamp?"

The girls at Aireyholme were not supposed to send letters without submitting them first to a mistress, but the rule was not very strictly enforced, and Gwethyn had no difficulty in answering by return of post. What she said to Mrs. Carter she did not reveal even to Katrine. Through the whole of that day and the next, she went about with a look of mingled anxiety and triumph on her face.

At four o'clock on the following afternoon, just when the girls were coming from their classes, there was a bustle at the side door. A porter with a hand-cart from the railway station was delivering a large hamper. Mrs. Franklin chanced to be passing at the moment, and stopped to make inquiries.

"A hamper? For whom? Miss G. Marsden! And labelled 'Live Stock, with Care'! What does this mean?"

Gwethyn, coming out of the Fifth Form room, caught sight of the hand-cart, and with a cry of ecstasy made a rush for the hamper.

"It's Tony! My darling Tony! Oh, my pretty boy! where are you?"

Pulling her penknife from her pocket, she cut the cords in a trice, and opening the lid, clutched her whimpering pet in her arms. A crowd of girls collected to see what was happening. Mrs. Franklin thought it high time to interfere.

"Gwethyn Marsden, whose dog is this?" she asked sharply.

"He's mine! We left him at a cottage when we shut up our house, but he fretted, so I told Mrs. Carter to send him here. He wanted his missis."

"You sent for this dog on your own authority? And without asking my permission?"

75

"He was breaking his heart!"

"You have taken the most unwarrantable liberty!" Mrs. Franklin was bridling with indignation. "I cannot allow you to keep this dog. It must be sent back."

"Oh no, please, please!" implored Gwethyn. "He'll die if he has to go back. I won't let him be one scrap of trouble. He'd sleep on my bed."

"Impossible!" said the Principal firmly. "Do you think I am going to relax all the rules of the school in your favour? You have been indulged too much already. There are thirty-six pupils here, and if each one wished to keep a pet the place would be a menagerie. I cannot make an exception in your case. It was most impertinent of you to write and arrange for the animal to be sent."

Matters had reached the point of tragedy. Mrs. Franklin for once was really angry. She considered that the Marsdens were not sufficiently amenable to school discipline at any time, but this breach was beyond all bounds. Gwethyn hugged Tony tightly, and wept stubborn tears. Then Githa Hamilton stepped to the rescue.

"Please, Mrs. Franklin, instead of sending the little dog back, might I take him home with me until the end of the term? My own fox-terrier died two months ago, and my uncle said I could have another dog."

It was such a splendid solution of the difficulty that even the Principal's face cleared. Gwethyn wiped her eyes, and beamed encouragement.

"Are you sure your uncle and aunt would consent?" asked Mrs. Franklin, hopefully but doubtfully.

"Oh, yes! They said I might take the first nice puppy that was offered me; so I know it's all right."

"Then I shall be very much obliged if you will accept the charge of this dog."

"I'll be only too glad."

"Githa, you absolute angel!" murmured Gwethyn, pressing her treasure into the Toadstool's hospitable arms as Mrs. Franklin, mollified at last, turned into the house.

"Angels don't have khaki-coloured complexions!"

"Yes, they do — the nicest sort! I don't care for the golden-headed kind. At this moment you're my beau-ideal of blessedness."

"Toadstools savour of elves, not angels!" Githa was well aware of her nickname. "But look here! I'll take good care of the little chap, and make him happy. I'll smuggle him to school sometimes, so that you can see him. I could shut him up in the tool-house, if I square Fuller."

"Your collie won't devour him?" Gwethyn asked, with a sudden burst of anxiety.

"Rolf never touches small dogs. He's a gentleman in that. Don't you worry. Tony'll be quite safe, and he'll soon fatten up with plenty of milk, and a garden to run about in. Bless him! He's taking to his new missis already. There, precious one!"

"I want him back at the holidays," cried Gwethyn jealously. "He's not to forget me."

"Right you are! Hold him while I get my hat and my bike. I don't think I can carry him and ride — he'd wriggle. I'll have to wheel my machine home. There, kiss his nose just once more, and let him go!"

CHAPTER VIII

An Adventure

THE transference of Tony cemented the friendship between Gwethyn and Githa. With such a precious bond to unite them, intimacy followed as a matter of course. On closer acquaintance the little Toadstool proved quite an interesting companion; she was humorous and amusing, and though not demonstrative, seemed to have a store of affection hidden behind the barrier of her reserve. She was seldom confidential, but every now and then she would open her heart the least little bit, and give Gwethyn a peep at her real feelings.

"Why did you take such a spite against me when first I came?" asked the latter in one of these rare moments.

"I don't know! I liked you and yet I hated you! I think it was because you and Katrine sprung yourselves so suddenly on me that morning in the orchard. You caught me in my old pinafore feeding the fowls. You both looked so smart, and you marched up so confidently asking for milk, and evidently taking me for a farm girl. I could have thrown stones at you! I thought you were conceited, and I'd try and take you down a peg."

"You certainly did your best. You were absolutely vitriolic!"

"Well, I'm sorry. No, I'm not! You were rather conceited at first. You and Katrine thought you'd just run the show at Aireyholme. You're ever so much nicer now. Don't be offended! I always say what I think. You know that by this time."

The Toadstool was certainly apt to carry the virtue of frankness beyond all bounds, and to allow it to degenerate into a vice. Gwethyn, however, was a very even-tempered girl, and instead of taking offence she only laughed good-humouredly at most of Githa's remarks, and told her not to be a little wasp. In the circumstances it was the best possible treatment. People who are fond of making smart and stinging remarks are always disconcerted if they fall flat. Gwethyn's good-natured toleration made Githa rather ashamed of herself. Insensibly she was catching her new friend's tone. The habit of perpetually sharpening her wit upon her companions began to slip away; not all at once, for habits are a strong growth, but by distinctly perceptible degrees. Even the girls noticed a difference. "Spitfire isn't half so venomous as she used to be," was the general verdict.

Though Githa might practise plain speaking where other people were concerned, she was extremely reserved on the subject of her own affairs. Only very occasionally would she wax confidential and talk about her home life. Even then the scraps of information seemed to escape her unwillingly. From the few hints thus dropped, and from what the other girls could tell, Gwethyn pieced together the main outline of her friend's childhood. It was a sad little story. Lilac Grange had been full of tragedy. Six years ago, when on a visit there, Githa's father, mother, and two elder sisters had fallen victims to a virulent outbreak of diphtheria, and had died within a few days of one another. The boy and girl, the sole survivors of the family, were adopted by their grandfather, and had lived with him at the Grange until his sudden death three years afterwards. Old Mr. Ledbury had often mentioned that he meant to make provision for his two grandchildren, but apparently he had allowed the months to slip by without fulfilling his intention. When his affairs were investigated, the only will which could be discovered was one dated ten years back, in which he left his entire fortune to his elder son, Wilfred Ledbury. At that time he had quarrelled with his daughter, Githa's mother, but a reconciliation had followed shortly afterwards, and the Hamiltons had stayed at the Grange on quite friendly terms. Mr. Ledbury had had another son, Frank, a headstrong, unsettled fellow, who had also quarrelled with his hot-tempered father and had gone away to America. That Frank should be entirely cut out of any inheritance, though unjust, was not surprising; but the neighbourhood agreed that to leave the orphan grandchildren penniless was an open scandal, and that old Mr. Ledbury had failed in his duty by neglecting to make a will in their favour.

Ill-natured people even whispered sometimes that Mr. Wilfred Ledbury, who had been on the spot at the time of his father's death, had spent the night hunting through his papers, and had probably suppressed any document that was not to his advantage. Such stories, however, were only in the nature of gossip. Nothing could be proved. Nobody had seen, or witnessed, a later will, and Mr. Wilfred Ledbury stepped unchallenged into his heritage. After all, it was not as good as he had expected. A number of securities, which he had believed his father to possess, turned out to have been disposed of beforehand, though what had become of the purchase-money it was impossible to tell. Old Mr. Ledbury had been fond of speculating on the Stock Exchange, and he had probably lost it in some unlucky venture. Mrs. Wilfred, thinking the Grange unhealthy, had refused to go and live there, so the furniture was sold, and the old house was to let, though so far no tenant had yet been found to take it. Mr. Wilfred Ledbury was a solicitor in Carford, and owned a pretty house in a much more open and airy situation four miles beyond Heathwell. His daughter was married (to his partner in the firm), and his sons were grown up, one practising at the Bar in London, and the other a professor at Cambridge. His whole interest was centred in his own children and their prospects. He had taken charge of his nephew and niece after his father's death, and gave them a home and education, but he let them feel that he considered them an encumbrance. The boarding-school which he chose for Cedric was not altogether suitable, but he would not listen to the boy's complaints, or inquire into the justice of his grievances. Githa he simply ignored. He paid the bills for her schooling and clothes, but took no notice of her. She kept out of his way as much as possible, and rarely spoke to him unless he asked her a question.

Mrs. Ledbury was not unkind, but did not care to be troubled with her niece. She left Githa almost entirely to her own devices. Except when her brother came back for the holidays the poor child led a lonely life at her uncle's home. She amused herself mostly out of doors. She was fond of animals, kept a few rabbits and white mice in a disused stable, and liked to help to look after the poultry. In the house she was suppressed and quiet, generally with her nose buried in a book. Her aunt said that she was a most unresponsive, tiresome, and unaccountable child, with no sense of gratitude for all that was done for her. The one person in the world whom Githa worshipped was her brother Cedric. She lived for his return from school, and the holidays spent with him were her landmarks for the year. At present she bestowed the wealth of her surplus affection upon Tony. He was a fascinating little dog, and so well-behaved that Mrs. Ledbury offered no objections to his temporary adoption. She was really kind to her niece in the matter of allowing her to keep pets. Tony took to his new mistress with an enthusiasm that would have disgusted Gwethyn, had she seen it. But Githa was discreet enough not to descant too much upon his blandishments, and keep his affection as a delightful secret between herself and him.

"I took you first of all to please Gwethyn, you precious!" she would say, kissing his silky head; "but now you're like my own, and what I'll do when I've got to give you up I don't know!"

Gwethyn, ignorant of the fickle Tony's lightly transferred allegiance, would ask eagerly for news of him each morning. She kept a snapshot of him on her dressing-table, and urged Githa to take the earliest opportunity of smuggling him to school for a day. But Githa, under the plea of the gardener's lack of connivance, and fear of Mrs. Franklin's wrath, always managed to find some excuse, and put the matter off to a future date.

The Marsdens had been again to the Grange with Miss Aubrey, and had finished their sketches of the dovecot. It was a pretty subject, and the result was quite successful. Katrine, contemplating her canvas in the studio on the following afternoon, was frankly pleased.

"We're both improving," she said to Gwethyn (the two girls had the room to themselves for once). "I like Miss Aubrey's style of teaching immensely. It's just what I wanted. She's helped me enormously. By the by, I lost my best penknife at the Grange yesterday. I must have dropped it somewhere by my camp-stool."

"What a nuisance! But you have another?"

"Not so good. I don't mean to abandon that dear little pearl-handled one. Will you come with me now, and we'll go and look for it?"

"Right-o! The Grange is out of bounds, but who cares?"

"Certainly I don't! Mrs. Franklin's rules are ridiculous for a girl of my age. Surely I can go and fetch my penknife? Besides, we needn't go by the road. If we climb the fence in the orchard we can cut across the fields as the crow flies, and get into the lane by the big gate of the Grange."

"I'm your girl! Let's toddle off at once. If any one croaks I'm sure we can call the fields within bounds."

"I'm not going to be bound by bounds. Mrs. Franklin is a bounder!" retorted Katrine grandly.

Nevertheless, she did not make her exit over the orchard fence until she was sure no one was watching. Choosing a suitable moment, the girls scaled the low bars, then skirted round by the hedge along the field till they were out of sight of Aireyholme. By this short cut it was only a few minutes' walk to the Grange.

The old house seemed more than ever like a story-book palace with an enchanted garden. The lilacs were fading, but the tangle of greenery had grown taller and wilder, and even the very windows were invaded and half covered by long trails of bindweed and traveller's joy that stretched out quickly spreading shoots and clinging tendrils, and threatened to bury everything in a mass of vegetation.

"How absolutely still and quiet it is!" said Katrine. "I don't suppose a soul ever comes near except ourselves. It doesn't look as if a footstep had been across the grass for a long time. Why, here's my penknife, on the walk. I must have dropped it out of my painting-bag. I'm so glad I've found it."

"It's well we came this afternoon. It would have rusted if it had lain there much longer. I wonder what the old house is like inside?"

"Probably very dark and damp, with the windows shaded and unopened."

"It looks gloomy — as if people had died there."

"It is sad to see it so neglected and overgrown. One feels Nature has been too exuberant, she doesn't care about our little lives and tragedies, it doesn't matter to her what has been suffered here. She just pushes that all to one side and forgets, and goes on making fresh shoots as if nothing had happened."

"I think it's kind of her to try and throw a lovely green veil over the place. It's like charity covering a multitude of sins. She's doing her best in her own way to soften down the tragedy. I'm going to lift her veil and take a peep inside," and Gwethyn pulled back a mass of succulent briony and peered through the dim glass.

"Can you see anything?"

"Yes, I can see a hall and long passage. It looks interesting. This window is not latched. I believe I could push it up if you'd help me. Heave-o! There, it's actually open."

The girls found themselves peering into a small room, which was apparently the vestibule of a hall. The window was not placed very high, so low indeed that Gwethyn scrambled without much difficulty on to the sill.

"I'm going in!" she declared. "It will be ever such fun to explore. I always wondered what the inside was like."

She dropped quite easily on to the floor within, and gave a hand to Katrine, who was not slow in following. Both felt it would be an adventure to investigate the interior of the old house. They stood still for a moment, listening, but not a sound was to be heard, so they ventured to go forward.

"I believe we have the place absolutely and entirely to ourselves, unless there are a few ghosts flitting about the passages! They'd seem moresuitable inhabitants than human beings!" proclaimed Gwethyn.

Several sitting-rooms led from the hall, which by their decorations proclaimed their use. The one with the rosewood fittings was undoubtedly the dining-room, the larger one with the big bow window could not fail to be the drawing-room, and the one to the back, with the oak panelling, must surely be a study or library. The wall-papers were very faded and dilapidated, and the paint dingy; there was an air of shabbiness about everything, the numerous damp-stains, the cobwebs, the odd heaps of straw and the thick dust helped to render it unattractive, and the general impression was forlorn in the extreme.

"I don't wonder nobody takes it," said Gwethyn. "I should say it will be to let for years and years. Why doesn't Mr. Ledbury tidy it up?"

"Perhaps he thinks it's no use spending the money unless he has a possible tenant. Even if he papered and painted it, it would soon get into the same state if no one lived here."

"He might have a caretaker."

"Yes, I wonder he doesn't. I expect it's so far away from the village that nobody would come without being very highly paid, and he couldn't afford that when he's getting no rent."

How large the place seemed! The girls peeped into empty room after empty room, their footsteps echoing in that strange hollow fashion that is only noticed in deserted houses.

"It gives me the shivers, it's so wretched," said Gwethyn. "I certainly shouldn't like to live here. I think we've been nearly all round. Shall we godownstairs again? Wait! There's just this one passage that leads somewhere."

"Haven't you seen enough?"

"My curiosity is insatiable."

Katrine hesitated. One room was exactly like another. It did not seem worth while to explore further. She half turned in the direction of the stairs; then noticing that the passage was panelled, and thinking that the room at the end might therefore be older and quainter than the rest, she changed her mind. After all, it was disappointing, as bare and empty as the others, with torn paper hanging in strips from the damp walls.

"There's a fine view of the dovecot though," said Katrine. "I can see the carving on the gable beautifully from here."

She flung the window open wide. The fresh wholesome outside air came rushing in. The draught banged the door, and a sound of something falling followed, but the girls were too occupied to take any notice. They were leaning out of the window trying to decipher the date on the worn piece of carving.

"It looks like 1600," opined Gwethyn.

"More likely 1690. The tail of the nine is cracked away. It's older than the house at any rate. I wish I had my sketch-book here, and I'd have copied it. Have you a note-book in your pocket?"

"No; and I shouldn't lend it to you if I had. We must be going at once, or we shall be late for prep."

Katrine consulted her watch, and turned to the door. Then she gave a cry of consternation. It was impossible to open it. The knob had been loose, and when the door banged the whole handle had fallen out into the passage. They were shut in as securely as if by bolt and bar. Here was a dilemma, indeed! They looked at one another in consternation.

"What are we to do?" faltered Gwethyn.

Katrine was trying to wedge the handle of her penknife into the empty socket, but the effort was useless. It went in a little way, but would not turn. Her attempt to slip back the catch with the blade was equally futile.

The unpleasant truth was hopelessly plain—they were prisoners in the empty house.

The prospect was appalling. The Grange was in such a secluded spot that nobody might come near for days. No doubt they would soon be missed at Aireyholme, but would Mrs. Franklin think of looking for them here? They shouted and called out of the window, but only the birds twittered in reply. They were in the upper story, a good height from the ground, and much too far to jump. The creepers were too frail to offer any adequate support.

They turned to the door again, and tried to break through one of the panels, but the wood was well-seasoned oak and resisted their kicks and blows. Were ever two girls in such a desperate situation? The tears were raining down Gwethyn's cheeks.

"Shall we have to stop here all night?" she sobbed. "I wish we'd never come near the wretched place!"

"We're trapped like rats in a cage!" declared Katrine, pacing distractedly up and down their prison. She paused at the window. "Gwethyn! I do believe somebody is in the garden! The blackbirds are making such a fuss!"

"Perhaps it's a cat or a hawk that's frightening them."

"Perhaps. But let us call in case it's a human being. Even a burglar would be welcome!"

"We're rather like burglars ourselves!" said Gwethyn, her sense of humour triumphing over her tears. "Only there certainly isn't anything here to burgle."

The girls leaned from the window and shouted with all the power of their lungs. Then they waited and listened anxiously. Was that a footstep crunching on the gravel.

"O jubilate! somebody's coming!" gasped Katrine. "Let's shout again! Oh, the angel!"

It was Mr. Freeman, sketching paraphernalia in hand, who stepped round the corner of the dovecot—a guardian angel in tweed knickers, smoking a most unangelic briar pipe. He looked about to see whence the noise proceeded, and, spying the girls, waved his hand.

"We're in an awful fix!" called Katrine. "We're locked into this room. Will you please climb in through the vestibule window—it's open—and let us out?"

"All right! I'll be up in half a jiff," replied Mr. Freeman, laying his painting traps on the dovecot steps.

In a few minutes they could hear him tramping up the stairs. He soon picked up the handle, fitted it in its socket, and opened the door. He regarded the girls with an amused smile of accusation.

"It strikes me you young ladies ought to be at school instead of exploring old houses on your own," he ventured in reply to their overwhelming thanks.

"We're going back now, and a jolly scrape we shall get into if we're not quick about it," said Gwethyn. "The Great Panjandrum will jaw us no end."

"Is your teacher capable of scolding?"

"Rather! You should just hear her!"

"She doesn't look it."

"Oh, you don't know her! She's all right in public, but she can be a Tartar in private!"

A shade passed over Mr. Freeman's face. He seemed disappointed.

"Oh, I don't mean Miss Aubrey!" put in Gwethyn quickly. "She's a darling. It's Mrs. Franklin I'm talking about. She's an absolutely different kind of person."

"Well, I'm glad to know somebody keeps you in order, for you seem to need it," laughed Mr. Freeman. "Have you heard from your father and mother again?"

"We had a letter on Sunday. They're getting on splendidly," replied Katrine. "Gwethyn, we must bolt!"

With renewed thanks and a hasty good-bye to their rescuer, the girls made their exit, and tore back over the fields to Aireyholme. They did not deserve any luck, but they managed to arrive in the very nick of time, and walked into their classrooms just as the preparation bell stopped ringing. The teachers, supposing them to be in the garden, had not noticed their absence. They had agreed to keep the adventure to themselves in case it should reach the ears of the monitresses, so Gwethyn heroically refrained from relating her thrilling experience to Rose or Susie. She had learnt by this time not to trust their tongues too far.

CHAPTER IX

The Tennis Championship

THE girls at Aireyholme did not go in for cricket, but concentrated the whole of their summer energies upon tennis. They practised constantly, and prided themselves upon their play. Dorrie Vernon was Games secretary, and calculated that she knew the exact capabilities of every girl in the school. Tournaments were the order of the term, sometimes — with handicaps — between different forms, sometimes "School versus Mistresses", for Miss Spencer and Miss Andrews were good players; and occasionally, when Mrs. Franklin entertained friends, a match was arranged for "Visitors versus Aireyholme". There were few schools in the neighbourhood against whom they could try their skill, but they had received an invitation to take part in a tournament at Carford Girls' College, and with Mrs. Franklin's sanction proposed to send two representatives. The choice of these champions was a subject of the very deepest importance. Dorrie went about the matter in a thoroughly business-like manner. She kept a tennis notebook, and carefully entered every girl's score, day by day, balancing the totals weekly. The results were discussed at the monitresses' meeting.

"Gladwin's play is fearfully off, this term," announced Dorrie. "Nan's a regular slacker, Tita is unequal — you never know whether she'll be brilliant or a dead failure. Coralie and Ellaline keep fairly well up to the mark; Hilda has improved simply immensely; our own record is satisfactory."

"May I see the notebook? Who has scored highest altogether?" asked Diana.

"Well — Katrine Marsden, by absolute points," admitted Dorrie, rather unwillingly.

The three monitresses scanned the book, and looked somewhat blank. It was an unpalatable truth that the new-comer had beaten the record. Katrine's swift serves were baffling; there was no doubt that she was an excellent player.

"It puts us in rather an awkward position," faltered Dorrie, wrinkling her brows.

"Not at all!" snapped Viola. "Katrine Marsden's out of the running for a championship."

"Well, I don't know — — "

"But I do know! She doesn't consider herself an ordinary pupil here, only what she chooses to call a 'parlour boarder'. Therefore she certainly can't represent the school — that's flat!"

"She played for Aireyholme against Visitors, though," objected Diana.

"Oh, well! That was different, of course. Miss Andrews played for Aireyholme too, but we couldn't choose her for a champion."

This was rather a convincing argument. Diana's face cleared. She was always ready to follow Viola's lead.

"We don't want Katrine, if we can help it," she agreed obediently.

"And yet we want to be sporting," vacillated Dorrie, who prided herself on strictest impartiality and fair dealing.

"Every committee has to have its rules. The school ought to be represented by its pupils."

"And that's the point. Is Katrine a pupil, or is she not?"

"Katrine says 'no'."

"But Mrs. Franklin says decidedly 'yes'."

"I think it's beyond argument," frowned Viola, "and, after all, I'm Captain, and final referee."

"Oh! if you put it that way, of course — — "

"I do put it that way. I consider it's only justice. If Katrine Marsden won't acknowledge herself on the same level with everyone else, she doesn't deserve to have our privileges. It can't be all take and no give on her part. There's no need for us to be so very tender about her feelings, I'm sure."

"Not the slightest need," echoed Diana. "It won't do her any harm to be passed over — good for her, in fact."

"We may as well pose as philanthropists while we're about it," twinkled Viola, suddenly seeing the humour of the situation. The three girls laughed.

"All the same, you're only looking at the matter from one side," contended Dorrie. "We've got the credit of the school to think about. The question is, who's likely to score highest for Aireyholme at the Tournament? We mayn't call Katrine an ideal champion, but we mustn't let ourselves be biased by private prejudice."

"I hope I'm above such a low motive as that," Viola answered stiffly. "No one could have the interests of the school more thoroughly at heart than I. For this very reason it seems to me folly to trust the championship to a girl who really hasn't much concern whether Aireyholme wins or not."

"Oh, surely she'd play up?"

"I don't know about that. If she were in one of her dreamy moods, perhaps she wouldn't. Better not risk it."

"Hadn't we better put the matter to the vote?" suggested Diana.

"By all means. I propose that Katrine Marsden is not eligible for the championship." Viola's tone was decisive, even slightly aggressive.

"I make a counter-proposition, to place her at least on the list of eligibles," returned Dorrie, stolidly keeping her temper.

Diana had the casting vote. She promptly plumped for Viola, partly from real conviction, and partly because she was chums with the Captain.

"So be it!" said Dorrie, shrugging her shoulders. She could not agree with the decision, but she did not take the matter much to heart. "You two will have to brace up, and practise for all you're worth. We mustn't let Carford beat us."

When the result of the monitresses' meeting became known, the school took it in various ways. Some girls sympathized with Viola, others hotly espoused Katrine's cause. The affair was very much discussed, and there were many lively arguments over the justice of the pronouncement. Katrine herself accepted it callously.

"I'm sure I don't want to be champion, thanks!" she responded to her sympathizers. "It would be an awful bore to go and play Carford. I'd rather stop in the studio and paint."

In spite of her assumed indifference, Katrine was rather piqued. She knew her play was good, and that it was mainly jealousy on Viola's part which caused her to be thus set aside. Although she had adopted a superior attitude, Katrine nevertheless rather liked to shine in the school. She had played tennis in a dilettante fashion before, just to amuse herself; now, in a spirit of opposition, she began to train. For once she would let these girls see what she was capable of. There were only five days before the tournament; she would devote them to tennis. Having arrived at this decision, she temporarily threw art to the winds. The studio knew her presence no more out of class hours: the whole of her spare time was given up to the courts. She had an immense advantage over the monitresses, for they were studying hard for their matriculation, and had very little recreation, while she had a double portion of leisure. Her play, good as it was before, improved by leaps and bounds. Soon not a girl in the school could compete with her upon equal terms, and win. Her handicaps were raised continually. There was a growing feeling that it was both unwise and unfair to exclude her.

"Someone ought to speak to the monitresses about it," said Jill Barton.

"It would be precious little use," returned Rose Randall. "Viola is so pigheaded, if once she says a thing, she'll stick to it."

"But is it fair that she should settle everything?"

"Well, she's Captain, and Dorrie's Games secretary; they have the authority between them."

"Dorrie has been overruled by Viola."

"No doubt; but I don't see what we can do, except call a mass meeting, and appeal."

"Um—that's rather a desperate measure. I hate upsets in a school. We ought all to pull together harmoniously if we can. Let us try and put the screw on privately, but don't have open ructions. Viola is a decent sort. We don't want to quarrel with her for Katrine's sake."

Most of the girls shared Jill's opinion. They might not agree with their Captain's views, but they liked her too well to proceed to extremities. After all, Katrine was a new-comer, and Viola was the bulwark of Aireyholme traditions. They tried to manage the matter by finesse. They understood their leader well enough to know that any alteration must be proposed by herself. She was not fond of entertaining other people's suggestions. So they forbore to revolt openly, and confined themselves to desperate hints and innuendoes. Viola was perfectly well aware of what was going on, and she ignored the hints. The situation amounted to a duel between herself and Katrine, and she trusted to her influence as Captain to come off conqueror. It was impossible not to acknowledge the superiority of Katrine's play, and Viola really stuck to her guns out of sheer obstinacy. Everybody wondered what was going to happen, and whether the difficulty could be solved without a quarrel. The time was painfully short.

It was now the very day before the tournament. The question must be settled that evening. The results of the scoring-notes were posted up by Dorrie on the notice board: Katrine headed the list by an overwhelming majority; Viola followed; Dorrie was only a few points behind, and Diana and Hilda, bracketed equal, came next. If Katrine were ruled out of competition, then the championship must fall to Viola and Dorrie. The strain waxed acute. Little groups of girls stood about in the hall and passages, discussing the pros and cons. It was evident that something must be done; the ferment of feeling was almost at effervescing point.

At this crisis Miss Spencer issued from the head mistress's study. She walked to the notice board, pinned up a paper, and marched away without a word. Everyone crowded round to read the notice. It was brief, but to the point, and in the Principal's own handwriting.

"In view of the forthcoming tournament, Mrs. Franklin requests that the Games Committee choose as champions girls who are not entered for the matriculation. No examination candidate will be allowed leave of absence to-morrow."

This was indeed a cutting of the Gordian knot. Viola, Dorrie, and Diana were absolutely disqualified. It was a totally unexpected dénouement, and for the moment they were utterly taken aback. As befitted monitresses, however, they pulled themselves together, and bore their disappointment with Spartan heroism. Perhaps they realized the cleverness of Mrs. Franklin's generalship. It was certainly a safe way out of an awkward predicament. Viola was an intelligent girl, and had the sense to climb down gracefully.

"Diana and Dorrie and I are out of it," she at once announced, "so I suggest Katrine and Hilda as champions. There has been some little doubt as to whether Katrine is eligible to represent the school, but I beg to propose that any disqualifying clause should be set aside in this emergency, and that she be requested to play for Aireyholme to-morrow. I'm sure she'll do us credit. All in favour of this proposition please say 'Aye'."

Such a universal chorus of assent rose from the assembled girls that Katrine, who had been inclined to refuse the proffered honour, was obliged to accede. Both she and Viola had saved their dignity, and in consequence each felt a more friendly disposition towards the other. They discussed the coming tournament quite amicably; and Viola even offered to lend her racket, which was superior to Katrine's own. Hilda was all smiles. With such a partner she hoped to do great things.

"Mrs. Franklin is a modern Solomon!" whispered Nan to Gladwin.

Katrine was secretly much gratified at being chosen champion after all, though she was far too proud to show it. Her affected carelessness, however, deceived nobody.

"She's as pleased as Punch!" was the unanimous verdict of the school.

Everybody sympathized, for each one would have been only too delighted if the happy lot had been hers. The two champions were the centres of congratulation. The various points of their play were eagerly discussed; they were the one topic of conversation.

In addition to the pair who were to take part in the tournament, twelve girls had been invited to Carford College as spectators. Those whose scores came next on the tennis list were chosen, and Gwethyn and Rose Randall were among the lucky number. They were to be escorted by Miss Andrews, whose athletic tendencies made her as keen as anybody on the event. Fourteen smiling girls stood ready on the following morning, all in immaculate white silk blouses, with their school ties and hats. Katrine and Hilda wore rosettes of pink, brown, and green — the Aireyholme colours — to distinguish them as champions, and most of the others sported patriotic badges. The school assembled on the drive to see them off, and they departed amid a chorus of good wishes. Some of the juniors even began to shout hoorays, but Mrs. Franklin suppressed them.

"It will be time enough to cheer if we win the tournament," she reminded them. "Remember that other schools are competing, whose play may be better than ours."

"Which is a polite way of saying, 'Don't crow till you're out of the wood!'" laughed Dorrie to Diana. "All the same, I'd back Katrine against anyone I know!"

Carford College was a big day-school, situated about a mile out of the town. The Aireyholme contingent was received by the head mistress, and at once handed on to stewards, who took Katrine and Hilda to the champions' tent, and the rest to the seats which had been reserved for them. The College prided itself on its Games activities; its courts were in excellent condition, and there was every facility for the comfort of spectators. Six other schools besides Aireyholme had been invited to compete, and bring twelve representatives each to witness the combat, so that, with the pupils of the College, there was a crowd of more than two hundred to watch the trial of skill.

Katrine and Hilda, inside the tent, were having a good time. They were regaled with lemonade, and introduced to the other champions. It was interesting to compare notes on sports and schools; if any of the strangers were inclined to be shy, the ice was soon broken, and all were chatting like old friends by the time the tournament began. The College Games Captain, a particularly jolly girl, made an admirable hostess, and put all her guests at their ease; she had herself been entertained in similar circumstances, so she had experience to guide her. As the train service from Heathwell to Carford was not very convenient, the Aireyholme party had come early; two of the other schools were in like case, and the rest turned up by degrees.

At last all the competitors had arrived, and the drawing took place. Aireyholme was not in the first set, rather to Katrine's relief.

"I hate to have to begin," she remarked to Hilda. "It's much more helpful if one can watch other people's play for a while."

The competitors who opened the tournament were fairly evenly matched. Oakfield House perhaps excelled in serving, but Summerlea possessed a champion who seemed able to take every ball, in whatsoever awkward spot it alighted; she was a short, freckled, ungainly girl (Katrine had mentally noted her plainness when they met in the tent), but her spread-eagle method of play was highly successful, and her side scored heavily.

"We shall have our work cut out for us if we're put against her," grunted Hilda. "Oakfield didn't do badly either, in the beginning, but they couldn't stand against this Doris What's-her-name!"

Pinecroft versus Arden Grange came next on the list, resulting in a narrow victory for the former.

Carford College had an exciting tussle with Windleness. Everybody, except of course the Windleness girls, wanted the College to win. It was felt that it would be too bad if the hostesses of the occasion were out of the finals. By almost superhuman effort Carford managed to score, but Windleness was accorded full honours of war by the spectators.

At last it was the turn of Katrine and Hilda. Aireyholme had been drawn to play Ashley Hall, a school, so it was rumoured, with a reputation.

"I'm horribly nervous! I know we'll never beat them!" whispered Hilda, with scarlet cheeks.

"Now don't work yourself up into a state! For goodness' sake, keep cool!" Katrine besought her. "If you let yourself worry, you'll play badly. Our salvation is to keep our heads. If you get excited, you're done for. Brace up, can't you!"

"I'll do my best," murmured Hilda, setting her teeth.

The Aireyholme girls had sometimes been inclined to sneer at Katrine's calm, imperturbable composure, but to-day it stood the school in good stead. In tournaments the level-headed, cool, self-controlled competitor generally has an advantage over an excitable, impulsive or nervous rival. The Ashley Hall champions were splendid players, but they were more brilliant than steady; one or two little things put them out; they lost their nerve and made a few bad strokes. Katrine, on the contrary, kept absolute self-possession; she calculated balls to a nicety, and it was chiefly owing to her all-round preparedness that the set was won. She and Hilda retired with sighs of relief.

"The foe was worthy of their steel — or rather, rackets," said Gwethyn to Rose Randall. "I'm glad I wasn't chosen champion; I never can keep cool like Kattie. She's always the same — never the least excited, while I'm gyrating all over the place like a lunatic!"

There was now a midday interval for lunch, and the crowd dispersed. Most of the College girls went home for their meal, but the visitors from the other schools were entertained in the big hall with coffee, plates of ham or tongue, buns, and fruit. At half-past one the finals were to begin. It was not desirable to waste too much time, as several of the schools must catch certain return trains.

"You played splendidly, Katrine, and Hilda backed you up no end!" declared the Aireyholme girls, anxious to congratulate their champions. "Go on in that style, and you'll do."

"Don't expect too much. The College will probably win a love set when we play them," returned Katrine. "You'd better be bracing your nerves."

"Oh, we're sporting enough to take our luck as it comes, but we pin our faith to you this afternoon!"

If the first sets had been exciting, the finals were doubly so. Summerlea, after a Homeric contest, vanquished Pinecroft, and was placed against Aireyholme. Katrine had anticipated a tussle with Doris Kendrick, their spread-eagle champion, and she had calculated correctly. Doris's play was magnificent, and Aireyholme only won by the skin of its teeth.

"We must tackle Carford too," whispered Katrine to Hilda. "Don't give in now."

The excitement among the spectators was intense. General sympathy was, perhaps, on the side of the College, but everyone admired Aireyholme's plucky play.

"Katrine is A1!" commented Rose. "Just look at that stroke! I never thought she'd take that ball! Forty-thirty. I believe we'll do it yet. Well done, Hilda! Good old girl! Keep it up! Keep it up! Oh! I say, it's ours! What a frolicsome joke!"

The College girls were disappointed at the failure of their champions, but they were magnanimous enough to start the cheer for Aireyholme. Katrine and Hilda were called up by the Principal to receive their prizes — two pretty bangles—and congratulations poured in from all sides. There was not time for much more than to express their thanks, for Miss Andrews was consulting her watch, and announcing that they must rush to the station if they wished to catch their train; so with hasty good-byes to their hostesses they made their exit. Their arrival at Aireyholme was a scene of triumph. Mrs. Franklin was immensely gratified at the good news, and the girls cheered till they were hoarse.

"We'll put it down in the school minutes under the heading of 'Victories'," purred Dorrie. "I'd have given up the matric. to be there. Anybody taken snapshots? You, Rose? Good! We'll develop them to-night, and if they come out decently, we'll paste them in the school album. I never thought we should really beat Carford College. It breaks the record. This is a ripping term for Aireyholme!"

"Kattie's scored in more senses than one to-day," whispered Gwethyn to her chum Rose Randall.

CHAPTER X

An Antique Purchase

AS the summer came on, bringing the climbing roses out on the cottages, and filling the village gardens with a wealth of flowers, Katrine's artistic soul revelled more and more in the picturesque beauty of Heathwell. Her sketching expeditions were an intense delight; she was improving fast under Miss Aubrey's tuition, and also picked up many hints from Mr. Freeman, who would always stop, if he passed their easels, and give her work the benefit of his criticism. Katrine often felt as if she were living in the past at Heathwell. Not only were the cottages antique, but the people also had an old-world atmosphere lingering among them. Many of the women wore sun-bonnets; they baked their bread in brick ovens, made rhubarb wine and cowslip beer, cured their own bacon, and pursued various homely little avocations which are fast going out of date in other parts of the country. Even the Elementary-school children were not aggressively advanced; some of them still bobbed curtsies, and wore clean white pinafores to go to church on Sundays.

Miss Aubrey was a great favourite in the village. Her painting brought her closely into touch with the people, and she had a ready sympathy for them, quite unmixed with patronage—a distinction which they recognized and appreciated. The patriarch in the picturesque weather-stained coat would slowly bring out his reminiscences during the hours she sat sketching him in his garden; the mothers would tell her their troubles; and the children swarmed round her like bees. It was an entirely new phase of life for Katrine, who had had no experience before of our sturdy English peasantry. She saw the people at first through Miss Aubrey's spectacles; then she learnt to like them on her own account, and acquired quite a number of village friends—the blacksmith who smiled at her from his forge, the crippled wife of the saddler, who waved greetings from her seat at the window, the fussy little spinster in charge of the post office, the six ancient pensioners who generally sat sunning themselves on the bench outside the almshouses, the cobbler who bobbed up his head and smiled as she passed his open doorway, the widow who baked the brown bread and the muffins, and the elderly dame at the crockery shop.

There were many quaint people in Heathwell—so many that Katrine often declared a list ought to be made of the village worthies and preserved in a local museum. There was Linton, a white-haired, bent old labourer, who supplemented his parish relief by breaking stones on the roadside. Katrine first made friends with him over a stile. It happened to be rather a high and difficult one, and he was sitting on the top of it, so she paused to allow him to descend. "Come on, missie, come on!" he cried in encouraging tones. "Though it do be a rare awkward stile for faymales. I telled Parson so, when he a-put it up; but says he to I, 'Faymales or no faymales, they'll have to be getten over it!'"

Linton was a character in his way, a self-taught antiquarian, a nature lover, a dormant poet, an incipient artist, and something of a philosopher round it all. Who knows what strange dreams he may have dreamed in his youth, of fame to be won and songs to be uttered? But life's obligations had proved too heavy a burden, and his was still a mute inglorious muse. His delight in Miss Aubrey's sketches was almost pathetic; he would toddle far out of his way to pass her easel, and take a peep at the progress of some roadside scene or cottage garden. He even volunteered, one evening, to find her a subject, and to please him, she and Katrine allowed him to escort them to the summit of a mound near the river. The place without doubt was an ancient grave, for it was close to Offa's dyke, the great eighth-century barrier between Saxon and Celt, and though from an artistic point of view it was not paintable, the romance of its situation was palpable.

To Miss Aubrey and Katrine the true subject was the white-haired, rugged old fellow himself, standing outlined against the glowing west, as with outstretched hand he showed where the slain in the forgotten battle-field had been heaped, and the earth piled high above them. His voice rang as he tried to picture the far-off scene, and there shone from his eyes just a gleam of the divine fire.

"Look around you!" he cried. "See where yon river's a-windin' down, and yon hills a-stand back as they did a thousand years agone. Aye! I often comes hither and thinks what a sight it will be for their uprising!"

Of all the quaint village folk perhaps the funniest was Mrs. Stubbs, who kept a little shop at the corner of the High Street. It was nominally a green-grocer's, but it included so many other things as well, that it might fairly claim to be a china store, a second-hand bookseller's, and a repository of antiquities. Though the counter was spread with cabbages and cauliflowers, the floor was covered with crockery, and the small parlour behind was overflowing with old furniture and all kinds of oddments picked up at auctions—eighteenth-century chairs, bow-shaped mirrors, ancient etchings and engravings, Wedgwood plates, Toby jugs, horn lanterns, tortoise-shell tea-caddies, blunderbusses, cases of butterflies, clocks, snuff-boxes, medallions, pewter dishes, and a vast number of other articles. Mrs. Stubbs had a genius for a bargain. She was a familiar figure at every sale in the district, where she would bid successfully even against hook-nosed individuals of the Hebrew persuasion, and bear off her spoils in triumph. She knew the marketable value of most of her antiques to the last halfpenny, and carried on a successful little business by disposing of them to London dealers, or to collectors in the neighbourhood, often at double the prices she had originally paid for them.

For Katrine this old curiosity shop held an absolute fascination. She had been brought up to appreciate such things, for her father's chief hobby was the collecting of antiques. Mr. Marsden revelled in carved oak furniture and Worcester china, and had communicated some of his enthusiasm to his daughter. Miss Aubrey sympathized with Katrine's tastes, and would often allow her to pay a visit to the shop, sometimes sending her there on small errands.

For the ostensible purpose of ordering peas for Aireyholme, Katrine entered Mrs. Stubbs's repository one memorable afternoon. The good dame had attended a sale on the preceding day, and her small establishment had received so many additions to its already large collection that it was almost overflowing into the street. She was superintending the rearrangement of some of these articles by Mr. Stubbs, a blear-eyed individual who proved a sad thorn in the flesh to his capable better half, and whose delinquencies formed a topic for much of her conversation.

"He's no more use nor a babe to-day," she confided indignantly, "with his legs that wobbly and his hand that shaky, I daren't let him lay a finger on the china, for fear he'd be dropping it. He took half a crown out of the till when my back was turned, and off he goes with it straight to the 'Dragon'. Well, he was a second-hand article when I married him, and I might 'a known he weren't up to much, if I'd had the experience I've got now."

Mrs. Stubbs spoke with warmth, evidently regarding her husband as a bad investment, which she unfortunately had no opportunity of passing on at a profit to anybody else. She hustled him out of the way at present, and telling him to retire to the kitchen, took Katrine into the crowded little parlour to inspect her latest purchases. The sale had been at the house of an old maiden lady who had possessed many antique belongings, including carved ivories and miniatures, as well as Sheraton furniture. These treasures were, of course, far beyond Katrine's pocket, though she regarded them with the covetous eye of a born collector.

"I'm afraid I can't afford anything old," she said at last. "I really came to order three pecks of peas for Mrs. Franklin."

"I've a little cupboard here I'd like to show you," urged Mrs. Stubbs, who always saw in Katrine a possible customer. "It went dirt-cheap at the sale, too, so I could afford to let you have it for one pound five, and clear a trifle of profit, just enough to pay me for the trouble of fetching it. What do you think of this, now?"

The cupboard in question was a small oak one, about two feet in height, with the date 1791 carved on its door. It was plainly intended for spices, for inside it had nine tiny drawers, surrounding a space in the centre. It was such a quaint, bijou, attractive little piece that Katrine promptly fell in love with it. She knew it would absolutely delight her father, and she determined to buy it, and give it to him as a birthday present.

"If you'd say a pound?" she ventured, remembering that all old-furniture dealers affect an almost Eastern habit of bargaining.

"Done!" declared Mrs. Stubbs promptly. "I wouldn't quarrel with you over a few shillings, and I'm so stocked up with things, I'll be glad to make room. This is as nice a bit of oak as you'd find in all Heathwell."

"I suppose it comes from Miss Jackson's family?" said Katrine. "What are those two initials carved under the date? They look like an R and an L."

"Maybe it might come from Mrs. Jackson's mother's. I didn't hear where she got it, but she'd a lot of fine stuff in her house, and thought a deal of it, too. I've seen her at auctions myself, buying a few odd trifles she fancied. Poor dear lady! it's sad to think she's dead and gone. She'd be sore upset if she could see her things all scattered. Well, missie, I'll send Stubbs round to Aireyholme this evening with the cupboard; but don't you give him the money for it, however he may ask. You call and pay me quiet-like, some other time when he ain't about. He's not fit to be trusted with a penny piece."

The delinquent Stubbs staggered round in the course of the evening, bearing the little oak cupboard in his arms; but, mindful of his failing, Katrine forbore even to give him a tip for himself.

"I felt horribly mean," she assured Miss Aubrey, to whom she had confided the particulars of her purchase, "especially as he hinted so desperately."

"You were right, for he would have gone straight to the 'Dragon' and spent it. Shall we carry your cupboard into the studio? Then we can all enjoy it while it's here."

"Oh, please do! Isn't it a little beauty? Dad will be simply delighted with it. I want to show it to Mr. Freeman. He's a very good judge of old oak, and will know if it's genuine."

"There can be no mistake about its genuineness. I think you are very lucky to get hold of it," replied Miss Aubrey, calling one of the servants, and telling her to take the cupboard upstairs.

A place was found for Katrine's treasure on the top of an oak chest, and it was admired to her heart's content. By special invitation Mr. Freeman came to inspect it, and congratulated her on her possession.

"It's a real antique—a very pretty little piece. It will just suit Mr. Marsden. In the meantime it's an ornament in the studio here. You'll find these small drawers most convenient to keep paints and bottles in."

Katrine always rode her hobbies hard. The acquisition of the oak spice-cupboard had started her in a new line. She now posed as a collector of antiques. She borrowed some books from Mr. Freeman, and after a brief study of their contents began to talk glibly of the Sheraton and Heppelwhite periods, Adams chimney-pieces, and soft paste Worcester china. She aired her new-found knowledge so ceaselessly, in season and out of season, that the girls, always ready to take offence at her superior attitude, began to make fun of her. They chuckled audibly when Mrs. Franklin, more mathematical than artistic, made her calculate the cubic contents of her cupboard as a problem in class, especially as her answer was wrong, and she had to work the sum again. All sorts of mock treasures were presented to her: rusty nails, old tins, scraps of leather dug up from the garden, or pieces of worm-eaten wood. One morning the following poetic gem was left on her dressing-table. The authoress was apparently too modest to sign her name, so the lines were anonymous.

"There was a collector of Oak,She knew more than ordin'ry folk!On pastes soft or hardShe'd hold forth by the yard,And now she's become quite a joke!"

Fortunately Katrine possessed a sense of humour that counterbalanced the strain of priggishness in her composition. She laughed at the effusion and took the hint. She was perhaps conscious that she had been "putting on side" rather too vigorously, and that it would be judicious to climb down.

"It's Viola who wrote it, I'm certain," she confided to Gwethyn. "Look here! I vote we play a joke on the school. I've thought of something rather fine."

The two girls put their heads together, and had a long confabulation. The result they confided to nobody, but during the afternoon they were observed to be hunting round the garden and orchard, apparently in search of something. Next day, Katrine studied the time-table carefully, and ascertained that the studio would be unoccupied by any classes from 3.30 to 4 p.m. Making the excuse that she wished to touch up some sketches there, she easily persuaded Miss Aubrey to excuse part of her outdoor work that afternoon, and returning to Aireyholme at half-past three, she secured undisturbed possession of the room for half an hour. She did not spend the time in painting, though she was extremely busy. When the girls trooped from their forms at four o'clock, they found a large and prominent notice posted up in the passage.

ART EXHIBITION

A choice and unique COLLECTION OF ANTIQUES AND CURIOS is now on view in the Studio, and forms an unparalleled opportunity of making acquaintance with the domestic arts and industries of the Middle Ages. Many objects of historic interest. Inspection Invited. Admission Free. Catalogues One Penny.

Proceeds given to the Belgian Relief Fund.

Everybody at once marched upstairs; even Dorrie and Viola, who were inclined to hold aloof, fell victims to Eve's instinct of curiosity, and followed the rest, excusing their weakness on the ground that as monitresses they felt obliged to be present at all school happenings, and were thus only fulfilling their duty.

Giggling a little, the girls entered the studio. The large table in the centre was spread with a variety of objects, neatly numbered as in a museum. By the door stood Katrine with a pile of hand-printed catalogues, and the Belgian Relief Fund Box from the dining-room chimney-piece. As the exhibition seemed unintelligible without a catalogue, the pennies rattled briskly into her box. The exhibits were as diverse as they were extraordinary, and according to the descriptions were both rare and historic.

No. 1. (Upper leather of a mouldy old boot.) Portion of the footgear of Simon de Montfort, worn before the Battle of Evesham, 1265.

No. 2. (A broken crock of china.) Valuable piece of soft paste Worcester from the Huntingdon Collection.

No. 3. (A rusty hairpin.) Pin worn in the head-dress of Queen Elizabeth at the Kenilworth Pageant.

No. 4. (A crooked nail.) Nail from the gibbet of Piers Gaveston, executed at Blacklow Hill, Warwick, 1312.

No. 5. (A dilapidated horseshoe.) Shoe worn by the horse of Charles I at the Battle of Nottingham, 1642.

No. 6. Glove button of Marie Antoinette.

No. 7. Needle used in embroidery by Mary Queen of Scots.

No. 8. Safety-pin employed in the toilet of Edward VI when an infant.

No. 9. Portion of feeding-bottle of Henry VIII.

No. 10. Do. fragment of rattle.

No. 11. (A worm-eaten piece of wood.) Relic of vessel of the Spanish Armada.

No. 12. (Rusty cocoa tin.) Remains of cup in which the Barons drank success to Magna Charta, 1215.

No. 13. (A small pebble.) Stone worn as a penance in the shoe of Henry II, on a pilgrimage to the shrine of St. Thomas à Becket.

No. 14. (A portion of wickerwork.) Fragment of guillotine basket used in French Revolution.

No. 15. (A rusty key.) Original key of dungeon in Berkeley Castle where Edward II was murdered.

No. 16. (A shabby quill.) Pen used to sign Magna Charta, 1215.

The girls laughed immoderately to see the various objects which they had presented in mockery to Katrine, described as such priceless relics.

"You haven't put in the soda-water bottle I gave you!" said Coralie.

"It's stamped with the maker's name, though I thought of breaking it, and preserving a portion as 'Roman Glass'," replied Katrine. "I'm going to write a book on collecting, next. I shall call it 'From Nine to Ninety, Reminiscences of the Fads of my First and Second Childhoods, by a Centenarian'. The introduction will contain 'Early Natural History Instincts—Preservation of Earth Worms and Dissection of Flies at the Age of Two'.It's to be published by subscription, 7s. 6d. per volume. Anybody who likes can give me the money now."

"We'll wait till we see the proofs, thanks!" tittered the girls.

"I like Simon de Montfort's shoe best," declared Githa; then drawing Gwethyn aside, she asked, "Where did Katrine get that little cupboard?"

Githa had been away from school for a few days, on the sick list, and had only returned that morning. She had heard the girls teasing Katrine about her oak treasure, but had not seen it until now. She examined it with much attention.

"Kattie bought it from Mrs. Stubbs," answered Gwethyn. "I believe she got it at a sale—a Miss Jackson's things."

Githa nodded.

"I know. She died last month. It used to be ours. The R and L are for Richard Ledbury. It stood on a table in the library at the Grange. Grandfather had promised it to me. He often called it 'Githa's cupboard'. I suppose Uncle Wilfred put it in with the rest of the things at the sale, and Miss Jackson must have bought it. I always wondered what had become of it. It's such a dear little cupboard."

"Oh! I'm sorry if we've sneaked it away from you."

"Never mind. It's not your fault; I'd rather Katrine had it than anyone else. I'm glad to see it again, and to know that somebody's got it who'll value it."

CHAPTER XI

Waterloo Day

THE girls at Aireyholme were nothing if not patriotic. They followed the course of national events with keenest interest. In common with most other schools they had sent their quota of knitted garments to the troops, and they kept collecting-boxes for both Prince of Wales and Belgian Relief Funds. These enterprises were good as far as they went, but not nearly sufficient to satisfy their martial spirit.

"We're not making any sacrifices," declared Viola Webster impressively. "We don't realize the war enough. We're letting our Allies outstrip us. If we were Serbian or Russian we should be doing far more."

"What sort of things?" queried Hilda Smart. Hilda was practical to a fault, though Viola liked vaguely to generalize.

"Oh! patriotic things, you know." (Viola was rather cornered when it came to matter-of-fact explanations.) "Tearing up our gymnastic costumes for lint, and — and — helping to make bullets, and all the rest of it."

"I thought bullets were made by machinery at ordnance works? And it would be rather silly to tear up our gym. clothes. They wouldn't make good lint, either!"

"Well, if not exactly that, we ought to be doing something."

"We have drill, and flag-signalling."

"I'd have liked rifle practice. I don't see why girls shouldn't shoot! At my brothers' school they have a Cadet Corps."

"Mrs. Franklin would have a fit if she saw us handling rifles," laughed Coralie. "A Girls' Cadet Corps sounds Utopian, but we'd never get the powers that be to allow it."

"All the same," interposed Diana, "I think Vi is right. We're not doing as much as we might. If we can't have a Cadet Corps, let us start a Girls' Patriotic League."

"Good! It would brace us all up. We'll plan it out. Have you a scrap of paper and a pencil? We'll call it 'The Aireyholme Patriotic League. Object — To render the utmost possible service to our country in her hour of need.' Let's make up a committee, and fix some rules."

"Best call a general meeting of the whole school," suggested Dorrie Vernon. "The kids will take to it far better if they have a hand in it from the beginning."

Dorrie was special monitress for the Fourth Form, and knew the mind of the juniors. She was always ready to take their part, and secure them their fair share in what was going on. Viola and Diana were inclined to use their prerogative almost to domineering point, but Dorrie stood as representative of the rights of the bulk of the school. After a short argument her counsel prevailed, and a general meeting was announced. The girls responded with enthusiasm. Everybody turned up, and all were ready to join the new society. Discussions were invited, and in the end the following rules were drafted: —

1. That this Society be called The Aireyholme Girls' Patriotic League.

2. That its object is to render service to our country and her allies.

3. That members pledge themselves to devote not less than half an hour a day to some patriotic duty, either drilling, signalling, Red Cross work, sewing, or the making of articles to be sold for the benefit of our soldiers and sailors.

4. That members cultivate the qualities of courage, self-reliance, and patience.

5. That each member agree to sacrifice some small luxury, and devote the money thus saved to the good of the cause.

6. That a particular effort be made to raise funds by giving an entertainment.

The idea of making some special self-denial for the good of their country rather appealed to the girls. Each promised something definite. Those who took sugar in their tea bound themselves to give it up, and ask Mrs. Franklin to place the money saved towards their fund; others agreed to relinquish chocolates, the buying of foreign stamps (the present hobby amongst the juniors), or the indulgence in various other little fads that involved the outlay of small sums. Further, it was unanimously agreed that Mrs. Franklin should be asked to give no prizes at the end of the term, but devote the money to patriotic causes.

Viola, who loved dramatic scenes, made all, with uplifted hand, take a solemn pledge to keep the rules; she exhibited a specimen badge which shehad designed — the initials A. G. P. L. worked in red, on a piece of white ribbon — and urged each member to copy it as speedily as possible. Having thus discussed broad details, she went on to particulars.

"We must get up some kind of a bazaar or entertainment to make money," she proposed. "Who can give suggestions? Oh, don't all speak at once, please! It's no use all jabbering together! Silence! Am I chairman or not? Anybody with a genuine and helpful idea kindly hold up her hand. The rest keep quiet. Yes, Gwethyn Marsden, what have you to say? Stand up, please!"

"I beg to suggest that 18th June is the centenary of the Battle of Waterloo, and that we ought to give our entertainment on that day."

A thrill passed round the room. Gwethyn sat down, covered with glory. Everybody felt that her idea was most appropriate.

"It would be glorious," hesitated Viola, "but how about the matric.? The exam. begins on 14th June, and lasts four days — 14th, 15th, 16th, 17th — why, we should just be free for the 18th! Of course it gives us a very short time to make arrangements, and Diana and Dorrie and I shall be too busy to help with anything until our ordeal is over."

"Never mind, the others must do the work. Waterloo Day would be just prime!" declared Dorrie, hugely taken with the notion. "We'd write and get our home folks to send us things. We can have stalls and sell fancy articles, and give entertainments as well. It will be ripping fun."

"We haven't asked Mother Franklin yet," objected Diana.

"Oh, she'll agree—don't you alarm yourself! She's as keen on the soldiers and sailors as we are. It's her saving virtue. The mother of the Gracchi won't refuse, you bet!"

The Principal, when approached on the subject, gave a cordial assent, but only on the understanding that the new undertaking should not interfere with the matriculation studies of the three monitresses. They might help when their examination was over, but not before. She approved of the League and its objects, promised to devote both sugar money and prize money to the funds, and set apart Waterloo Day for a special entertainment to which the neighbourhood should be invited. She moreover graciously consented to act as President of the society, and accepted a badge in token of membership. The A. G. P. L.'s set to work with red-hot enthusiasm. Scarcely more than a fortnight was at their disposal for preparations, so it behoved them to waste no time. Urgent letters were dispatched home, begging for suitable things to furnish the stalls, and to provide costumes for the entertainment, while all available recreation was spent in the fabrication of such articles as they could make at school. An extra spur was given to their patriotic ardour by stirring news which Mrs. Franklin, with shining eyes, announced one morning. Her son at the front had performed a splendid and heroic deed in guarding an outpost against almost overwhelming odds. His brave action was recorded in the newspapers, which also published his portrait and a brief account of his career. He was practically sure to receive the Victoria Cross. Poor Mrs. Franklin could not restrain her pride in her first-born, though there was anxiety mixed with the triumph, for he was lying wounded in a French hospital as the result of his gallantry. She cut the account from the newspaper, and pinned it on the school notice board for the girls to read, and did not check them when they raised noisy cheers on behalf of the hero.

"I wish we knew where Hereward is!" sighed Katrine to Gwethyn. "It's fearfully tantalizing just to be told that his regiment is moved, and not a hint allowed as to where it's going. I'm sure he'll win a Victoria Cross too, before the war is over. Wouldn't Mumsie be proud?"

"She'd be ready to worship him," agreed Gwethyn.

The Marsdens heard from their parents as frequently as circumstances allowed. They looked forward immensely to mail days, and devoured the long letters that arrived, full of descriptions of the doings of the Conference at Sydney, where Professor Marsden was winning laurels by his lectures on Geology and Antediluvian Mammalia. "Mumsie" gave bright accounts also of her adventures in Australian society, and of various excursions to see the sights of the country. She spoke warmly of the hospitality that had been accorded them, and the agreeable impression they had formed of the colony. The girls in return had plenty of school doings to relate. Katrine waxed enthusiastic over her sketching experiences, and Gwethyn described her chums, and descanted on the fun enjoyed by her form. Both acknowledged that they were happy at Aireyholme, and that the term was passing very much faster and more pleasantly than they had anticipated.

It was, of course, impossible for the Marsdens to ask their mother to send gifts for their Patriotic Bazaar; the whole affair would be over before the letter could reach Australia; but they wrote to various aunts and cousins, and pleaded their cause so well that they had quite a nice little collection of articles to offer as their contribution. Everybody at school was working, as well as begging from friends and relations. All kinds of dainty trifles were fabricated by willing fingers, and the Entertainment Guild seemed to be practising incessantly. Miss Aubrey was a great help in planning and arranging costumes, and Katrine even boldly tackled Mr. Freeman, and persuaded him to paint a scene background to be used for the tableaux. A few of the village youngsters were requisitioned to take parts which

114

needed child actors, for none of the Aireyholme girls were under twelve, and even the youngest in the Fourth had reached a leggy and lanky stage quite impossible for the infantine rôles that were required. There was no lack of volunteers from the Council school; the picturesque little Gartleys were delighted to be chosen, and such keen rivalry was shown among the other cherubs to secure the honour of helping in the entertainment, that Miss Aubrey found it difficult not to include the whole of the Infant Standard.

Invitations were sent to everybody in the neighbourhood who was likely to come; a poster was nailed up outside the market hall, and another by the church, so that all the village might know what was happening. They were designed by Mr. Freeman and executed by Katrine, with a little assistance from Nan and Gladwin, and very temptingly set forth the attractions of the Bazaar.

It was a great scramble to get everything finished in so short a time, and Miss Aubrey and the other mistresses bore the brunt of the burden of the arrangements. Thanks to their energy and clever management, there were no hitches, and the goods for sale and the entertainments were in equal readiness when the great day came.

On the Monday, Tuesday, Wednesday, and Thursday, Viola, Diana, and Dorrie had attended the local centre at Carford to take their matriculation examination. Their ordeal being over, they were able with free minds to devote their energies to the League.

Mrs. Franklin was not particularly fond of remitting classes, but she had the wisdom to grant a whole holiday for the occasion. Perhaps she realized that it would be futile to attempt to set her pupils to work in the morning, when so much was to happen in the afternoon.

"I couldn't have tackled one single problem!" averred Rose Randall. "It would have been cruelty to animals to expect us to do maths. Besides, we've got to set out our stalls, and that's no end of a business. It'll take hours. I'm glad we're French—I think our costumes are much the prettiest."

The stalls were to represent various nations; they were lavishly decorated with flags, and upon them were displayed goods representative of the countries of the Allies. The Sixth had chosen "The British Empire", and had an assortment of all kinds of articles of a patriotic description. Photos of Lord Kitchener, General French, and Admiral Jellicoe were of course largely to the fore, and as memorials of the Waterloo centenary, portraits of Wellington and of Napoleon also figured on the stalls, with picture post cards of the famous battle-field. It was astonishing how many purposes the Union Jack was made to serve. Its familiar red, white, and blue stripes were reproduced on pin-cushions, Bradshaw covers, nightdress cases, blotters, work-bags, handkerchief sachets, and toilet tidies. The shamrock also was a favourite design, and the Red Dragon of Wales and the Scotch Thistle had been attempted. Coralie's aunt had sent a few Indian contributions, bought from the "Eastern Department" at the Stores, and Ellaline Dickens had managed to procure a number of post cards of Egypt, to help to represent the Empire. Perhaps the most striking feature of the stall was an exhibit which was not for sale. Colonel Harvey, an elderly gentleman who lived within a few miles of Heathwell, had lent some swords and bullets taken from the Battle of Waterloo, where his great-grandfather had commanded a regiment. I am afraid the girls giggled a little as they arranged them on the stall, for it reminded them of Katrine's mock exhibition. These, however, were genuine and certified antiques, of whose authenticity there could be no possibility of doubt.

The stallholders were dressed to represent various typical members of the Empire. Britannia, with helmet and trident, stood for England, and wasimpersonated by Diana Bennett. Gladwin Riley made a sweet Irish colleen, Tita Gray wore the Scotch plaid, and Nan Bethell the tall Welsh hat. Viola Webster was a Hindu Zenana princess, and Coralie Nelson a Canadian squaw.

The French stall run by the Fifth was an equal success. The girls had chosen to wear the picturesque Breton costume, and looked charming in their

116

velvet bodices, white sleeves, and quaint caps. It had been most difficult to provide articles that were specially French, so they had fallen back mainly on refreshments, and sold numerous dainty cakes and sweetmeats, and cups of café au lait. Yvonne and Mélanie de Broeck, the two little Belgian refugees who were being educated at Aireyholme, were naturally much in request on this occasion, and chattered French to the guests very winningly.

But perhaps the prettiest of all was the Fourth Form stall, which was intended to depict a scene in Old Japan. Coloured lanterns were hung up, and branches of fir and clumps of lovely iris were carefully arranged in artistic Japanese fashion. A number of cheap and tasteful articles had been procured from the Stores — tiny cabinets, cups and saucers, teapots, vases, lacquered goods, paper kites, native dolls, and queer little books, all of which found a ready sale. Six brunette members of the form were attired in Geisha costumes, and made quite creditable little Oriental ladies, with their dark tresses twisted into smooth knots, and their eyebrows painted to give them the required slant. They sold fruit and flowers in addition to their other wares, and waxed so persuasive that their stall began to be cleared the earliest of the three, rather to the envy of France and the British Empire, who had not expected the juniors to do so well.

In addition to providing a stall, each form gave a special entertainment, for which a separate admission was charged.

The Sixth made great capital with patriotic songs: "Drake's Drum", "Your King and Country Want You", "The Motherland's a-Calling", and "O England, Happy England!" were received with much applause, and all the audience joined in the chorus to "Tipperary". A very pretty picture accompanied the song "In a Child's Small Hand". Wee Ruth and Rose Gartley, dressed in the Greenaway costumes they had worn on May Day, and looking sublimely cherubic, stood holding out their fat little fingers while Ellaline sang:

"In a child's small hand lies the fate of our land,It is hers to mar or save,For a sweet child, sure, grows a woman pure,To make men good and brave.We English ne'er shall kiss the rod,Come our foes on land or sea;If our children be true to themselves and to God,Oh, great shall our England be!"

Special emphasis was laid, in the entertainment, on the fact that it was Waterloo Day. Hilda Smart, in a white dress of the fashion of 1815, recited Byron's famous lines: "There was a sound of revelry by night"; and Nan Bethell gave "Napoleon at St. Helena", and "Nelson's Motto". Some pretty English, Scotch, Irish, and Welsh folk dances were highly appreciated, together with national ballads. But the pièce de résistance of the Sixth was the Pageant of Empire at the end. Britannia as the central figure grasped the Royal Standard, and was surrounded by representatives of the Colonies, holding native products in their hands. Canada bore a sheaf of corn, Australia offered fruit, India showed silks and sandalwood, South Africa a bunch of ostrich feathers. Various emblematical characters added to the effect, and little Hugh Gartley as "The Midshipmite" evoked special applause.

The Fifth Form was not to be outdone by the Sixth. Their French and Belgian entertainment had been prepared with equal care. They commenced appropriately by singing "The Marseillaise". Yvonne and Mélanie were placed in prominent positions in the front, holding the Belgian flag, and followed with "La Brabançonne" in English, as a duet. It was rather an affecting performance, as the two little refugees sang in their pretty foreign accent:

"O'erpast the years of gloom and slavery,Now banished by Heav'n's decree.Belgium upraises by her braveryHer name, her rights, and banner free.Loyal voices proclaim far and loudly:We still are unconquered in fight.On our banner see emblazon'd proudly:'For King, for Liberty, and Right!'"

Some spirited Breton peasant dances followed, and Jill Barton and Ivy Parkins recited a short piece entitled "Two Little Sabots", founded on an actual incident, and describing how an English officer, arriving on Christmas Eve at a half-shelled Belgian farm, still tenanted by its peasant proprietors, found the wooden shoes of the children placed hopefully on the hearth, and acted Santa Claus by filling them with the biscuits, raisins, and chocolate that he had in his pockets.

Beatrix Bates, the champion reciter of the form, gave an English version of "Chantons, Belges, chantons!" Mr. Harper, the music master from Carford, who had very kindly come to help with the entertainment, accompanied her by playing a piano setting of Elgar's famous "Carillon", based upon the poem. The chiming of bells and the rolling of drums were a fitting prelude and interlude to the inspiring words. Beatrix rose to the occasion; her cheeks flamed and her eyes were flashing as she declaimed:

"Sing, Belgians, sing!Although our wounds may bleed, although our voices break,Louder than the storm, louder than the guns,Sing of the pride of our defeats'Neath this bright autumn sun;And sing of the joy of honour,When cowardice might be so sweet!"

The Fourth Form entertainment was of a different type. A Japanese festival was represented, and most pretty it proved to be. A number of tiny village children were dressed as Japanese dolls, and posed as in a toy shop; but to the great delight of the audience, the "dolls" suddenly came to life, stood up, and played a Japanese game very charmingly. "Tit-willow" and other appropriate songs were sung, and a patriotic touch was given to the affair by the inclusion of some Russian peasant dances and the Russian National Anthem:

"Lord God, protect the Tsar!Grant him Thy grace:In war, in peace,O, hide not Thou Thy face!Blessings his reign attend,Foes be scattered far,May God bless the Tsar,God save the Tsar!"

The afternoon was a huge success. The neighbouring gentry and the villagers came in full force, and sixpences literally poured in. The articles for sale were all inexpensive, and the stalls were almost cleared.

"We've made twenty-four pounds, three and twopence!" chuckled Viola, when Mrs. Franklin and the monitresses had counted the proceeds. "We'd better decide to divide it between the Prince of Wales's Fund and the Belgian Relief Fund. I never expected we should do so well at a little school affair in a country place like this. We shan't forget Waterloo Day in a hurry. I think we may consider the A. G. P. L. has scored no end!"

CHAPTER XII

Katrine's Ambition

KATRINE undoubtedly had a very decided vocation for art. She was full of enthusiasm, and ready for any amount of hard work in connection with this, her favourite study. Moreover, she was ambitious. In secret she cherished a very precious dream. She did not dare to confide it to anybody, not even to Gwethyn, but she thought about it constantly in private. Her scheme was no other than to get a picture into some public exhibition. The Royal Academy, she realized, was beyond her; also it was at present open, so that there could be no chance of competing for it until March in the following year. When you are seventeen, eight months seem an eternity; it was impossible to wait so long before trying to place her work in the public gaze. She knew that autumn exhibitions were held in some of the large provincial cities; Mr. Freeman was at present busy with pictures destined for these galleries, and Miss Aubrey also was a member of several art societies which had held local shows. Katrine's idea was to try and paint a really good sketch, then to have it framed, and entreat Mr. Freeman to allow it to be dispatched with his pictures when he sent them to the Liverpool exhibition. Of course it might not get in — the Hanging Committee would very possibly reject it — but there was always the chance of its acceptance, and surely there could be no harm in trying her luck. To have a picture in a public exhibition would place her entirely above the level of schoolgirl, and raise her to the delightful rank of artist. In imagination she saw her picture already hung — not skied, but in an excellent position on the line — perhaps even with a red star in one corner (that summit of artists' hopes!) to mark it as sold. How delightful to go to the gallery and see it for herself! How she would revel in the catalogue in which her name would be printed as an exhibitor! She would certainly turn up her hair for the occasion. It would be ridiculous to wear it in a plait.

But before these golden visions had any chance of realization she must produce her masterpiece. She did not think Mr. Freeman would countenance submitting any of her present sketches to a Hanging Committee. His criticisms of them, though kindly, had not spared their faults. A really good subject was half the battle of a picture in her estimation, so she turned over many ideas in her mind.

One day she had an inspiration. Miss Aubrey had engaged as a model an old village woman, who came three days in the week to sit in the studio. She was a picturesque figure in lilac cotton dress, white apron, and sun-bonnet, and Miss Aubrey posed her with Katrine's own cupboard as an accessory. Katrine's notion was to complete the picture by the addition of a child holding outstretched hands, as if to ask Granny Blundell for something from the cupboard. Little Hugh Gartley was the very one! His flaxen curls would look lovely against a background of old oak. Moreover, he was the school mascot. Twice before, his portraits had secured luck to their fortunate painters. Why not a third time? In anticipation her name was already in the catalogue. She thought of several appropriate titles: "Please, Granny!" "Grandmother's Cupboard"; "I want some!" and "I'm a Good Boy!" but could not decide which she liked the best. She easily persuaded Miss Aubrey to allow her to have Hugh as a model, and the little fellow came for a short time every day after his school-hours to stand for his portrait. Katrine took an immense amount of pains over her sketch. It was decidedly the best she had done, and Miss Aubrey commended it.

"The thing it chiefly wants is a really suitable background," said Katrine. "I ought to paint a cottage interior with a little window and a flowerpot on the sill. May I take my sketch to the Gartleys' cottage, and finish it there?"

"Certainly, if you like. I can't go with you, for there wouldn't be room for two easels, but you will be all right there alone."

Gwethyn laughed when Katrine announced her intention.

"I don't envy you painting in the midst of a close circle of Gartleys," she said.

122

"Never mind, I shall have to stand it. One must pay the price for one's efforts. Perhaps the mother will keep them in order."

"Put on your oldest skirt, then, for they'll smear sticky fingers over it! 'We are seven' is a nice sentiment in a poem, but one prefers a lesser number in a cottage, especially when the family is so addicted to treacle. I call you a martyr to the cause of art. I like the dilapidated, tumble-down, picturesque exteriors, but I draw the line at sitting inside some of them."

"That's where your enthusiasm falls short of mine!"

"Yes, I should want the Gartley residence spring-cleaned first. But tastes differ—you can always overlook every inconvenience for the sake of the picturesque; so go, and my blessing go with you!"

"Don't rag!" murmured Katrine. "It's not so bad as all that."

When Katrine arrived at the cottage, and proffered her request to Mrs. Gartley to be allowed to make a sketch of the kitchen, she thought just a shade of doubt passed over the care-worn face, and that the assent, though ready enough, was not quite so cordial as she had expected. She saw the explanation of the woman's hesitation at once when she entered. Seated by the fireside, with his boots on the fender and a clay pipe in his mouth, was a hang-dog-looking individual whom she had no difficulty in guessing to be Bob Gartley, though she had never chanced to come across him before.

"You won't mind he?" said Mrs. Gartley apologetically, under her breath. "He's biding at home to-day, instead of at his work. It's a poor place for you to sit, but I'll try and keep the children off you. Hugh? Oh yes, he'll stand if you want him! Go and fetch him, Mary! Get away, Tom! Would you like a chair, miss?"

"I've brought my camp-stool, thank you," replied Katrine, unpacking her sketching materials, and placing her canvas upon her easel. "You see, I've already put Hugh into the picture. I only want to finish him off, and paint a background."

"Why, there he be to the life! And if it isn't old Mrs. Blundell, too! Oh, isn't it beautiful? Might Bob take a look? Bob, come and see how nice the lady's painted our Hugh!"

Bob heaved himself up rather diffidently, and approached the easel. He was apparently modest at receiving visitors. He stared hard at the canvas, bending down, indeed, to examine it more closely. Katrine thought he was mentally appraising the portrait of his child, but when at last he spoke, his criticism was totally unexpected.

"Where did you get yon cupboard?" he grunted.

"This little spice cupboard in the picture? Why, I bought it from Mrs. Stubbs."

"You bought it? Off Mrs. Stubbs? How did she come to get hold of it, now?"

"I believe she got it at a sale."

"And you've drawed it just as it is? You haven't made up they letters and figures and things as is on it?"

"Oh, no! I copied them exactly."

"And where is it now?"

"I have it safely at Aireyholme, in the studio."

"What do you want to know for, Bob?" interposed his wife.

"Never you mind, it's no business of yours, nor of anyone else's, so far as I can see. Hugh? Oh, yes! It's like enough to the brat, I dare say. They're a noisy set, all on 'em!"

And without vouchsafing any further information, the head of the Gartley family stumped out of the cottage in the direction of the "Dragon".

"Well, it's the first time as ever I've known Bob take so much notice of anything!" exclaimed Mrs. Gartley. "What's he got to do with cupboards?"

"Perhaps he's fond of old furniture," ventured Katrine.

"Him! He's fond of his pipe and his beer, and that's all! I'd like to know what be up?"

"Why, I suppose anyone can feel a little natural curiosity when he looks at a picture," said Katrine, who saw nothing unusual in the incident.

"Natural curiosity, indeed! He's a deep 'un, is Bob!"

"Well, perhaps he'll tell you at tea-time."

"Not he; he don't tell me naught. But there! what's the use of talking of him? A young lady like you won't want to be thinking of such as he."

Probably Mrs. Gartley was right. Katrine went on with her sketch, and forgot all about Bob and his temporary burst of inquisitiveness. She painted the little window and the pots of geraniums, and a part of the doorway with a peep of the village street showing through the open door. It was exactly the background she wanted for her figures. The whole made quite a charming picture.

At half-past four she packed up her traps, and went back to school rather reluctantly, for she had spent a pleasant afternoon. It was not until after she had gone that Mr. Bob Gartley sauntered back from the "Dragon" to join his family circle.

By occupation he was a farm labourer, a blacksmith's assistant, a bricklayer, or a carter as the case might be, but he never stuck long to any job.Owing to the exertions of his wife and his numerous olive branches at haymaking, bean-picking, or in the harvest field, he generally managed to get through the summer without any undue expenditure of energy on his own part—a state of affairs which he regarded as highly satisfactory.

"Let the kids work!" he remarked on this particular evening, after pocketing the sixpence which Katrine had left for Hugh. "It's good for 'em. Develops their muscles, and teaches 'em punctuality and perseverance and order, and all they things the Parish Magazine says ought to be instilled into 'em while they are young. I was set at it soon enough myself, and clouted on the head if I didn't keep it up. I don't hold with these Council schools, keeping the children shut up for the best part of the day, when they ought to be a bit of use in the fields at a job of weeding or such-like."

"I suppose they must get their schooling. Mary is learning to recite Shakespeare, and she can do vulgar fractions, so she tells me," replied Mrs. Gartley, who was proud of her first-born's talents.

"Shakespeare and vulgar fractions is all very well, but they don't earn nothing. Didn't I take first prize myself for reciting when I were a boy at school? And much good it's done me! No; if I'd a voice in public affairs I'd drop education, and spend the money on giving allotments to decent working men with big families — men who'd train their kids not to be idle, and keep 'em at it. What's the use of sendin' a child to school for a matter of nine years, to cram it with head-learnin' when it's goin' to get its livin' with its hands afterwards? Let it stop at home, says I, and copy its father."

"A nice example you'd make, for sure!" sneered Mrs. Gartley. "You only want 'em at home so that you can have some 'un to send errands. Why, if there isn't Mrs. Stubbs at the door! Whatever's she come for, I'd like to know?"

Though she might not feel undue delight at the advent of a visitor, Mrs. Gartley nevertheless hastened to admit the old-furniture vendor, and usher her into the kitchen.

Most poor people are very much afraid of giving one another offence, and suffer greatly from the intrusions of their neighbours. It is impossible to say "Not at home" when they must answer the door in person, and the plea of being busy would be regarded as a mere excuse. Bob Gartley did not rise to greet the new-comer, neither did he remove his pipe from his mouth; but Mrs. Stubbs was unaccustomed to be treated with ceremony, so she did not notice such trifling omissions.

"I came to see if you could spare half a day to help me with some cleaning, Jane," she announced. "I've had a fresh lot of furniture in last week, and it do be in such a state, I must tidy it up a bit before I let folks look at it.

There's a gentleman wrote to me from London about it—a dealer in a big way, he is—and he may come down any day, so I want it to have a rub with the polishing-cloth."

"You do a nice little bit of business in your line, Mrs. Stubbs," remarked Bob Gartley. "And a pretty quick turnover, too, from what I hear."

"Well, things be just tolerable, like. Sometimes I make a profit, and sometimes I don't," admitted Mrs. Stubbs cautiously. "It takes knowing, does the buying of old furniture; but I may say I've got a reputation for spotting what's genuine. All the best people about comes to me for things. I've had Mrs. Everard, and Captain and Mrs. Gordon, and Mr. Jefferson, and even Sir Victor White his own self!"

"Bless me! Can't they afford to buy their furniture new?" exclaimed Mrs. Gartley in much astonishment.

"That shows you don't know anything about it, Jane. Gentlefolks has a great liking for old things, and will pay almost any fancy price for 'em. No, I don't mean plain deal tables and chairs like these," intercepting Bob's hopeful glance at his property; "but oak dressers and chests and cupboards that have come down through a generation or two."

"Well, it's a queer taste. If I was a lady I'd go into Carford and get a velvet sofa, and a sideboard with glass at the back of it."

"Ah! that's not the present fashion," said Mrs. Stubbs, shaking her head wisely. "You'd be amazed how everybody has took a craze for what's old. The young ladies at Aireyholme is always in and out of my shop, lookin' at bits of china, and samplers, and such-like."

"Didn't one of 'em buy a cupboard of you a while ago?" inquired Bob.

"So she did; but I don't know how you come to hear of it."

"I seed it in a picture she were making of our Hugh."

"And she put in Granny Blundell as well," added Mrs. Gartley.

"I remember the cupboard well enough," said Mrs. Stubbs. "I was sorry afterwards I'd let her have it, for I could have sold it for ten shillings more to someone who came in the very next day."

"Where did you get it?"

"At Miss Jackson's sale."

"Had it always been at The Elms?"

"No; I remember Miss Jackson buying it about three years ago, when there was that sale at the Grange. I'd a fancy for it myself then, but she outbid me; so I was quite pleased to get hold of it in the end."

"I reckon it belonged to old Mr. Ledbury, then?"

"No doubt, though I can't say where he got it from. What do you want to know for?"

"I don't want to know. It's no business of mine."

Katrine's sketch was greatly admired by the girls at Aireyholme, but Miss Aubrey, in her capacity of art teacher, criticized it sternly. To rectify the faults thus pointed out, Katrine toiled very hard, and completely repainted the two figures. Granny Blundell was a patient model, and (as the sittings resulted in shillings) expressed her willingness to pose any time for the school. Several of the other girls sketched her at the life class, though none of their efforts were as successful as Katrine's. Noticing the old woman's interest in the progress of the portrait, Gwethyn made her a present of the oil-sketch she had just finished. Her gift was hardly as well received as she had anticipated.

"The old body scarcely said 'Thank you!'" complained Gwethyn, much aggrieved.

"Perhaps she doesn't think it flatters her; it's one of the worst daubs you've ever perpetrated!" laughed Katrine.

"Oh! I should hardly imagine her an art critic! Besides, she's so very plain, in any case. No picture in the world could make her look handsome."

Though Mrs. Blundell might not be the belle of the village, a little vanity lingered nevertheless under her striped sun-bonnet. Katrine happened to visit her cottage alone next day, and found her in a state of much discontent over her likeness. She plainly did not consider that it did her justice.

"It makes me look all speckly!" she remonstrated. "And I'm not speckly, am I, now? I was thinkin' of askin' her to touch it up a bit. I wouldn't mind payin' her a trifle, if she don't want to charge too much for her time. I was that set on sendin' it to my gran'darter at Chiplow, but I'd be 'shamed to let her think I'd a face like a dough dumplin' stuck wi' currants."

Fearing it would be impossible to idealize the portrait to the sitter's satisfaction, Katrine solved the problem by taking a snapshot of her standing in the doorway with her favourite cat in her arms; and though the photo did not flatter her, it presented her with a smooth countenance, at any rate. It apparently satisfied her craving for immortalization, and preserved a remembrance also of her pet, who unfortunately met with an untimely fate soon afterwards. Mrs. Blundell had lamented the disappearance of Pussy for some days; then one afternoon when Katrine arrived with her easel, she discovered the good dame in the garden, busily engaged in washing her pans and kettles.

"Why, what a turn-out!" exclaimed Katrine. "Is it a spring cleaning or a removal?"

"Oh, miss," returned Mrs. Blundell, "I've just found the pore cat drownded in the well! I drew her up myself in the bucket, and it gave I such a shock I went all of a tremble. She must have been there the whole time, and somehow now I can't quite fancy the water."

"I should think not!" exclaimed Katrine, horrified at the idea.

"I sometimes wish I lived in a town, with water laid on, and gas-lamps in the streets," continued Mrs. Blundell. "I can't think what you see to paint in these old cottages. The creepers lovely? Why, they helps to make 'em damp! They don't be fit for decent folks to live in. They did ought all to be pulled down."

Poor Mrs. Blundell evidently held strong views on the deficiencies of her residence, to judge from a conversation which Miss Aubrey and Katrine heard wafted through the door as they sat sketching in her cabbage-patch. The minister appeared to be paying her a visit, and was trying to count up her blessings for her—a form of consolation which, from her tart replies, she keenly resented.

"You've got a roof over your head," he urged.

"The rain comes through in the corner," she sniffed. "It don't be right as I should be in this place, and some in such comfort! Folks as live soft here didn't ought to go to Heaven!"

"But wealthy people can live good lives as well as poor ones," objected Mr. Chadwick, the minister.

"Easy enough for 'em, when they've all they want; but it don't be fair! They be gettin' it at both ends," she answered bitterly.

"Doth Job serve God for nought?" quoted Miss Aubrey, as they listened to the querulous old voice. "I quite grasp her point, poor old soul! I dare say it's much easier to watch the wicked flourishing like a green bay tree, and anticipate his retribution, than to see the righteous in such prosperity, and think he's skimming the cream off both worlds. I admire Mr. Chadwick's patience. I think he'll talk her into a better frame of mind before he leaves her."

Whatever her notions might be on the subject of future rewards or punishments, Granny Blundell made a picturesque model, and that for the present was Katrine's main concern. She finished both figures and background, then left the canvas to dry, so that she might add some last high lights. Would it ever hang in an exhibition? she asked herself. She had not yet dared to broach the subject to Mr. Freeman.

She looked at it often, hopefully and wistfully. At present it was the focus round which her dreams centred, a matter of the utmost importance. The rest of the girls would have laughed at her had they realized her ambition in connection with it; yet, after all—so strangely do things happen in this life—the painting of this very amateur sketch was a link in a chain of circumstances, and if it did not bring artistic success to herself, was to lead to wider issues in other respects than she could imagine.

CHAPTER XIII

Githa's Secret

WITH Tony as their bond of union, the amenities between Gwethyn and Githa still continued. They could hardly be called chums, for they were never on absolutely familiar terms such as existed between Gwethyn and Rose Randall. The poor little Toadstool's natural disposition was too reserved for the frank intimacy common in most schoolgirl friendships. She rarely gave any confidences, and though she evidently admired Gwethyn immensely, it was with a funny, dumb sort of attachment that did not express itself in words. On the subject of her home and her own private affairs she was generally guarded to a degree. Once only did she break the ice. In a most unwonted and unusual burst of confidence she admitted to Gwethyn that she was unhappy about her brother.

"Cedric is at such a horrid school. The head master is a brute! None of the boys like him, and he's taken a particular spite against Ceddie, and is absolutely hateful to him. You see, it's mainly a day-school, and there are only fourteen boarders. Cedric is the eldest of them by three years, and he thinks it's very hard he should have to keep exactly the same rules as the little chaps. But Mr. Hawkins won't make any difference. He treats Ceddie as if he were at a preparatory school. He's a blustering, bullying, domineering sort of man, very fond of using the cane. Well, you know a boy of sixteen won't stand all that! Especially Cedric. He's frightfully proud and independent, and he answers old Hawkins back, and then there are squalls. Sometimes it gets to such a pass that Cedric says he'll run away. I really believe he will some day! It's past all bearing."

"Can't your uncle interfere?" asked Gwethyn.

"It's no use telling Uncle Wilfred. He always says he's not going to listen to complaints, and that Cedric is quite as well treated at school as he used to be, and that boys are a soft set nowadays, and haven't the grit their fathers used to have, and that he doesn't think anything of a lad who comes whining home after a few strokes with a cane, which are probably only too well deserved. That stops Cedric's mouth. He can't bear Uncle to think him a coward. All the same, he's often in a very tight fix, and I wish we could see some way out of it."

"I suppose your Uncle Wilfred is his guardian?"

"Yes, unfortunately. There's nobody else. We have another uncle, but he went out to America years and years ago, and we've heard nothing of him. I wish I knew his address. Perhaps Cedric might have gone to him in America. Uncle Wilfred is decent enough to me, because I'm a girl, but he says it's wholesome for boys to be knocked about a little. Sometimes Aunt Julia says Mr. Hawkins is too strict, but Uncle always stands up for him and takes his side against Cedric. Aunt is quite kind; she sends Ceddie cakes and hampers of jam every now and then, but those don't make up for Mr. Hawkins being such a beast. He and Cedric just hate each other."

Gwethyn was deeply interested, but could suggest no remedy. There seemed, indeed, no way out of such a difficult situation. Her warm sympathy, however, quite touched Githa.

"I never thought you'd care about my affairs," she faltered.

"Care! You silly child! Of course I care," protested Gwethyn. "I'm as sorry about it as I can be! Why didn't you tell me before?"

"It never struck me to tell you. Uncle Wilfred and Aunt Julia don't care to hear things, so I thought other people might be the same. Ceddie and I are nothing to you."

"Yes, you are, and please to remember that in future. I don't want to be inquisitive and pry into your private concerns, but I'm very interested in anything you may wish me to know. We can't be friends when you're such an absolute oyster!"

The poor Toadstool sighed and smiled at the same time. She had been too afraid of snubs to open her heart readily. Her present outpouring, though in a sense a relief, was also an effort. Perhaps she thought she had revealed too much of her home atmosphere, for she closed up again, and for days

Gwethyn could get nothing at all out of her. Fortunately Gwethyn had the tact to leave her alone and make no attempt to force her confidence. She realized that such an odd, prickly little character must be treated with discretion, and that the sympathy which she was burning to offer was — incertain moods — as likely to offend as to please her peculiar friend.

For the last three days Githa had been more than usually what the girls called "toadish". She would speak to nobody, or if baited into words, her retorts were of a stinging quality, not encouraging to further conversation. She was late for school one morning, and went off in a great hurry in the afternoon. In class she seemed preoccupied, and was several times reprimanded by Miss Andrews for not attending to the lessons. She took the reproofs rather sulkily. Her form-mates had many wrangles with her about quite trivial matters.

"You always were a cross little toad, but your temper's got worse than ever!" declared the outraged Novie Bates, after an unprovoked push from Githa in the classroom.

"You shouldn't stand in my way then! I wanted to get to my desk!" retorted the Toadstool snappily, opening the lid about two inches to slip in a book.

"You're very surreptitious about your precious desk," bantered Lena Dawson, for the mere sake of teasing. "What have you got inside it?"

For once the pale little face was fiery.

"If you dare to touch my desk!" stamped Githa, in a perfect fury.

Lena had never intended to touch it, but thus challenged, she thought it rather fun to — as she expressed it — "make Githa let off squibs".

"Hi-cockalorum, what a to-do!" she exclaimed. "I'm janitor this week, my child, so I've a right to look into anybody's desk if I like, and report its condition. It's my solemn duty to examine yours now, and see if it reaches the standard of neatness required — ahem! — in this very select scholastic establishment. Naturally you don't wish to risk the loss of an order mark, but duty is duty, my hearty!"

"You blithering idiot!" flared Githa, holding down the lid of her desk, and pushing Lena away with her elbow.

"Now that's equivalent to assaulting the police! I must trouble you to show me the inside of this. Will someone please help me?"

Novie Bates and Jess Howard, giggling their hardest, came to Lena's aid. The three easily pulled Githa aside and flung open the desk. Within were several paper bags, into which Lena, on a plea of "ex officio", insisted on peeping.

"Hello! What have we got here? Bread-and-butter! Scraps of meat and potatoes! Cake! By the Muses, you're having a good old feast! Do you come and refresh during recreation?"

Githa's flush of colour had faded. Her cheeks were drab again as the fungus to which Gwethyn had originally compared them. Her dark eyes were inscrutable.

"It's no business of yours if I do," she parried.

"Oh, certainly not! Munch away as hard as you please, if you like. It doesn't affect us. We'd willingly spread honey on the bread-and-butter if it would sweeten your temper."

"There, Lena, let her alone!" pleaded Jess, who thought the teasing had gone far enough. "If you weren't so touchy, Githa, nobody'd trouble to bother about you. It's your own fault if you get ragged! Don't be absurd; we're not going to run away with your precious parcels. You needn't stand guarding them like an old hen cackling over its eggs."

"Go and have a picnic with them in the garden!" jeered Lena. "Tell Mother Franklin she doesn't give you enough at dinner-time, and you have to bring extra supplies to school. She'd not refuse you a second helping if you asked. Some people have big appetites. It's a silly secret to make such a fuss about."

"I call it greedy!" scoffed Novie.

On that very same afternoon, between four and five o'clock, Katrine and Gwethyn were walking together in the orchard. The two often liked to have a private chat; though Gwethyn chummed with Rose Randall, Katrine had not made any special friendship among the Sixth, and mostly counted upon her sister for company. They had kept their adventure at the Grange to themselves, and they talked of it now as they sauntered between the apple-trees.

"It's a quaint old house," said Katrine. "We didn't half examine it when we were there. I should like to look again at that panelling in the library, and take a rough pencil sketch of it. I believe it's just what I want for one of my pictures. Shall we scoot and go across the fields?"

"Yes, by all means, if you'll guarantee we'll not get locked up! Mr. Freeman mightn't be handy a second time."

"Oh, we'll be very careful, and inspect all the door-knobs before we venture into the rooms! Come along; it will be rather sport!"

Needless to say, Gwethyn acquiesced. The mere fun of dodging the school authorities and paying a second surreptitious visit to the old Grange appealed to her; she did not care very much about the artistic merits of the panels or wish to sketch them. So again the girls climbed the fence and manoeuvred across the fields under cover of the hedges.

"It looks as if a bicycle had been here lately," said Katrine, examining some tracks on the gravel as she opened the gate. "Perhaps we shan't have the place to ourselves to-day."

"Keep a look-out, then. We can soon scoot if necessary."

Observing due caution, they entered the house by the same window as on a former occasion. Very softly they stole down the passage past the dining-room. The library door stood ajar, and Katrine pushed it open. She stopped with an exclamation of surprise. On some upturned boxes at the far end of the room sat Githa and a boy, who was eating something hastily out of a paper bag. At the sight of strangers he jumped up with a wild, hunted look on his face, and unlatching the French window, disappeared into the garden in the space of a few seconds. Githa had also sprung to her feet.

"Katrine! Gwethyn! Are you alone, or is Miss Aubrey or anyone with you?" she faltered.

"All serene! We're quite by ourselves!"

Githa ran promptly to the window.

"Right-o!" she called. "Come back, Ceddie!"

The boy did not reply, and after waiting a little, Githa turned again to her friends.

"You've plumped upon my secret, so I may as well tell you. I know you won't give me away?"

"We'd be burnt at the stake first!" protested Gwethyn.

"Well, I dare say you guess that was my brother. Poor old Ceddie! He's been in fearful trouble, and he's run away from school. He always said he would, and now he's done it at last. I told you Mr. Hawkins was a beast. He caught Ceddie smoking a cigarette, and said he meant to make an example of him. He was just white with passion. He hauled Ceddie into the big classroom, and made the janitor hold him over a chair, and then thrashed him simply brutally, before all the school. He gave him seventeen strokes. Ceddie didn't care so much about the pain — he bore it like a Stoic; but it was such an indignity to be caned like that — a tall fellow of sixteen, before all those little boys! He took the first opportunity and bolted that very evening. He says he'd rather die than go back to school. I'll try and get him to come in and speak to you."

Githa ran into the garden and apparently used her powers of persuasion successfully, for after a short time she came back accompanied by her brother, whom she introduced to her friends. Cedric was rather a nice-looking lad, painfully shy, however, and much oppressed by the awkwardness of the situation. He did not seem disposed to talk to the

137

visitors, and stood with his hands in his pockets looking out of the window, and whistling softly. As their presence only seemed to embarrass him, Katrine and Gwethyn had the tact to go away. Githa walked with them down the passage.

"He's been here three days," she confided. "He knew there'd be a frightful hue-and-cry after him, so he's lying low until it's over. Of course we daren't let Uncle know where he is. There's ever such a hullabaloo going on about it all at home, but I look absolutely stolid and don't breathe a word. I come every day and bring him food, and he sleeps on some straw in the attic. He'd rather do that than be sent back to old Hawkins's tender mercies."

"Does your uncle know how he was thrashed?"

"I'm not sure. Probably Mr. Hawkins only told his own side of the story. I daren't ask anything. I'm so afraid of letting out the secret."

"But he can't stay here for ever!"

"No, he's just waiting until things blow over; then he'll do a bolt at night, and walk to Settlefield and try and enlist. He's wild to join the army."

"But he's too young!" gasped Katrine.

"He's very tall for his age, and of course he'd pretend he was eighteen."

Katrine was aghast at such a plan. It seemed pre-doomed to failure. Cedric might be tall, but his boyish figure and youthful face would proclaim to any recruiting sergeant that he was below the age for enlistment. She stated her opinion emphatically, and urged Githa to persuade him to give up so foolish a notion.

"Oh dear! Whatever are we to do then?" sighed the worried little Toadstool. "We'd both counted on his getting into the army. I'm at my wits' end. I suppose he'll have to tramp to Liverpool, and get on a ship as a cabin-boy or a stoker, and work his passage to America. Perhaps he'll find Uncle Frank there."

"I'm afraid that would be worse still," said Katrine gently. "Couldn't you trust your Uncle Wilfred? Perhaps if he really heard Cedric's side of the case, he would take him away from this school, and see about fitting him for what he's to be in the future. After all, he's his guardian."

"And a very harsh one! No, I daren't tell Uncle Wilfred. Ceddie must try to get to America. Other boys have run away and made their own fortunes."

"But how many have done the opposite?" urged Katrine. "Don't let him throw away his life like this! Have you no friend you could ask to help him?"

Githa shook her head forlornly.

"Nobody cares to bother about us."

"I wish Father and Mother were in England!" said Gwethyn.

"Oh, how I wish they were!" exclaimed Githa, with a flash of hope on her face that faded as suddenly as it arose. "But what's the use of wishing, when we know they're in Australia?"

The suggestion had given Katrine an idea, however.

"Would you trust your secret to Mr. Freeman?" she asked. "He's one of the kindest men I know, and perhaps he'd be able to think of some way out of the matter. I needn't tell him that Cedric is hiding at the Grange" (as Githa hesitated); "I'd simply state the facts of the case, and ask for his advice."

"Oh! Dare we trust him? He wouldn't let Mr. Hawkins get hold of Ceddie?"

"I promise he wouldn't."

Having wrung a somewhat unwilling consent, Katrine hurried away before Githa had time to change her mind. In defiance of all school rules she and Gwethyn went straight to the village, and called at Mr. Freeman's lodgings. They found their friend painting in his studio, and, having first pledged him to strictest secrecy, poured out their story.

"Whew! Poor little chap!" he exclaimed. "He seems to have got himself into a precious mess! Sleeping on straw, did you say? And living on scraps his sister brings him? No, no! He mustn't think of running off to America. So Mr. Ledbury is his uncle? The solicitor at Carford? Well, as it happens, he's doing some legal business for me at present, so I fancy I might open negotiations with him, very diplomatically, of course. Don't be afraid! I'll stand the boy's friend. It's high time they were thinking what to make of him. Leave it in my hands, and I'll see if I can't talk the uncle round."

"Oh, thanks so much!" exclaimed the girls. "You don't know what a relief it is to hand the matter over to you. Now we must scoot, or we shall get into trouble at school ourselves."

On this occasion, Katrine and Gwethyn went straight to Mrs. Franklin's study, and reported themselves for having broken bounds. The Principal glared at them, entered the offence in her private ledger, and harangued them on its enormity; but as they had made voluntary confession, she gave them no special punishment. On the whole, they considered they had got off rather more easily than they had expected.

"I can't bear to think of that poor laddie sleeping all alone in that dismal old house," said Katrine, as the sisters went to bed that night. "It gives me the creeps even to imagine it. He looked a jolly boy. He and Githa seem to have hard luck. It was too bad to leave them utterly to their uncle's charity."

"The grandfather ought to have provided for them properly," agreed Gwethyn. "People should make just wills before they die."

Githa came to school the next morning with dark rings round her eyes. She admitted having lain awake most of the night, worrying about her brother.

"If Mr. Freeman can't help us, Ceddie means to start to-night for Liverpool," she whispered to Gwethyn during the interval.

The three girls spent an anxious day. They wondered continually if their friend were working on their behalf, and with what success. At about half-past three, Mr. Freeman called at the school, and asked Mrs. Franklin's permission to speak to Katrine. He had good news to report. He had seen Mr. Ledbury and had spoken to him about Cedric, without betraying the boy's whereabouts, which indeed he did not himself know. He found that Mr. Ledbury exhibited the utmost relief at hearing tidings of the runaway. He said he had been making inquiries, and discovered, through information given him by one of the under masters, that the school was not what he had thought it to be, and that the punishment given to his nephew had been excessive and brutal in the extreme. He was sorry that he had ever placed the boy in Mr. Hawkins's charge, and should at once remove him. He sent a message to Cedric, telling him to return home, and that all would be forgiven. He seemed anxious to do his best for his nephew, and to give him a good start in life.

"I was able to make a proposition," added Mr. Freeman, "which opens a way for the boy's immediate future. My brother is in the Admiralty Department, and I am almost sure that I can persuade him to give Cedric a nomination for the navy. They want lads of his age at present, and I should think the life would just suit the young chap. So let his sister tell him to go home. I don't suppose his uncle will exactly kill the fatted calf for him, but he won't be thrashed or sent back to school. I'll guarantee that."

Githa's eyes shone with gratitude when Katrine told her the result of Mr. Freeman's kind offices as peacemaker.

"Oh! I am so relieved — so thankful! Ceddie would love to get into the navy! It would be far nicer than enlisting as a private. How proud I should be of him in his uniform! I'll fly now on my bike to the Grange, and get Ceddie to come straight home with me. I believe Aunt Julia will be glad. Oh, how ripping to have Cedric at home again! You and Gwethyn are just the biggest trumps on earth!"

As Mr. Freeman had prognosticated, the runaway was not received with any great outward demonstration of joy by his uncle and aunt, though both were secretly much relieved at his reappearance. Matters took an unexpected turn, however, for the poor lad had caught cold by sleeping ondamp straw in the empty house, and was confined to bed with a sharp attack of rheumatism. His illness brought out all the kindness in his aunt's nature. She had always had rather a soft corner for him, though she had not been willing to admit it, and had generally persuaded herself that the two children were a burden. She nursed him well now, and was so good to him during his convalescence that Githa's manner thawed, and the girl was more at ease with her aunt than she had ever been before — a wonderfully pleasant and unusual state of affairs.

Mr. Freeman's representations at the Admiralty had the desired effect. Cedric received his nomination, and in due course, when the doctor would pronounce him fit, was to go up for his examination. He was wild with enthusiasm.

"If I can only get quickly into the fighting line," he declared, "won't I just enjoy myself!"

"Get well first," commanded Githa, whose sisterly pride seemed to think her brother destined to become at least an admiral.

CHAPTER XIV

A Midnight Alarm

MR. BOB GARTLEY had not the best of reputations in Heathwell. He had more than once been convicted on a charge of poaching, and had served time in Carford jail. Of late his aversion to work had become so marked that his presence in the bosom of his family seemed a doubtful benefit to his wife and his olive branches. The numerous young Gartleys learnt rapidly to scuttle out of reach of the parental fist, and spent a great portion of their time sitting upon curb-stones or playing under hedgerows, oblivious of damp or dirt, while poor Mrs. Gartley, who received the brunt of her spouse's ill-humour, covered up her bruises and put the best face she could on the matter towards the world. Her labours had to provide for the household; her better half's uncertain and occasional earnings being liable to be forestalled at the "Dragon".

"Why they gives him credit passes me!" she confided to Mrs. Stubbs, who, having gone through similar experiences, was loud in her condolence.

"It be a speculation on Stephen Peters's part," replied the worthy vendor of antiques. "He knows he can get it in kind, if not in cash, and he be fond of a pheasant for his Sunday's dinner. But Bob had best be careful, for the keepers are on the watch more than ever, and if he is taken again so soon, he'll get an extra hard sentence."

"I'm sure I've warned him till I'm hoarse, but it seems no use. He never listens to I."

One Sunday morning, the obdurate Bob Gartley might have been found sitting by the fireside in his own kitchen. He was attired in his shirt-sleeves, and had not yet had the temerity to attempt either washing or shaving, but he consoled himself for these deficiencies by puffing away at his pipe, and taking an occasional glance into a saucepan whence issued a savoury odour strongly suggestive of hare, or some other unlawful delicacy. The seven little Gartleys, having found their father in a very unsabbatical frame of mind, had wisely removed themselves from his vicinity, and were at present scrambling about in the road, awaiting with impatience the arrival of the dinner-hour, coming to the door occasionally to indulge in anticipatory sniffs, but being promptly scared away by a warning growl from the arm-chair.

"Keep they brats out of my sight!" roared Mr. Gartley fiercely, turning to his wife, who was making a slight endeavour to tidy up the cottage. "Why can't you pack 'em off to Church and Sunday School? I were always sent regular when I were a boy."

"Much good it's done for you!" retorted Mrs. Gartley scornfully. "Not but what I'd send the children if they'd any decent clothes to their backs. I'd be 'shamed to let 'em go, though, in the same rags they wears week in and week out, and their toes through the ends of their boots!"

"It don't be fair as we poor folks should have to take the leavin's of everything," remarked Mr. Gartley, waxing sententious. "Why shouldn't my children be dressed as well as Captain Gordon's?"

"Because you can't buy 'em the clothes, I suppose. What's the use of askin' such questions?"

"I'd like to see 'em in white dresses and tweed suits," continued Mr. Gartley, who might have been a model father as far as aspirations were concerned; "a-settin' off proper and regular to Church of a Sunday."

"Precious likely, when all you've got goes at the 'Dragon'."

"It's a shame as some should be rich and some poor. There were a man come round last election time, and said as how everything ought to be divided up equal, share and share alike, and the workin' classes wouldn't stand bein' oppressed much longer. They'd rise and throw off the yoke. Those was his very words. Some as is doin' nothing now would have to set their hands to work."

"If you mean yourself, it might be a good business."

"No, it's the idle rich I be talkin' of, like Mr. Everard or Captain Gordon, or even Parson; for what does he do, I should like to know, beyond preach, and that's an easy enough job. What right have Captain Gordon or Mr. Everard to the hares and pheasants? They be wild things, and I says let anybody take 'em as can catch 'em. The folks in Scripture went out huntin', and we're not told as it was called poachin'. They didn't bring Esau up before the magistrates for gettin' his venison."

Mrs. Gartley shook her head. Such reasoning was utterly beyond her powers of argument.

"I reckon times was different then," she ventured. "They be cruel bad for us poor folks just now."

"We'd be as good as anybody else if we had the money," urged her husband. "You're a fine-lookin' wench still, Jane, if you'd a silk dress and a big hat with feathers like Mrs. Gordon's."

"What's the use o' talkin'?" replied Mrs. Gartley, amazed at the unwonted compliment. "I'm never likely to wear a silk dress this side o' the grave."

"Unlikelier things has come to happen than that! We might be somebodies if— —"

"If what?"

"If something I've got in my mind was to come off."

"What do you mean?"

"Oh, nothing particular! Only it would be uncommon nice to set up as fine as other folks — in a new country, where no one knowed what we had been."

"I don't understand."

"Wouldn't you like to go out to America or Australia, and start afresh?"

"Why, yes; but we haven't got a penny to go with."

"No more we have, that's true," chuckled Mr. Gartley. "You say uncommon clever things sometimes, Jane. No, we've not got a penny-piece to pay our fares — at present."

"What are you drivin' at?"

"Nothing. Don't you begin askin' questions. You'd best keep a still tongue in your head and shut your eyes, as far as I'm concerned."

"Oh, Bob! You're never going to be at some of your old tricks? I tell you it's not safe. A stray hare now and again is bad enough, but when it comes to — —"

"Shut up!" commanded Mr. Gartley angrily. "I'll mind my own business, and you may mind yours. Go and turn those squalling brats off the door-step, they send me mad with their noise. I'll make 'em go to Church another time, clothes or no clothes. Parson may put 'em in clean pinafores, if he's so anxious to have 'em at Sunday school."

Mrs. Gartley fled to disperse her family, and wisely refrained from any further inquiries about her husband's intentions; arguments, she knew, were wasted upon him, and it was useless to distress herself with too close a knowledge of his devious methods of acquiring a living.

"I can guess what he's after," she thought. "And if he's caught, they'll give he seven years. It'll mean the poorhouse for I and the children. Well, it's no use talkin', for once Bob's set his mind on a thing, do it he will."

When his wife was safely out of the way, Mr. Gartley retired upstairs to the bedroom, where after moving a heavy oak chest, he laid bare a loose plank in the floor. This he lifted, and from some receptacle below he drew a dark lantern and one or two tools of peculiar workmanship. He stored these treasures in his pockets, then, replacing the plank, he lifted the chest back into its accustomed position.

"She's no idea where I keep 'em," he muttered, "and it's best as she shouldn't know. I may as well try to-night, folks be always abed early and sleep sound on Sundays. Parson would say it was their good conscience.

My old granny had a sayin': 'The better the day, the better the deed', so good luck to my work to-night, and may we soon be off to America!"

On this identical Sunday it happened that a few of the Aireyholme girls, taking a walk with their Principal in the afternoon, met Mr. and Mrs. Ledbury and Githa, who were also out for exercise. Now Githa had brought Tony, and Gwethyn, who was with the school party, fell upon her pet with the rapture due to long separation. Mrs. Franklin was not at all fond of dogs, but on this occasion she was in a singularly gracious and generous mood. She had had a pleasant little chat with Mr. and Mrs. Ledbury, and when turning to go, she noticed Gwethyn's unwillingness to part with her darling Tony.

"It's very kind of Githa to take charge of your dog," she remarked. "If you like, you may bring him home with you this afternoon, and keep him until to-morrow."

Gwethyn walked away cuddling her treasure closely. To have her pet to herself even for twenty-four hours was an indulgence sufficient to make her forgive Mrs. Franklin for many other strictnesses. Master Tony was the idol of the school at tea-time; he was a vain little dog, who loved admiration, and that afternoon he was cosseted to his heart's content. He held almost a royal reception, everybody declaring him "perfectly sweet".

"I wish we'd even a yard dog at Aireyholme," said Rose Randall. "It's a pity Mrs. Franklin detests them so."

"She was quite kind to Tony to-day. How well he looks, the darling! He's almost too fat now, instead of being too thin. Precious one! Are you going to sleep with your own missis to-night?"

Evidently Master Tony had no intention of being left alone, for when nine o'clock came he trotted upstairs with Gwethyn, and promptly installed himself on her bed. Miss Andrews, coming her duty-round at half-past nine, noticed the silky head peeping from under the dressing-jacket that covered him, but she kindly took no notice. For once he was to be privileged.

"Everyone seems to go to bed early on Sunday night," remarked Katrine, taking a glance through the window at the silent village at the bottom of the hill below the school. "Perhaps it's the mental effort of listening that exhausts their brains. I dare say on week-days many of them are like the agricultural labourer in Punch, who said he thought of 'maistly nought'. People seem far more tired with two services than with a day's work in the fields."

The girls had been sound asleep for a long time, when Gwethyn was suddenly disturbed by an uneasy whimper from Tony. Wideawake in a moment, she sat up.

"What's the matter, my precious?"

The room was in complete darkness, but she could tell from the dog's warning growl that he was all on the alert.

"Do you hear anything?"

Tony's low grumble was a sufficient answer in his own language.

"Is it rats?"

"Be quiet, Gwethyn, and let us listen too," said Katrine, who was also aroused. "I thought I heard a queer noise."

In dead silence the girls waited. For a minute or two all was still, then came a curious subdued sound like the very gentle working backwards and forwards of a file.

"What is it?" whispered Gwethyn.

"I don't know."

"It seems to come from downstairs."

"Yes, most certainly."

"Is it a rat gnawing?"

"That's no rat."

"Has a bird got into the chimney?"

"No, it sounds quite different. I believe it's outside."

"Shall I strike a match?"

"Better not. I want to listen at the window."

Katrine crept out of bed, and groped her way across the dark room to the open casement. It was a cloudy night, with neither moon nor star in the sky, and the view was one uniform mass of blackness. The silence was almost oppressive; none of the ordinary country noises were to be heard, not a cow lowed nor a solitary owl hooted — all the world lay hushed in quiet sleep. The darkness seemed to hedge them round and cut them off from the rest of the slumbering humanity in the village.

Tony had followed Katrine, and pushed his cold moist nose into her hand. As she bent down to pat him, she could feel his whole body quivering with tense agitation.

"He knows something is wrong, or he wouldn't be upset like this," she thought.

Again from the darkness outside came that curious subdued scraping sound. Their bedroom was over the porch. Could a strange dog be scratching at the door beneath? Or some wild animal — a weasel or a stoat, perhaps — be seeking an entrance?

She leaned cautiously from the window, trying in vain to distinguish any object. Her heart was beating fast, and she was trembling with nervousness. The noise ceased again, there was a moment's pause, and for one second she saw a gleam of light in the garden below. Instantly a sudden illumination swept over her mind: it was neither rat, bird, dog, stoat, nor weasel, but a human being that was disturbing their peace.

"Gwethyn," she breathed in a panic-stricken whisper, "somebody is trying to break in through the dining-room window!"

At the very suggestion of burglars Gwethyn gave a shriek of terror, which set Tony barking loudly enough to have disturbed the Forty Thieves. So furious was his anger against the unknown intruder, that he would have leaped through the window if she had not held him by the collar. All his doggish instincts urged him to defend his mistresses, and he was ready to fly at the throat of whoever had set foot in the garden below.

The noise disturbed the other occupants of the landing. The girls came running from their rooms to inquire the cause of the upset. Mrs. Franklin appeared upon the scene with the promptitude of fire-drill practice. On grasping the fact that an attempt was being made to break into the house, she ran to the big school bell, and tolled an alarm signal calculated to waken the whole village. She went on ringing vigorously until shouts and running footsteps outside assured her of help.

Mr. White, from the farm near at hand, and some of his boys were the first to arrive, but they were followed almost immediately by the blacksmith, the saddler, and a number of cottagers, till quite a little crowd had collected in the drive. Mrs. Franklin hastily explained the situation, and some of the men, taking lanterns, made a thorough examination of the premises.

This midnight alarm caused a great stir in Heathwell. Such a thing as an attempted burglary had hitherto been absolutely unknown, and the inhabitants felt that it was a reflection on the village. The policeman paid a solemn call at Aireyholme, produced his notebook, and asked a multitude of questions, particularly of Katrine and Gwethyn; but the girls could give little or no information. Beyond the fact that they had heard a noise and seen a light in the garden, there was not a shred of evidence, or the faintest clue to lead to the identification of the thief. The inspector examined the frame of the dining-room window, which certainly bore marks as if an effort had been made to force it with some sharp tool, and he carefully measured the footprints in the flower-bed; but as many of these had undoubtedly been made by the stalwart boots of Mr. White and other assiduous helpers in the ardour of their search, it would have been impossible for even a Sherlock Holmes to gain any enlightenment from them. Nobody in the village had seen any suspicious characters about, and everyone seemed to have been sound asleep in bed until roused by the ringing of the Aireyholme alarm bell. In the end the policeman wrote a formal report to the effect that some person or persons unknown had made an attempt to commit a felony, but had been interrupted in the act by the barking of the dog.

"All of which is absolutely self-evident, and didn't need a whole hour's investigation," said Gwethyn. "Still, I suppose poor old Whately had to write something in his notebook. The chief credit seems to be due to Tony. I'm sure he scared the wretch away. I don't know what we should have done without him."

Tony was undoubtedly the hero of the occasion. If he had been petted before, he was lionized now. Even Mrs. Franklin admitted that a dog in the house was a great protection, and offered to let Gwethyn keep Tony at Aireyholme for the rest of the term.

The Principal had been more alarmed at the attempted burglary than she would confess to her pupils. She tried to reassure the girls, telling them it was very improbable that any thief would make a second attempt on the premises; but for many nights everybody in the school slept uneasily, and woke at the least sound.

The only person in Heathwell who did not exhibit much excitement at the news of the attempt to break into Aireyholme was Mr. Bob Gartley, who received his wife's very enlarged version of the story with an imperturbable countenance.

"There was a gang of them, was there?" he remarked. "All armed with pistols and bludgeons, and bent on murder? Where be they a-gone to, then? And why ain't Whately tracked 'em out? Seems to me as if he don't know his business, and he'd best retire. I think I'll apply for the job! How would you like me as a police inspector?"

"I've no doubt you'd be up to a trick or two, if you was! It's a comfort, though, as you're not mixed up in this, for you was over in Captain Gordon's preserves at Chiselton, though you couldn't bring that in as an alibi!"

"Yes, at Chiselton, and that be four miles from Heathwell. If I likes to take a little midnight walk to admire the moon, I don't see what call anyone has to go interferin' with me. Everyone has their hobbies, and mine's for enjoyin' the beauties o' nature."

"But there weren't no moon last night," objected his wife.

"What business is that o' yours? A man may be a bit wrong in the calendar, and go out to look for what ain't there. Why can't you get on with your washin', instead o' standin' idlin' and talkin'?"

"It were a nearish shave," reflected Mr. Gartley, as his wife beat a retreat. "I'd only just nipped over the wall afore John White come runnin' out. I thought I should 'a managed the trick that time. I were a fool not to find out first as they kept a dog! 'Twouldn't be safe to venture it again for a goodish bit, at any rate, so good-bye to America for the present. It's hard luck on a workin' man who's tryin' to do the best for 'is family!"

CHAPTER XV

Amateur Artists

FLOWERY June had given place to blazing July. The pink roses were fading on the cottage fronts, and the laburnums had long been over. Tall white lilies still bloomed in the village gardens, and geraniums were beginning to show their scarlet glory. The fresh green of early summer had yielded to darker tones, the trees were thick masses of foliage, the hedges a tangle of traveller's joy. If the landscape lacked the inspiration of spring, it was nevertheless full of rich beauty, especially to eyes trained to appreciate the picturesque. Miss Aubrey's sketching class was at present quite a large one, for it had been augmented by the addition of Viola, Dorrie, and Diana. Now that their matriculation examination was over, they no longer needed private coaching, and Mrs. Franklin transferred their spare hours to her sister. The three monitresses were glad of the change; after the hard brainwork and the very close application that had been required from them, they turned to painting with the greatest relief. Every afternoon a procession of enthusiastic students, bearing camp-stools and easels, wended its way from Aireyholme. At first Miss Aubrey had led her artistic flock to the village, but with July days came a change of plans. The Council school broke up for six weeks, and Heathwell was suddenly over-run with children. Although according to statistics the population of England might be on the decrease, here it certainly showed no signs of dwindling. Small people were everywhere, as the amateur artists found to their cost. No doubt it was most unreasonable of the Aireyholme girls, who liked their own August vacation, to object to other schools having holidays, but they did not appreciate a crowd of spectators, and grumbled exceedingly.

"Good-bye to the last remnants of peace and quiet!" said Dorrie. "We're simply haunted by these wretched infants. They seem to think us fair game. I had the whole of the Gartley family, including the baby, sitting round my feet to-day."

"I like children singly or in pairs, or even up to half a dozen," protested Diana, "but when it comes to having them wholesale like this, I feel as if I were minding a crèche. Oh, what a nuisance they are!"

"It all comes of being too attractive, as the old lady said when she was struck by lightning!" laughed Gwethyn.

The class was sketching the street and the market hall. Some of the girls were making very good attempts at the subject, and Miss Aubrey was most anxious for them to finish their paintings, so for two more afternoons they braved their fatal popularity. It was impossible to escape the too friendly juveniles. Scouts were generally waiting to convey the news of their arrival, and they would walk down the village followed by a long comet's tail of small fry, who would encamp close to them on the market-hall steps, bringing babies, puppies, or kittens, eating bread and treacle, munching green apples, and singing deafening school songs in chorus. It was not the slightest use to tell the youngsters to go away; they would only retreat to a distance of about ten yards, and then edge gradually nearer again.

"I've tried to look cross and savage," said Gladwin Riley, "but they only grin."

"I've been trying to civilize them," sighed Nan Bethell. "I suggested to one youth that it would be an improvement for him to wash his particularly grimy little fingers. He looked at me, and then at his hands for a moment or two—apparently it takes some time for the agricultural brain to turn over a new idea—then he remarked briefly: 'I likes 'em dirty!' and transferred them to his pockets. Any further arguments on my poor part would, I felt, be superfluous."

Though the girls laughed over the humour of their experiences, they really found the children very trying, and both teacher and pupils were thankful when the sketches of the market hall were successfully finished. One final incident seemed the coping-stone of their annoyances. A child, even more eager than the rest to press near, was jostled by the others off the raised pathway where she was standing, and fell with a crash on to the road, almost upsetting Katrine's easel, and smashing a bottle of vinegar which she had been holding clasped in her arms. A woman, who proved to be the delinquent's mother, came out from a cottage, and after first administering a vigorous smack to her offspring, offered hot water wherewith to sponge the damaged clothing.

"She was really very kind," said Katrine afterwards, "but I could see that she was all the time regretting such a waste of good vinegar, more than sympathizing with me for absorbing it. I don't believe this skirt will ever be fit to wear again. I know I shall feel like a pickled herring if I put it on!"

It was not at all an easy matter for Miss Aubrey to choose a suitable subject for a large class. The girls were at different stages of ability, and the beginners must not be sacrificed to the cleverer few. While Katrine, Gladwin, and perhaps Diana could manage a sketch of trees, hayfield, or reedy river, the others demanded something more palpable in the way of drawing. A cottage, where you could reproduce the lines of roof, door, windows, and chimney, was far easier than a misty impression of sky and foliage. But where there were cottages there were nearly always children to stand and stare, so again Miss Aubrey found herself in a difficulty. She solved it by taking her class to sketch a picturesque, tumble-down little farm, about a mile and a half away from Heathwell, where, for a marvel, not even a solitary specimen of childhood resided.

The mistress of the place was an attraction in herself. She had established a considerable reputation in the neighbourhood as a herb doctor, preparing various nauseous and ill-smelling brews for sick cows or horses, or for human sprained ankles, bad legs, toothaches, headaches, or other ailments. She charmed warts and cured agues, and was even held by many to be somewhat of a witch. She was credited with the evil eye, and awestruck neighbours told dark tales of terrible misfortunes having befallen those who were unfortunate or rash enough to cross her will. As it is rare in this twentieth century to meet anybody with even the shadow of a reputation for the black arts, the girls were thrilled at the accounts they heard, and much disappointed that the old dame never vouchsafed them an exhibition of her talents.

One day she invited them to enter, and they persuaded her to explain to them the various treasures that adorned her parlour. Certainly the collection was unique. Two stuffed cocks stood on the window seat, each covered with an antimacassar, whether to preserve them, or merely to display the crochet work of which an example adorned every chair, it was impossible to decide; while a third chanticleer on the mantelpiece was generally used as a stand for the good woman's best bonnet. They had no doubt been fine birds in their time, and had won never-to-be-forgotten prizes at a local show, but their present value as ornaments was a matter of opinion. A marvellous sampler representing the Tabernacle in the Wilderness hung over the sideboard; carefully worked flames were depicted rising from the altar, and two cherubim with black beads for eyes and white Berlin-wool wings hovered at either corner, a few sizes too large for the building. On the mantelpiece lay two extraordinary objects which the girls at first took to be shells, but as they corresponded with no known specimen of conchology, inquiries were made.

"Ah, well!" said the old woman, taking them down tenderly. "These are my poor Richard's heels, the only thing I have left of him now. They came off all in a piece like that, when he was peeling after the scarlet fever. Indeed, I've always kept them to remember him by. They're the best weather-glass I have. I can generally tell by them when it's going to rain."

Thirty years—so Miss Aubrey hastened to ascertain—had passed since the memorable illness, therefore they might reasonably hope that no germs yet lingered in the relics; but they shuddered to think of the infection which must surely have been spread in the earlier days, when these treasures were examined and handled by curious neighbours.

An old illustrated Bible, with the date 1807, containing many crude woodcuts, occupied the little round table under the window. Mrs. Jones declared she never did anything without consulting it; and the girls were just going to express appreciation of her pious attention to Scripture, when she explained that her method was to shut her eyes, and opening the book at random, to insert the door key, and close it again. It had then to be turned over seven times, and whatever text the key pointed to, was sure to be appropriate. Once, so she declared, she had applied to it for advice as to whether to go to law with a farmer who had encroached upon her plot of land. She had struck the words: "Him will I destroy", and being thus encouraged to pursue her suit, she had won her case in triumph.

"Indeed, it's always right," she said, putting it carefully back on its wool-work mat. "I call it my conjuring book, and I wouldn't part with it for anything you could offer me."

"One gets odd peeps at life in the course of one's painting adventures," said Miss Aubrey. "An artist has the opportunity of becoming a good student of human nature. Sketching somehow brings one into touch with people in a way which no other hobby can emulate. I have had many funny experiences since I first took up the brush."

"Mrs. Jones beats even Granny Blundell at queerness," decided the girls.

One afternoon, as a very special treat, Miss Aubrey decided to take her three best pupils with her on an expedition by river to Chistleton. The landlord of the "Dragon Inn" owned a boat, and would row them there and back, waiting several hours for them in the town, while they saw the sights. They were to start after an early lunch, and have tea at a café in Chistleton. Katrine, Diana, and Gladwin were the chosen ones, and their luck was the envy of the rest of the sketching class, who implored to be included also. Miss Aubrey, however, stuck to her original plan. She could not take more than three girls in the boat, and told the others they must be content to wait until some future occasion. There was much to be seen in the old town; the walls were still extant, and two of the ancient gateways remained; the almshouses were show places, and the castle was the glory of the neighbourhood. Miss Aubrey wished to encourage the girls in rapid sketching, and made them take quick pencil impressions of all the principal sights. She had refused to allow them to bring cameras.

"People are too ready to make snapshots nowadays," was her verdict. "They are putting photography in the place of drawing. I grant that your kodaks will give a perfectly accurate picture, but a photo can never have the artistic merit of a sketch. In my mind it corresponds to a piece played on the pianola; it is correct, but has no individuality. Look at some of the pencil sketches of the great masters: how beautiful is the touch, and how much is conveyed in a few lines! Nothing gives a better art training than the habit of continually jotting down every pretty bit you may see. Hand and brain learn to work together, and you begin to get that facility with your pencil which nothing but long practice can give you."

Miss Aubrey's own drawings were delightful; the girls watched with admiration as her clever fingers in a few minutes transferred some picturesque corner to paper. They tried their best to emulate her, and filled several pages of their sketch-books with quite praiseworthy attempts. At the castle especially they secured some charming little subjects. It was a grand old Norman building, half in ruins, with ivy-clad towers, grass-grown courtyard, and the remains of a moat. The guard-room with its vaulted roof, the oratory with its rose window, and the banqueting-hall were almost intact, and a winding staircase led to a pathway round the battlements. The girls wandered about, drawing first one bit and then another, going frequently to Miss Aubrey for good advice. They were pleased with their efforts, which, as well as being good practice, would make delightful reminiscences of the place. It was perhaps a weakness on their part to purchase picture post-cards of the castle; but then, as they elaborately explained to Miss Aubrey, they only bought them to send away to friends, not to shirk sketching on their own account.

Katrine, always on the look-out for antiquities, listened to the voice of an old post-card vendor of guileless and respectable appearance, who mysteriously intimated that for a consideration he would transfer from his pocket to hers a few broken tiles out of the oratory, the removal of such keepsakes by the general public being strictly forbidden. She yielded to the temptation, pressed a shilling into his ready hand, and pocketed the fragments. She brought them in great triumph and secrecy to show to Miss Aubrey.

"It's lovely to have some real old pieces!" she exclaimed ecstatically. "These will go with some Roman tiles that I have at home. I shall get a museum together in course of time! I had to give the old chap some backsheesh, but I think he deserved it."

"Let me look," said Miss Aubrey, examining the treasures. "My dear girl, I'm grieved to blight your hopes, but I should certainly like to know how one of these antique crocks has the Doulton mark on the back of it!"

"It hasn't!" gasped Katrine.

"There it is, most unmistakably. I'm sorry to undeceive you, but I'm afraid it's no more mediæval than I am."

"Oh, the craft of the old villain!" mourned Katrine. "I wonder how often he's tried this trick on innocent and unsuspecting visitors? If I could only catch him, I'd upbraid him, and demand my money back!"

"You wouldn't get it, you silly child! He has conveniently vanished, and is perhaps boasting of his cleverness to a circle of envious and admiring friends. You must be very cautious if you want to go in for collecting; false antiquities are, unfortunately, more common than genuine ones, and clever rogues are always ready to lay traps for the unwary."

After having tea at a café, Miss Aubrey and the girls made their way to the wharf, and found Stephen Peters, the landlord of the "Dragon", ready at the trysting-place. In excellent spirits they took their seats, anticipating with much pleasure their return trip on the river. "They hadna' gane a mile, a mile", as the ballad says, before they began to wish themselves back on dry land. Miss Aubrey had not particularly noticed their boatman's condition before they started; but they had not rowed far when she made the unpleasant discovery that he was hardly fit to handle the oars. He was in a jovial mood, and insisted upon bursting into snatches of song.

"He was perfectly sober coming from Heathwell; he must have spent the whole afternoon at the inn on the wharf while he was waiting for us," thought poor Miss Aubrey, trying to conceal her fears from her pupils.

The girls were very naturally alarmed, for Mr. Peters was rowing in a particularly crooked fashion, continually bumping into the banks, and running into clumps of overhanging willows, perhaps under a mistaken impression that he was arriving at his own landing-place.

"I believe the rudder's wrong," said Diana, who had an elementary knowledge of matters nautical, and had undertaken to steer. "He must have partly unshipped it before we left Chistleton. It's not the slightest use. I wish we hadn't come!"

The landlord's rowdy hilarity was shortlived, and rapidly turned to pessimism; he now shipped his oars, and regarded his frightened passengers with a baneful glance.

"It will be best if I send us all to the bottom!" he announced.

"Oh, no! Come, come, Mr. Peters, I'm sure you won't do that!" said Miss Aubrey persuasively, hoping to change the tenor of his mood again.

"I'll do anything to oblige a lady," was the maudlin response; after which, apparently finding the situation too much for his failing senses, he lay down comfortably in the bottom of the boat, and fell asleep. It was safer to have him thus out of harm's way; but the little party was in an extremely awkward strait. None of them, except Diana, had the slightest experience of rowing, and the rudder was undoubtedly half unshipped. Katrine and Diana each took an oar, but their efforts were of a most amateur description, and they could make little progress against the current. Poor Miss Aubrey sat very white and quiet in the stern, giving what directions she could, though she was practically as helpless as her pupils. She reproached herself keenly for having exposed them to such danger. What was their joy, on rounding a bend of the river, to see an easel on the bank, and the familiar figure of Mr. Freeman working at a canvas. They all halloed loudly to him for help, and he soon grasped the situation.

"Can you manage to turn her, and paddle to the bank?" he shouted. "Be careful! That's right—never mind where she lands, just get her ashore anyhow!"

The boat, after wobbling round in a rather unsteady fashion, finally ran aground in a bed of reeds. By taking off his shoes and stockings, Mr. Freeman contrived to wade out and board her, much to everyone's relief.

"We thought we should never get home safely," said Miss Aubrey. "Peters has been dreadful! He threatened to send us to the bottom! We were thankful when he collapsed."

"The drunken sot!" exclaimed Mr. Freeman, looking with disgust at the prostrate figure. "He ought to have his licence withdrawn! He has no right to take out pleasure-boats. We'll leave him where he is, and I'll row you back to Heathwell. I'll fetch my sketching traps. Oh no, please don't apologize! I couldn't think of doing otherwise. I'll come again to my subject to-morrow; I'm in no hurry to finish it."

"It has been a most horrible experience," said Miss Aubrey to the girls, when they were at last back in safety at Heathwell. "I hope Stephen Peters will be thoroughly ashamed of himself when he recovers. I shall never hire his boat again, and shall warn other people not to trust him. I certainly thought we were going to be upset. If we hadn't fortunately come across Mr. Freeman, I don't know what might have happened."

"The Fairy Prince always turns up at the right moment!" whispered Diana to Gladwin, causing that damsel serious inconvenience, for she wished to explode, but was obliged to suppress such ill-timed mirth in the presence of the mistress.

CHAPTER XVI

Concerns a Letter

THE Girls' Patriotic League never for a moment forgot that it was wartime. Though the quiet village of Heathwell was little affected by the European crisis, echoes of the conflict often reached Aireyholme from relations at the front. All the school grieved with Jill Barton when her brother was reported missing, and rejoiced when he turned out to be safe and sound after all. They did their best to comfort Jess Howard, whose cousin's name was added to the Roll of Honour, and shared Hebe Bennett's anxiety when her father was in a Red Cross Hospital. As a practical means of showing their patriotism, they had grown vegetables instead of flowers in their school gardens, and sent the little crops of peas and onions and cabbages to be distributed among the soldiers' and sailors' wives at a Tipperary Club in Carford. Katrine and Gwethyn heard rather irregularly from Hereward. They looked forward to his letters as uncertain but delightful events, and sat in eager expectation every morning when Mrs. Franklin distributed the correspondence. News that he was wounded came as a sore blow, though a letter in his handwriting followed immediately, assuring them of his convalescence in a Base Hospital.

"I am doing splendidly," he wrote, "and hope soon to be at those Huns again. I am very comfortable here, and as jolly as a cricket, so don't bother yourselves over me. There's a fellow in the bed next to mine who says he knows Heathwell. We got talking, and I told him you two were at school there, so that's how it came up. He used to live at a house called the 'Grange'. His name is Ledbury—an awfully decent chap—he's in the Canadian Rifles. He's had rather a nasty shrapnel wound, and will probably be sent home on sick leave. We've a jolly lot of books and magazines here, and sometimes there's a concert in the ward. I can tell you we all yell the choruses to the songs. We don't sound much like invalids."

When Katrine and Gwethyn had finished joying over the happy fact that Hereward seemed to be in no danger, and was apparently enjoying himself in hospital, it occurred to them to consider the item of news which he had mentioned concerning his fellow-patient. They showed the letter to Githa. She was immensely excited.

"Why, surely it must be Uncle Frank!" she exclaimed. "It couldn't possibly be anyone else! He's been away for years and years, and no one knew what had become of him. I haven't seen him since I was a tiny tot, and I shouldn't remember him at all. How splendid that he's joined the Canadians! Oh! I'm proud to have a relation at the front. It's glorious! How I'd love to write to him! If I did, would you enclose it with yours to your brother, and ask him to give it to him? Of course it mightn't be Uncle Frank after all, but I think I'll chance it!"

"Write straight away, then," said Katrine, "for we shall be posting our letters to Hereward to-day. I'll lend you some foreign paper."

"Oh, thanks so much!"

Githa spent the whole of her recreation time at her desk. Her epistle, if rather a funny one, had at least the merit of being spontaneous, for she put exactly what came into her head at the moment, without pausing to think of the composition.

"DEAR UNCLE FRANK,

"At least, I'm not at all sure that you really are my Uncle Frank, but I do hope you are. It's just splendid that you are in the Canadians. I am dreadfully sorry you are wounded. I hope you will soon be quite well again. If you come back to England, do please come and see me, that is to say if you are really Uncle Frank, but I expect you are. I want to see you most dreadfully. Cedric and I have often talked about you, and planned that we would go and live with you. Cedric tried to run away to you in America two weeks ago, but it is a good thing he did not go, for he would not have found you there. I am quite sure you are nice, and I should so like to see you. Nobody is living at the 'Grange' now, and it looks so wretched. I wish you would come and live there, and ask me to come too. I should like

163

to live at the 'Grange' again, and Cedric could come for the holidays. He is to go to-morrow to stay with a gentleman in London, who will coach him for the Naval Examination. I must stop now, as the bell is just going to ring, and I have no more time. I have written this letter in school.

"From your loving Niece,

"GITHA HAMILTON.

"I hope I really am your niece, after all."

Githa folded and addressed her letter, and ran to give it into Katrine's safe keeping. Her eyes were dancing, but clouded as a sudden apprehension struck her.

"Suppose he's left the Base Hospital?" she queried.

"Hereward will send it to him. He'll easily find out where he's gone. I'll undertake it shall reach him somehow."

"What a trump you are! Oh! I wonder if it is really and truly Uncle Frank, or only somebody else?"

"I wish somebody could send me news of my uncle," said Yvonne de Boeck wistfully. "It is now five months since we hear. Is he alive? we ask ourselves. My aunt and my two cousins remain yet in Holland."

Yvonne and Mélanie had been at Aireyholme since the preceding November, and though when they arrived they could speak nothing but French and Flemish, they were now able to talk English quite fluently. Indeed, Mrs. Franklin complained that they had picked up many unnecessary expressions, and often scolded the girls for teaching them so much slang. They were favourites in the school, partly because everybody was so sorry for them, but also because they were really jolly, friendly children, and had adapted themselves so readily to their new circumstances. Yvonne's twelfth birthday was celebrated with great rejoicings; the many presents she received and the English iced birthday-cake which made its appearance on the tea-table caused her little round rosy face to beam with smiles, and she exclaimed for the hundredth time: "Mesdemoiselles, you are too good towards me!" Yvonne evinced the utmost admiration for Tony; nothing delighted her more than to help with his toilet, to brush his glossy coat, wipe his paws when he came in from the garden, and assist at his Saturday bath. She was even found tying her best hair ribbon as a bow on his collar. "C'est un vrai ange!" she would declare ecstatically.

One afternoon, when most of the girls were at the tennis courts, Yvonne happened to stroll to the bottom of the garden to look for a lost ball. While hunting about under the laurels she could see plainly into the road, and she noticed Tony trotting through the gate. She called to him, but, intent on errands of his own, he ignored her, and crossed to the opposite hedge, where an abandoned bone claimed his interest. He was still busy gnawing it and growling over it, when tramping from the direction of the village appeared an old ragman, with a sack slung over his back. As he passed Tony he stopped, and set his bag down on the ground, apparently to rest himself, though he glanced keenly round with such a strange vigilant look on his face that it immediately attracted Yvonne's attention. Hidden under the laurels, she watched him carefully. The ragman, finding himself the only occupant of the road, and believing he was safe from observation, opened his bag, and drawing out a piece of meat, offered it with a few cajoling words to the unsuspecting dog. Tony had a friendly disposition, and also, alack! a tendency towards greediness. He was always ready for something tempting. He left his bone and came up inquiringly. The moment he was within reach, the ragman snatched him up and crammed him unceremoniously into the sack, then shouldered him, and walked off at a rapid pace. It was all done so quickly that Tony had not even time to yelp, and once in the interior of the sack, his protests were smothered to suffocation point.

Yvonne, overwhelmed by the extreme suddenness and unexpectedness of the occurrence, could only give a gasp of horror; the dog had seemed to vanish as if by a conjuring trick. Luckily she was possessed of a certain presence of mind; she raced up the shrubbery, found George, the garden boy, and poured out her news, pointing the direction in which the ragman had gone. George flung down his spade, hurried out by the side gate, and ran along a short lane that led to the road. By thus cutting off a long corner, he almost fell into the arms of the ragman, who, no doubt, had been congratulating himself upon the speed with which he was escaping with his booty, and who certainly did not expect to be intercepted in so prompt a manner.

"You rascal! Let's have a peep inside that bag," exclaimed George, and dragging the sack from the man's shoulder he opened it, and revealed poor Tony, who crawled out, looking the most astonished dog in the world. The thief did not wait to explain matters. He took to his heels, leaving his sack behind him.

The thrilling tale of Tony's adventure soon spread over the school. Gwethyn was almost in hysterics at the danger her pet had escaped. Yvonne, proudly conscious that for once she had acted as a heroine, received congratulations on all sides with a pretty French air of graciousness. Coming so soon after the attempted burglary, the episode made an even greater stir than it would perhaps otherwise have done. It seemed as if bad characters were abroad in the neighbourhood, and property must be guarded with unusual vigilance. The girls had allowed their fears to be calmed a little since the recent midnight alarm, but now their anxiety broke forth again in full force. They went to their rooms that night in a highly nervous condition. They looked carefully underneath their beds and inside their wardrobes, to make sure that no thieves were concealed there.

"I wish Mrs. Franklin would let us have night-lights," sighed Rose Randall. "Directly the room's dark, I know I shall be just scared to death. Suppose a man climbed in through the window!"

166

"I'm more afraid of someone being hidden inside the house, waiting for his opportunity when every one's asleep," said Beatrix Bates. "Don't you remember that dreadful story of the pedlar's pack? Oh, yes, you do! It was at a lonely farm-house, you know; the father and mother were away for the night, and at dusk a pedlar called, and asked if he might leave his pack there till the next day. The girl said yes, so he carried it in, and put it down in the parlour; then he went away. It seemed fearfully heavy, so the girl was curious and went to look at it, and then" — Beatrix' voice was impressive with horror — "she saw it move! She guessed at once that a man was concealed inside it!"

"Oh! a big parcel came to-day by the carrier — I saw it arrive!" interrupted Prissie Yorke, in visible consternation.

"What did the girl do with the pedlar's pack?" asked Dona Matthews.

"She stuck a knife into it," continued Beatrix, "and there came out — blood!"

"Oh! had she killed him?"

But at this most sensational point of the narrative Miss Andrews came into the dormitory, scolded the girls for being slow in getting to bed, and absolutely forbade further conversation. The penalties for breaking silence rule were heavy, and might involve suspension of tennis on the following day, so Beatrix' story, like a magazine serial, must perforce be left "to be continued in our next".

Rose could not help thinking about it as she lay in bed. She wondered if groans came from the pack, and what the girl did next — whether she ran to a neighbour's for help, or called the dog, or locked the parlour door, or went out of her mind with terror. "It would have driven me stark staring mad!" she shuddered. She felt too nervous to go to sleep. All the tales she had ever heard or read about murders and burglaries rushed to her remembrance with startling vividness.

The night was very hot, and the window, of course, was wide open. How easy it would be for somebody to creep up the ivy, and climb across the sill!

The more she thought about it, the more terrified she grew. For a couple of hours she tossed restlessly, lying perfectly still every now and then, so as to listen intently. Were those stealthy footsteps in the passage? Was that the sound of a file on the window below? How could Beatrix, Dona, and Prissie sleep so peacefully? The whole house was absolutely quiet; there was no moon, so it was perfectly dark. Again Rose longed for a night-light. It would be reassuring, at least, to be able to see for herself that the room held no intruder. What—oh! what was that? Through the dead silence came a sound like a pistol-shot. She sat up in bed, trembling in every limb. The noise had wakened the other girls. Again it rang through the quiet, so near that they were convinced it must be in the room. Dona was whimpering with terror, Prissie buried her head in the bedclothes; Beatrix, more courageous than the rest, stretched out her hand for the matches that lay on a small table near her bed, and lighted a candle. The girls looked fearfully round, fully expecting to see a masked figure covering them with a revolver. There was nobody at all. They stared into one another's panic-stricken faces. A third time, close at hand, came the ringing report.

"It's in the cupboard!" quavered Rose.

At the end of the dormitory two steps led to a small store-room where Mrs. Franklin kept spare blankets, curtains, and a miscellaneous assortment of articles. The door was always locked, and the girls had never even seen inside. It had often excited their curiosity: to-night it was a veritable Bluebeard's chamber. They remembered that a big parcel had been delivered that day by the carrier. Had Mrs. Franklin stored it in the cupboard? Could it—oh, horrible idea!—be a repetition of the pedlar's pack? Very white and trembling, Beatrix got out of bed, and, candle in hand, crossed the room. From under the cupboard door, down the white-painted steps, ran a stream of something dark and red. The shriek which she uttered was followed by piercing screams from her companions. That a tragedy was being enacted in the store-room they had not a shadow of doubt. At any moment they expected the door to open and the murderer to show himself. With an instinct of self-preservation they fled from the dormitory, and ran along the passage shouting for help.

Instantly the house was aroused. Alarmed faces peeped from other dormitories, timorous voices asked what was the matter. Several girls began to weep hysterically. Mrs. Franklin, armed with a poker, came hurrying up, followed closely by Miss Andrews, grasping a hockey stick. Taking the candle from Beatrix, the Principal proceeded to No. 7, the girls marvelling at her courage.

"There's blood oozing out of the cupboard!" Prissie and Dona assured the audience in the passage.

"What nonsense! Nothing of the sort!" declared Mrs. Franklin's firm, matter-of-fact voice, as after a moment of inspection she emerged from the dormitory. "What has really happened is this. I had left half a dozen bottles of elder syrup there; the very hot weather has no doubt caused them to ferment, and I suppose they have popped their corks. I'll fetch the key. Yvonne and Novie, stop crying this instant! There's nothing whatever to be frightened about!"

Mrs. Franklin's supposition proved to be correct. When the cupboard was unlocked, three corkless bottles and a sticky pool of elder syrup were revealed. Miss Andrews wiped up the mess with a towel, and carried the bottles downstairs, removing also the three which were intact, in case of further accidents. The general alarm had changed to mirth. In their revulsion of feeling the girls laughed uproariously at their scare. The elder syrup was used in winter-time to doctor colds, and they were rather fond of it. It had never played such a gruesome prank before.

"It's a good thing we didn't ring the school bell again, and send for Mr. White," said Mrs. Franklin. "We should have looked extremely foolish if he and half the village had arrived."

"But how can you tell whether it's a real scare or a false one?" objected Dona, who felt that there was ample excuse for their alarm.

The Principal, however, was not disposed to argue that point, and packed the girls back to their rooms. In half an hour, even Rose Randall was sleeping the sleep of the just.

CHAPTER XVII

The Wishing Well

MR. LEDBURY, feeling rather doubtful whether Mr. Hawkins's tuition had been up to the required standard, had decided to send Cedric to receive some special coaching before going in for his naval examination. The boy departed to London in high spirits, leaving his sister visibly depressed at his absence. Mrs. Ledbury had lately been far more sympathetic with Githa, and noticing that the girl seemed to be moping, she suggested inviting a school-mate to spend Friday to Monday with her. Her aunt had never before made such an amazing proposition. Much as Githa would have liked to entertain an occasional visitor, she had not dared to ask to be allowed to do so. She looked so utterly delighted that Mrs. Ledbury, who generally saw her most undemonstrative side, was frankly astonished.

"It's good for you to make friends of your own age," she remarked. "Tell me which girl you would like to have, and I will write a note to Mrs. Franklin."

Githa's choice promptly fell on Gwethyn. The invitation was sent, and Mrs. Franklin, after an interview in the study, gave majestic permission forits acceptance. The proposed visit caused much amazement in the school. Mr. and Mrs. Ledbury had been looked upon rather as bogeys by the girls. Githa had been so guarded in her information about her home life that it was always presumed she was unhappy. How she spent her spare hours she had never divulged. Her doings, away from Aireyholme, had always been more or less of a mystery.

"I hope you'll have a tolerable time!" said Gwethyn's friends to her in private, their tone clearly expressing anticipation of the contrary. "I suppose Mrs. Ledbury's most frightfully strict. You'll have to be 'prunes and prism' personified."

"I'll worry through somehow without shocking her more than I can help," returned Gwethyn. "It's ever so decent of her to ask me."

"Well, of course you couldn't refuse," decided her chums.

If Gwethyn had any misgivings upon the subject, the sight of Githa's pathetic eagerness was sufficient to nerve her to brave a hundred strict and particular aunts. The poor little Toadstool had been so friendless, that it was an immense event in her life to be able to bring a companion back with her on Friday afternoon. Gwethyn had really grown to like her, so the visit was one of inclination, and not, as her chums insisted, sheer philanthropy. Perhaps a little curiosity was mixed up with it. She would certainly be the first Aireyholme girl to see the Ledburys at home. There was much debating as to whether Tony should accompany them, but in the end they reluctantly decided to leave him at school. He could not keep pace with bicycles, and it was almost impossible to ride and nurse him, so that to take him would necessitate wheeling the machines the whole way. He possessed such a host of admirers that they could not honestly flatter themselves that he would pine for their society. Yvonne would be only too proud to give him his Saturday bath, and he could sleep on Katrine's bed. Gwethyn's luggage was sent by the carrier, and when school was over on Friday afternoon she and Githa started off to cycle.

Gwethyn laughed as she reminded her companion how she and Katrine had first approached the Gables on the morning of their unauthorized ride. The house, which from the back had looked like a farm, proved a very different building when viewed from the front. It was a handsome modern residence, with beautifully kept grounds and immaculately rolled gravel drive.

Mrs. Ledbury received Gwethyn very graciously; if her manner was not expansive, she evidently intended to be kind. She was not at her ease with young girls, that was plainly to be seen, but she made some efforts at conversation, to which Gwethyn responded nobly. Tea, served in the garden, was rather a solemn business, for Githa scarcely spoke once before her aunt, and there were long pauses of silence, during which Mrs. Ledbury seemed conscientiously endeavouring to think of some fresh remark to address to her youthful visitor. All three were secretly relieved when the ordeal was over, and Mrs. Ledbury went into the house, leaving her niece to entertain her friend alone.

Githa had much to show to Gwethyn, and they adjourned at once to inspect the menagerie of pets which she kept in a disused stable. Gwethyn loved animals, and was ready to wax enthusiastic over the waltzing mice, the guinea-pigs, the rabbits, the silk-worms, and the formicarium with its wonderful nest of ants. The latter especially fascinated her, when Githa removed the cover, and she was able to watch the busy little workers running hither and thither at their domestic operations.

"How do you feed them?" she asked.

"I put honey inside this doorway, and water inside the other; that's all they need."

Rolf, the collie who had given Gwethyn so churlish a reception on her former visit, was now ready to make friends, and a grey stable cat also condescended to be petted and stroked. Githa took a deep interest in poultry, and was anxious to show the flock of young turkeys, the goslings, the chickens, and ducks, all of which she had helped to rear.

"Of course I can't look after them altogether when I'm at school all day, but I get up very early, so that I can give them their morning meal, and I feed them in the evening too. They know me as well as they know Tom. I just love taking care of them. When I grow up, I'd like to have a poultry farm."

Gwethyn had to see Githa's garden, the seat she had made in the apple-tree, the field where she often found Nature specimens to bring to school, and the bushes where the nightingale sang in spring. Indoors also there were her books and picture post-cards to be inspected, and some fancy work upon which she had been busy. Mr. and Mrs. Ledbury dined at seven, and the two girls had supper by themselves in the morning-room.

"I do my lessons here in the evenings," Githa explained, "but, thank goodness, we've none to-night. What would you like to do now? Shall we play tennis, or go for a walk down the fields?"

Gwethyn, knowing from school experience that Githa's tennis capabilities were not of a very high order, chose the walk. It was a greater change for her; she loved exploring, and Aireyholme rules did not give her as much scope in that direction as she would have wished. Mr. Ledbury owned some of the land near The Gables, and Githa proposed that she should take her friend to see the church, and that they could then come back through her uncle's plantations. It was a lovely summer evening, with a fresh little breeze that was most exhilarating after the heat of the day. They strolled down a lane where wild strawberries were still in their prime, and could be found for careful searching. Through cornfields and across a pasture, then down a deep lane, a very tangle of traveller's joy, their way led to the church, the object of their expedition. It was a beautiful old Norman building, standing solitary and apart, with no hamlet or even a farm near to it. It had a neglected appearance, for the porch was unswept, the walk a mass of weeds, and grass grew high over the graves.

"It seems such a lonely place for a church," said Githa. "I often wonder if there used to be a village here in the Middle Ages. It's a chapel of ease now to Elphinstone; we only have service here on Sunday afternoons, except on the first Sunday in the month. Not many people come, only a few of the farmers about. I wish I could take you inside, but the door's locked, and the clerk lives too far off for us to go and borrow the keys."

By peeping through the windows they could see the ancient carved choir stalls, and some tattered flags, placed as memorials of long-ago battles. A few sculptured tombs, with knights in effigy, were also dimly discernible in the transept.

"They belong to the Denham family," explained Githa. "They used to be the great people of the neighbourhood once, and they still own Malbury Hall, that quaint old place with the moat round it. No, they don't live there; it's let to some Americans. The Denhams are too poor now to keep it up. This is their coat of arms over the porch—a griffin holding a sword. Once they used to come to church with all their followers; it must have been a grand sight. I often wish I could shut my eyes and catch a vision of it. They tied their horses to those yew-trees; the rings are still there. Then they would come clattering with their spurs up the paved path, and the ladies would come too, with little pages to hold up their Genoese velvet trains, and the very same bell would be ringing that rings now, and perhaps some of them would sit in the same places that we do. They were all baptized, and married, and buried here."

"And do they haunt the church?" asked Gwethyn with a little shudder.

"Many people say they do. I don't think anyone cares to come here after dark. Sir Ralph is supposed to walk, and Lady Margaret. They go down that path, towards the Wishing Well."

"Really a 'wishing well'?" queried Gwethyn.

"So folks say. It's very, very ancient. Shall we go and look at it? Oh, we shan't meet Sir Ralph and Lady Margaret! Don't be afraid — it's hardly dusk yet."

Githa led the way along an overgrown little path among the bushes. In a corner of the churchyard, overshadowed by thick trees, lay the well, a pool of water about six feet square, with walls like a bath. A few broken pieces of masonry lay about.

"It's sometimes called the Black Friar's well," continued Githa, still acting as guide. "He lived during the great Black Death in the reign of Edward III. The church was closed then, because the rector and most of his flock had died of the plague; but one of the Dominican friars used to come from Cressington Abbey and preach in the churchyard to the few people who were left, and baptize the babies in this well. There was a sort of little chapel over it once, but that's supposed to have tumbled down long before the time of the plague, perhaps even before the church was built."

"What have Sir Ralph and Lady Margaret to do with it? Did they die of the plague?" asked Gwethyn.

"No, that's quite another story. They lived in the time of the Civil Wars. They were on the side of the King, and after Charles's execution, Sir Ralph was considered a rebel by the Commonwealth. A troop of Parliamentarian soldiers was sent to arrest him. They stopped at Cressington Abbey, which was then the country house of Sir Guy Meldrum, a Roundhead. His wife, Dame Alice, was cousin to Sir Ralph, and though of course they were on opposite sides, she was anxious to save him. She did not dare to write him a letter, or even to send him a verbal message, but she wrapped a feather in a piece of paper, and made a stable-boy run across the fields with it to Malbury Hall, while she delayed the troopers as long as she could at Cressington. People in those troublous times were very quick at taking hints. Sir Ralph guessed that he had better fly, but the difficulty was where to go. No one would be anxious to receive him, and get into trouble with the Parliament. In desperation he fled to the church, and hid himself in the crypt underneath the chancel. It was a horrible, dark, gruesome place to take refuge in, and of course he needed food while he was there. The troopers had established themselves at Malbury Hall, and kept close watch, but Lady Margaret, his wife, used to steal out at night, and go to visit her husband in the churchyard. It must have been terrible for her to walk there all alone, and she was afraid of being followed by the soldiers. Her fears were only too well justified. In spite of all her precautions, the captain of the troopers was too clever for her.

"One night she stole to the crypt as usual, bringing food and wine for her husband, and as all seemed safe and quiet, he came up into the churchyard to get a little fresh air and exercise. They were walking together along the path that leads to the well, when suddenly there was a shout, and they found themselves surrounded by the band of troopers. Their captain had discovered that someone left the house at night, and had keptwatch with extra care. He had caused his men to tie cloths over their boots, so that they could walk very silently, and when Lady Margaret was seen vanishing down the garden, they had followed her. They tried to make Sir Ralph prisoner, but he was determined not to be taken alive, and fought desperately, with his back to the little bit of stone wall left near the well. One man had no chance against a troop of soldiers, however, and he was soon despatched. When they found he was dead, they laid him down beside the well, and left him until they could return by daylight and carry his body away. They arrived the next day with a stretcher, and there, lying close by his side, with her arms flung round him, they found Lady Margaret—quite mad. They treated her gently, and took her back to Malbury Hall, and she lived there many years; but she never recovered her senses, and whenever she could escape from her keepers she would try to run by night to the churchyard. They guarded her as carefully as they could, but she was cunning, and at last she managed to evade them, and get a start. When they discovered her loss, they followed her, and found her lying drowned at the bottom of the well. They buried her beside her husband, in the transept, and a beautiful monument was erected over their grave."

"I don't wonder they're supposed to haunt the place," commented Gwethyn. "I vote we go. This churchyard is too spooky for my taste. I don't want to meet either Cavaliers or Roundheads, thank you!"

"You mustn't go before trying your luck at the well," said Githa. "Everybody who comes here goes through the ceremony. It's most ancient."

"What have I got to do? Will it raise ghosts?"

"Certainly not. You utter a wish, then you throw a stone into the water, and count the bubbles that rise. If they are an odd number, you'll get the wish, but if they're even you won't!"

"All right—here goes! I wish Mother may bring me back an Australian cockatoo from Sydney. What a splash! Now, how many bubbles? One-two-three-four-five-six-seven-eight! Oh, what a sell! I suppose she won't, though I've asked her in several of my letters. It's your turn now. What are you going to wish?"

"That some time I may go and live at the Grange again. My stone went in with a plop, didn't it? One-two-three-four-five-six-seven! O jubilate! I shall get it."

"Please invite me when you're settled there."

"You bet I will!"

"Now I'm not going to stay in this haunted hole two seconds longer," proclaimed Gwethyn. "It's growing ever so dark, and Sir Ralph and Lady Margaret may come promenading out any time. I'd rather have burglars than ghosts."

"Right-o! We'll go across the stile here, and take a short cut home through the plantation," agreed Githa, leading the way.

CHAPTER XVIII

A Discovery

IT was indeed high time for the girls to go home. The sun had set nearly an hour ago, and the dusk was creeping on to that particular stage when the law of the land requires cyclists to light up. They climbed the stile and plunged into the thick copse of young oaks and beeches. It was dim and mysterious and gloomy under the trees, a slight breeze had arisen, and the rustle of the leaves sounded like gentle footsteps.

"It's rather spooky and creepy," said Gwethyn. "I wish there were a moon."

"There is; but it's a new one. I saw it—a tiny thin crescent—when we were in the lane."

"Don't you feel rather like the Babes in the Wood? It's getting darker and darker. If we met the two villains I should certainly 'quake for fear'."

"We're not likely to meet anyone. It's Uncle's wood."

"I thought I heard footsteps."

"I think it's nothing but the wind rustling the branches."

"Oh no, Githa! It is somebody! Do stop and listen. I can hear voices, and they're coming towards us. Suppose they're poachers! Let us hide quickly behind these bushes, and let them pass without seeing us. I wish we'd brought Rolf."

Since the midnight adventure at school Gwethyn was disposed to be much alarmed at all doubtful characters, and would have gone considerably out of her way to avoid a tramp. She seized Githa's arm, and drew her aside now, in nervous haste, and together the pair crouched behind a thick sheltering group of bramble bushes. In the dim light they were just able to distinguish the features of the wayfarers who advanced; one was unmistakably Bob Gartley, and the other they recognized as a carter whom they had sometimes noticed hanging about the "Dragon". The errand of the two men seemed of a doubtful nature, and might well justify Gwethyn's

179

suspicions. They stopped opposite the very bush where the girls were concealed, and taking various pieces of wire and string out of their pockets, commenced to set traps with much care, and a skill worthy of a better cause. They were so near that the unwilling listeners behind the brambles could overhear every word that was spoken.

"Things aren't the same as they used to be," remarked Bob Gartley sulkily. "It's hard work for a poor man to get even a rabbit nowadays. Look out, Albert, you're spoiling that noose!"

"It was very different when I was a boy," returned Albert. "Mr. Ledbury didn't own the shooting in these woods then, and they weren't so strictly kept. One had an easy chance of a pheasant or two."

"Aye, it all belonged to the Grange, and it always went with the house in those days."

"Pity it's changed hands."

"Yes; old Mr. Ledbury never used to trouble much, and if one took a walk in his woods there was no particular questions asked."

"This lawyer chap's too sharp."

"He got more than his share. When the old man died, everyone in the village said it was a shame those two Hamilton children should have been overlooked and left nothing. Some folks went so far as to say there must have been a later will, and gave Mr. Wilfred the credit of suppressing it. There was a lot of talk at the time. It seems there was a big sum of money, thousands of pounds it was, that old Mr. Ledbury was known to have received only a day or so before his death. It had been paid over to him in notes. He hadn't put it in the bank, and after his death it never turned up. He was a queer chap was old Ledbury; fond of gambling, and the tale went that he must have lost it at play."

"Now you speak of it, I've heard some talk in the village myself. They say old Ledbury was a miser as well as a gambler, and hoarded things like a magpie. It was a queer thing what he'd done with that money."

"It was uncommon queer," replied Bob, "and between you and me, Albert, I could tell you a thing or two about that."

"What do you mean?"

"Something I saw once," admitted Bob cautiously. "But so far it's not been worth my while to let on about it, and I ain't been able to takeadvantage of it myself. I sometimes think if I'd a pal now — — "

"You and me was always thick, Bob," put in Albert eagerly.

"I dare say. But you go clacking like an old hen, when you've a drop of drink in you!"

"I wouldn't touch aught—leastways not more than my usual pint at supper."

"If I thought you could keep a still tongue, the two of us might manage a pretty big deal. It 'ud be a risky enough job, but I know you don't stop at a trifle."

"Not me!" chuckled Albert.

"Well, I don't mind tellin' you that I was peepin' in under the blinds at the Grange on the very night before old Mr. Ledbury died."

"And what did ye see?"

"Never you mind what I saw exactly, but all they panels aren't solid like the rest. There be one as takes out."

"Wheer?"

"Ain't I tellin' you? In the room at the Grange, plump opposite the fireplace it were. There's a knob as twists. Look here, if you've a-set that noose proper, why can't you be comin'? Do you expect me to be waitin' on you same as if you was Captain Gordon? If we ain't quick the keepers will be comin'. That Morris always takes a round about dark, that's what brought me out so early."

"All right, but as you was a-sayin'——" grunted Albert, his voice sinking to a murmur as he rose and followed his estimable friend farther into the wood, where more snares might be set with advantage during the progress of their conversation.

When they judged the two men to be at a safe distance, Githa and Gwethyn emerged from behind the bush, and scurried away along the path as fast as the gathering dusk would permit. So anxious were they to get out of the wood, that neither spoke a word until they had reached the farther side, and, climbing the fence, found themselves once more in the fields below The Gables.

"It was the Gartley children's father," exclaimed Gwethyn, taking Githa's arm, not so much for protection as for a sense of companionship in the dark. "I've always heard he's a dreadful poacher. I think he's such a hateful, insolent kind of man. I'm thankful he didn't see us."

"So am I. It will serve them right if the keepers catch them."

"Could you understand what they were talking about?"

"You mean what they said about Grandfather and the Grange? It was most mysterious."

"Gartley certainly dropped a hint about a panel."

"Yes, but I couldn't make out the rest, or what he wanted Albert to help him with."

"You don't think that your grandfather could have hidden some money in the panelling, and that Bob Gartley saw him do it?"

"If he did, the money certainly wouldn't be there now! Considering the house has been empty for about three years, Gartley must have had every opportunity of going in and taking it, and I scarcely think he'd be restrained by conscientious scruples."

"Hardly!"

"No, there was something more—some secret that he didn't want to tell even to 'Albert'."

"If only they hadn't gone away just at that identical minute!" groaned Gwethyn. "It was too tantalizing, when we seemed on the very point of learning something. It must be important, or he wouldn't make such a mystery of it, and talk about its being to his advantage. Do you think his wife knows, and that we could get her to tell us?"

"No, she's too much afraid of him."

"But if we tried bribery and corruption? He himself might perhaps be induced to part with the information."

"He spoke of a 'risky job', which certainly means something dishonest. In that case I'm sure he wouldn't reveal a word."

"If we were to tell the police, could they make him confess?"

"No, he'd simply deny everything flatly."

"Then what can we do?"

"Nothing as regards him, I'm afraid. We might as well investigate at the Grange, though. Shall we get up early to-morrow, and ride over on our bikes before breakfast? I don't suppose we shall find anything, but if you like we'll go and look."

"I'm your man!" responded Gwethyn eagerly.

Of the two girls Gwethyn was the more excited. Her romantic imagination at once made her plan all sorts of delightful possibilities. They were to find an immense fortune at the Grange, of which her friend would be the heiress! Who knew what treasures might be hoarded somewhere behind the panelling? Githa, whose natural disposition was not sanguine, and who had already tasted some of the hard experiences of life, shook her head at herschool-mate's golden dreams, and stuck to her former contention—if Bob Gartley was aware that money was hidden in the old house, he certainly would not have let it remain there for long.

Nevertheless, Githa was anxious to explore, just to satisfy herself that there was really nothing to find. She would not admit the weakness, however, and pretended that the early morning expedition was a concession to her friend's impatience.

The girls decided not to tell a word to anybody of what they had overheard. They did not mention to Mrs. Ledbury that they had been in the plantation; and Githa, when reproved by her aunt for staying out so late, merely explained that she had been showing Gwethyn the church. With an injunction to keep to the garden in future after supper, Mrs. Ledbury passed the matter over.

Githa was a habitual early riser, but next morning she excelled herself, and called her friend almost as soon as it was light. At five o'clock they were getting their bicycles from the stable. Githa, mindful of her pets' healthy appetites, chalked a notice on the door asking the gardener to feed them as soon as he arrived.

"I haven't time now, but they may be getting hungry for their breakfasts before we are back," she said; "and the fowls ought to be let out. Tom will attend to them, I know."

The ride through the fresh morning air was very pleasant. The girls felt so fit that they raced along, making nothing of hills, and covered the distance in record time. The dew was still heavy on the grass as they went up the drive to the empty old house. Since Cedric's sojourn there neither had been near the place, and apparently nobody else had disturbed the solitude. In spite of agents' tempting advertisements no possible tenant had even come to look at its attractions. The vestibule window still stood open; an enterprising piece of clematis had made entrance, and had grown at least a yard inside, and a robin was flying about in the passage. The girls went at once to the wainscoted room that had been old Mr. Ledbury's library.

"Now I wonder if Bob Gartley was telling the truth or not?" queried Githa.

"He said 'exactly opposite the fireplace', and 'a knob that twists'," said Gwethyn, tapping the panels critically with her knuckles. "What does he mean by knobs? There aren't any."

"Unless he called these rosettes in the scrollwork knobs!"

Part of the panelling was beautifully carved, with a twisting conventional design: no part of it protruded sufficiently to merit the title of knob, but at intervals there were round objects, possibly intended to represent roses. They did not look encouraging, but, beginning with the end near the window, Githa carefully tested each one. The first eleven were part and parcel of the solid woodwork, but the twelfth moved; it turned round fairly easily when she twisted it, evidently unlatching some catch, for the panel below fell open like a door, revealing a small hole or cupboard. Not altogether surprised, the girls peeped eagerly inside.

"Nothing—as I thought!" exclaimed Githa. "Only a thick coat of dust. I never imagined there would be anything. Certainly not if Bob Gartley knew anything of it."

"No, it hardly seemed likely," faltered Gwethyn, "but I'm disappointed all the same. Move just an inch, and let me put in my hand. Oh yes, I know it's useless, but I'm an obstinate person and like my own way. I want to feel the inside. It's uncommonly dirty—and it's absolutely empty. No! What's this? Why, Githa, look! I actually have found something after all."

The object which Gwethyn had discovered in the dust of the cupboard behind the panels was neither beautiful nor important, only a small key of such an ordinary pattern that it evidently could not claim any interest on the score of antiquity.

"Not much of a find, I'm afraid," she mourned. "Just something that has been overlooked when the place was cleared out. I don't suppose the panel was a very dead secret; it opens so easily that the servants would probably find it when they polished the woodwork."

"I never knew of it," said Githa.

"I wonder how Bob Gartley knew of it, though, and why he seemed to think it rather a valuable piece of information?"

"Yes, that's decidedly puzzling, except that sometimes uneducated people like to make an absurd mystery over simple things, just to increase their own importance. Perhaps he wanted to rouse Albert's curiosity."

"He succeeded in rousing ours, at any rate."

"And we haven't gratified it. A key without a lock is a rather useless discovery. I shall take it, though, and keep it carefully, in case it ever turns out to be of any use."

"Well, we've found the precious panel, but no fortune! It's rather a swindle!"

"Only exactly what I expected. I wanted to come just for the satisfaction of seeing there was nothing."

"We've had a ripping ride, at any rate!"

"Yes; and we'd better be going home again now. Come along and get our bikes."

CHAPTER XIX

An Accident

AFTER breakfast Githa and Gwethyn, having the whole of Saturday morning at their disposal, resolved to go mushrooming. The warm weather had brought out a fairly plentiful crop, and they hoped, by diligent searching, to be able to fill at least a small can. The pastures were generally scoured early by people from the village, who sold the mushrooms in Carford at a good price.

"We ought to have thought of it first thing, when we were riding to the Grange," said Githa. "I'm afraid we shall find the best places have been cleared. To get mushrooms one almost has to sit up all night and watch them grow. Everybody's so keen on them just now. Still, I think I know of one or two fields that are worth going to, on the chance that no one else has been there already."

The meadows which Githa proposed to visit lay near the river, about half-way between The Gables and Heathwell. The prospect of finding mushrooms there was rendered more promising on this particular day because most of the village children were helping to gather the bean harvest, and would therefore be busily employed elsewhere. The July heat was already ripening some of the corn, and before long the reapers would be at work.

"It's a pity gleaning has gone so completely," said Gwethyn; "it must have looked so delightfully romantic. None of the village people are half so picturesque as those in the old pictures. Even Mrs. Gartley wears a dilapidated but still fashionable hat, which she bought at a rummage sale, and Mrs. Blundell's daughter makes hay in the relics of a once gorgeous evening blouse and a voile skirt, instead of a print bed-gown and striped petticoat. I suppose people must keep pace with the times, but from an artistic point of view I wish their clothes were more suitable to their occupations."

"It's no use mourning over vanished customs. We don't defy the fashions and appear in Sir Joshua Reynolds costumes. Granny Blundell, at any rate, is picturesque in her apron and sun-bonnet. She made a splendid model for Katrine's picture of the old spice cupboard."

"The cupboard she's stolen from you!"

"No, no! She bought it fairly and squarely from Mrs. Stubbs. As I told you before, I'm glad for her to have it, since I can't have it myself. How hot it's getting! I believe I'm tired with going out riding so early. I shall feel in better spirits when I've found some mushrooms. A penny for the first who sees any!"

"And who's to give the penny?"

"Why, the other, of course!"

"Suppose one sees the mushroom and the other picks it. What then?"

"Oh, I don't know! It would be like the fable of the two boys and the walnut."

"And what do 'toadstools' count?" asked Gwethyn mischievously.

"A penny on the wrong side, decidedly."

The best and richest meadows for mushrooms lay a little distance from the highroad, in a hollow not far from the bank of the river, and beyond a coppice which was enclosed with wire-fencing and strictly preserved. A pathway led through the edge of this wood, and the girls, anxious to avail themselves of a short cut, turned their steps in that direction. Githa, who was walking first, stopped for a moment to admire a lovely clump of silver birches which, with gleaming white stems and shimmering leaves, stood as outposts of the wood. A blackbird—always the sentinel of the wild—flew from the hedge, clattering a noisy warning of her approach, and roused a cock pheasant, that whirred almost over her head in his flight for the open. Laughing at the start it gave her, she climbed lightly up the steps of the stile, but at the top she paused, and suddenly drew back, all her merriment gone in a flash. From the farther side of the fence, down among the bracken and the brambles, she had heard a groan, an unmistakably human groan, with a faint cry after it that sounded something like "Help!"

"Gwethyn," she said, with a decided tremble in her voice, "I believe there's somebody lying down there!"

"Is there? Let me look! Oh, I say! It's a man, and I'm afraid he's hurt."

Gwethyn did not delay a moment to hop after Githa over the stile. A figure in corduroy trousers and an old tweed jacket lay prostrate in the hedge bottom. At first sight the girls feared he was drunk, but one glance at his white face showed that he needed their help. He raised himself rather shakily upon his elbow as they made their appearance. His cheeks were drawn with pain, and his eyes were like those of a snared animal; but they had no difficulty in recognizing Bob Gartley.

"What's the matter? Have you hurt yourself?" asked Githa briefly.

"Oh! Thank goodness anyone's come! I believe I've broken my leg," he moaned.

"Did you fall?"

"Yes, and I can't move an inch, not even to drag myself along. I've been lying here all night, and I thought I was goin' to die like a rabbit in a trap. I shouted and shouted, but there weren't no one to hear, and then I couldn't shout no more. I'd give the world for a drop of water," he added feebly, sinking back on the bracken, and half-closing his eyes.

"I'll fetch some directly," cried Gwethyn, seizing the can which they had brought as a receptacle for the mushrooms, and rushing frantically in the direction of the river. She was quite unused to illness, and had never seen an accident before, so Bob Gartley's haggard face filled her with alarm. Suppose he were to die out there in the wood, before any aid could be secured! The horror of the thought lent wings to her feet. Without stopping to consider her dread of bulls, she climbed a high fence, and plunging recklessly through a drove of formidable-looking bullocks, reached the bank, and dipped her tin in the river, returning to the stile as quickly as she had come. Bob Gartley was still alive — that was a mercy — but he was lying groaning in the most terrible manner. Githa, looking very scared, was supporting his head with her arm. She seized the can from Gwethyn, and held it to his blue lips. A long draught of the water seemed to revive him, and he opened his eyes again.

"How be I a-goin' to get home?" he asked plaintively.

The question roused Githa to energy.

"We must do something to your leg first," she replied. "Gwethyn, remember our Red Cross work, it's a case for first aid. Help me to find some sticks, and we'll make splints. I shall want your handkerchief, and that scarf off your hat. I'm so glad I put on a soft belt this morning — that will help!"

It was easy enough to find sticks in the coppice for amateur splints, and Githa set to work with the best skill she could, binding the pieces of wood firmly on each side of the broken leg, with handkerchiefs, Bob's neck-tie, Gwethyn's scarf, and her own belt. The patient moaned considerably during the operation, but he seemed on the whole grateful.

"I might 'a died if you hadn't chanced to come by," he remarked. "I've had a night of it!"

"How did you manage to fall?" asked Gwethyn.

"I don't know. I suppose I caught my foot in the dark, gettin' over yon stile."

Githa forbore to ask for what purpose he had been visiting a game preserve at nightfall, and turned her attention to the more imminent and practical consideration of how to convey him home.

"I must fetch help at once," she said. "I believe we're quite close to Mr. Cooper's poultry farm. I'll run there, and try and get somebody to come."

"Do. I'll stay here, then, with Mr. Gartley, for I don't think he ought to be left alone, in case he turns faint again," agreed Gwethyn.

This poultry farm was within sight, at the top of a small hill. It was certainly the nearest place at hand. Githa made a bee-line for it, through hedges and over hurdles. If she tramped across the corner of a cornfield, her errand was her excuse. Arrived at the house, she seized the knocker, and gave, in her nervousness, a tremendously rousing rap-tap. The door was opened by Mr. Cooper himself.

"Oh, please, there's been an accident!" gasped Githa in tones of tragic staccato. "Bob Gartley has broken his leg. He's down in the wood there, and we don't know what to do. Can you come?"

"Whew! That's a bad job. Of course I'll come. Perhaps I'd better bring a little brandy with me. Yes, and something to carry him on, for it will be the dickens to move him. My man will help; he's round now with the hens. Between us, I should think we ought to be able to manage it; and if not, we can fetch somebody from Pratt's farm."

"Perhaps I can carry something," said Githa. "Could I hurry back first with the brandy?"

"No, no! If you don't mind waiting a second, I'll come with you. I don't know where the fellow is."

"He's lying just by the stile that leads into the wood. You couldn't miss the place."

"Right-o! Hello, Jack! Are you there? I want you. Bring two long broom-handles, and follow me down to the birch coppice. No, never mind the hens at present, they'll have to wait."

Leaving Githa for a moment on the door-step, Mr. Cooper darted into his farm-house, emerging in an incredibly short space of time with a flask in his hand and a blanket flung over his arm.

"It's Bob Gartley, you say?" he commented. "Oh, yes! I know the fellow well enough—a disreputable scamp he is, too! He was in the coppice for no good, you may be sure. Still, of course, we can't leave him there, though it will be a doubtful benefit to his wife and family to cart him back with a broken leg. If you consulted the gamekeeper, I expect he'd prefer nailing him to a corner of the lodge, in company with a choice collection of stoats, hawks, and owls. He certainly classes poachers under the head of vermin."

They found Gwethyn looking out anxiously for them, and much relieved at their arrival. Her patient had fainted after Githa left, and she had been obliged to fetch more water from the river to revive him. He was conscious now, but very weak, and scarcely able to speak.

"We'll soon have him home," said Mr. Cooper, pouring a few spoonfuls of the brandy between his lips. "This will bring him round a little, you'll see. Oh! There you are, Jack! Got the broom-sticks? That's all right. Now we must manage to make a litter."

Mr. Cooper undoubtedly had a head upon his shoulders, and knew exactly how to manage in the circumstances. He spread the blanket on the ground, and with Jack's assistance lifted Bob Gartley on to it; then rolling each side tightly along a broom handle, he contrived a kind of hammock, on which it was possible to carry the unfortunate man. The first and greatest difficulty was to get him out of the wood. It was hopeless to think of lifting him over the stile, so they were obliged to beat down the hedge, and make a gap sufficiently wide to admit their ambulance.

"We must explain it to the keeper afterwards," said Mr. Cooper. "It will be comparatively easy now across the fields. Step with me, Jack, and perhaps we shan't shake him so much. The poor chap's in awful pain. Now then— left, right, left, right! We'll get him to the road, and then call at Pratt's farm, and ask them to lend their cart. It would be difficult to carry him all the way to Heathwell. The sooner he's home and the doctor can set his leg the better, though I must say this first aid has been splendid. If one of you young ladies don't mind taking the flask out of my pocket, you might moisten his lips with the brandy; he looks as if he were going to faint again."

The people at Pratt's farm were busy haymaking, but they put down their rakes in stolid astonishment at the news of the accident, and after turning the matter over for a short time in their rustic brains, agreed to lend their horse and cart to convey the invalid home.

"We'll put a good layer of straw for him to lie on," said Mrs. Pratt. "It'll save him from the jolting a bit. Yes, he be too big and heavy to carry all the way to Heathwell on that blanket. My goodness! He do look bad. I shouldn't be surprised to see him took. Lor'! It'll need be a warning to him if he pulls round."

"So it will, for sure! It's sent as a judgment without doubt," agreed Mr. Pratt, gazing with contemplative interest at the moaning victim, laid temporarily by the roadside.

"I wish they'd think less about warnings and judgments, and be a little quicker with the cart," whispered Githa.

"I'll offer to help them get it ready, that will probably hurry them," replied Mr. Cooper. "Country people have no idea of the value of time in these cases, or, indeed, in any matter at all, as I often find to my cost."

After what seemed an incredible waste of precious minutes, the cart was at last brought out, and Bob lifted on to the pile of straw. Sending his man back to feed the hens, Mr. Cooper decided to ride himself with the invalid, while Githa and Gwethyn ran on to warn Mrs. Gartley of what had occurred. They found the poor woman in a state of indescribable muddle, doing some belated washing. Gwethyn, with a promise of sweets, managed to cajole all the little ones from the cottage, while Githa broke the news as gently as she could to the mother.

"I knew it 'ud come to this some day!" exclaimed Mrs. Gartley, flinging her apron over her head, and collapsing in tears on to a chair. "I've told him fifty times, if I've told him once, there'd no good happen from the way he was carrying on, but he never would listen to I!"

"Have you got everything ready for him?" asked Githa. "He ought to lie on a mattress, not a soft bed, Mr. Cooper says. I can hear the cart coming now. As soon as they've brought him in, we must send a messenger for the doctor."

It was such a limp, moaning burden which was carried upstairs, that Mrs. Gartley broke into frantic hysterical sobs at the sight, and was no more use than the children, who, scenting the fact that for some reason they were being kept out of the way, evaded Gwethyn's blandishments, and tore back into the cottage. The men, however, made the poor fellow as comfortable as they could, and so many neighbours began to arrive that there was soon far more help than was necessary.

"We may as well go," said Mr. Cooper to the two girls. "We've done all we can, and he'll have to wait now for the doctor."

Bob was lying quite still, with his eyes shut, and his face as white as his pillow, but he evidently heard that, for he roused himself.

"If it hadn't a-been for you, I'd ha' died in the wood," he said. "I shan't forget."

Githa and Gwethyn had gathered not a single mushroom, but they were much too excited even to think about them. They ran up to Aireyholme to tell their news before they walked back to The Gables, and Miss Aubrey promised to go at once to the Gartleys' cottage, to render what aid she could. Mrs. Ledbury also was much concerned when she heard the girls' report of their morning's adventure, and sent during the afternoon to inquire about the invalid.

"He's a bad lot, that Bob Gartley," said Mr. Ledbury; "I have more than a suspicion that he comes poaching into my woods. I've seen him skulking about once or twice. Still, in the name of humanity, you're bound to help a man, even if you find him with a hare in one pocket and a cock pheasant in the other. You can't let him lie with a broken leg. I'm sorry for his wife, poor thing!"

CHAPTER XX

Bob Gartley Explains

THE prospects of the Gartley family at present were certainly not of a rosy description. With her husband in bed, Mrs. Gartley could not go out to work, and her household was obliged to subsist as best it could on charity. The parish allowed some outdoor relief, which was supplemented by doles from the Church funds, and neighbours, now that there was the excuse of real sickness, were kind in giving practical help. There was no danger of actual starvation, though luxuries were out of the question.

Laid by the heels, with no exciting expeditions to break the monotony of his days, Mr. Bob Gartley alternately pitied himself and railed at fate. He was a fractious invalid, and spared his wife neither time nor trouble in attending to his wants.

"He be worse nor a baby!" she complained to her friends. "I've only to get him settled and go downstairs and begin a bit o' washin', when there he is hollerin' for me again, and all about naught. I fair lose my patience sometimes, but he keeps a boot handy under his pillow, ready to fling at I if I crosses him, and he be such a good shot he never misses, duck as I will."

The exactions of her lord and master kept Mrs. Gartley so busy that her family lived more than ever in the road, escaping passing motors by a miracle, and receiving chance meals from anybody who had fragments to spare—a practice rather sniffed at by some of the neighbours.

"Not as I've any wish to see 'em go wantin'," remarked Mrs. Blundell, "but I think they're doin' better now than when their father had his health. Hungry? Why, yes—they'd always be ready to eat sweet stuff at any hour of day. That don't prove they be in need. As for Bob Gartley, he must be livin' like a fightin' cock with all they basins of broth and pots of jelly. He'll want to break his leg again when times is bad."

Lying in his stuffy little bedroom, Mr. Gartley had leisure to consider his circumstances and air his views. He carefully compared the various viands that were sent him, with criticisms on the culinary skill of the donors.

"Don't bring me no more broth!" he said to his wife one afternoon; "I'm sick of the very sight of it. Might as well be in hospital. Why can't you get me a scrap of liver and bacon?"

"Doctor said we wasn't to give you that on no account," objected Mrs. Gartley. "I wish they had taken you to hospital while they was about it. If it had been I, I'd have jumped at goin'."

"Shows how much you knows about it! Why, when I was in the infirmary they washed me all over every day! Yes, it's the truth I'm tellin' you! And they left windows open all day long, and wouldn't allow me a smoke, or even a chew of 'baccy. No more hospitals, says I! Take that broth away, can't you? Ain't there any jelly in the house?"

"No, the pot's empty."

"Then you've let those brats get at it!"

"I ain't. You've had it all yourself."

"Maybe they'll be sending some more from somewheres."

"Like enough; but you won't get much more from Aireyholme."

"Why not?" asked Mr. Gartley much aggrieved.

"Because the young ladies is going away next week."

"Oh, it's their holidays, is it?"

"Aye; the school's always shut up in holiday time. Miss Aubrey and Mrs. Franklin goes away too."

The news appeared to make Bob thoughtful, and he pondered over it for a few moments.

"I suppose that young lady'll be takin' that little cupboard with her," he remarked at last.

"What little cupboard?"

"Why, you stupid, the one as she put in the picture with Granny Blundell and our Hugh. She'd bought it from Mrs. Stubbs."

"Oh, I remember. Yes, if she's bought it and paid for it, of course she'll be takin' it with her."

"It's hard for a poor man to be tied to his bed as helpless as a log!" groaned Bob. "Goodness knows what she'll do with it if she takes it away! Sell it again, maybe. Anyways, I shall be off the track of it."

"What do you mean?" queried his wife. "I can't see as you've got aught to do with Miss Marsden's cupboard."

"You never could see farther than your nose, Jane. Some of they young ladies has been very good to a poor man. I'd a-died if they hadn't found me in the wood."

"Why, yes, I know that!" exclaimed Mrs. Gartley, immensely amazed at such an unwonted outburst of gratitude.

"It might be good for a fiver," murmured Bob. "That's little enough, but it would be better than missin' everything. Look here, Jane. Send Mary across to Aireyholme, and tell her to say I'd like to see Miss Hamilton on a bit of special business."

"What's it all about?" asked Mrs. Gartley inquisitively.

"Never you mind. Leave that to me, and send the child as I tell you."

Little Mary Gartley arrived with her message soon after four o'clock, just as Githa was leaving school. Gwethyn was walking with her down the drive, being in fact on her way to the Gartleys' cottage to leave a basketful of fruit from Mrs. Franklin. Both girls were much astonished at the summons.

"Are you sure your father wants me?" asked Githa.

"Yes, miss. He said most particular as it was Miss Hamilton."

"Come with me, Gwethyn!" begged Githa. "You have to call at the door, in any case. I'm sure Mrs. Franklin wouldn't mind your going in. Perhaps Mr. Gartley wants to thank us for our 'First Aid'. I don't like going alone."

"All serene!" returned Gwethyn, whose curiosity was considerably aroused.

"He do be askin' for you," said Mrs. Gartley, who greeted the girls at the door. "What's come over him passes me, but he's set on seein' you. It's a poor place upstairs, and I've not had time lately for cleanin'; still, if you wouldn't mind steppin' up— —"

"Oh, it's all right!" said Githa, stopping the apologies. "Will you go first to show us the way? Well, Mr. Gartley," as they entered the room, "you look a little better than when we saw you last."

"I might easy do that," replied Bob; then turning to his wife, he whispered: "Chuck they brats downstairs, we don't want 'em listenin' here."

Mrs. Gartley hastened to put to flight five of her offspring who had followed the interesting visitors, and having administered chastisement, and locked them out of the house, returned panting from the fray, fearful of missing the least detail of the conference.

When his audience was ranged conveniently round his bedside, Bob Gartley, greatly enjoying the sense of his own importance, opened the conversation.

"I sent for you, Miss Hamilton," he began, "because there's a something I've had on my mind. You done me a good turn, and I'd be ready to do a turn back. Suppose, now, as I had a bit of information that might mean a deal to you, I reckon as you'd be glad to get hold of it?"

"I've no doubt I should," replied Githa, "if it's anything worth knowing."

"It be well worth knowing. Don't you have no fear on that score. It might be the makin' of you, and it would clear up a mystery, too."

"What do you mean?" asked Githa quickly.

"I'm a poor man," returned Mr. Gartley evasively. "I've a big family to keep, and I wears myself out with strivin' for 'em. It 'ud be worth anybody's while to know what I knows, but the question is whether it 'ud be worth my while to let on. Maybe I'd best keep my information to myself."

"Suppose it were made worth your while to tell it?" returned Githa, grasping the situation.

"Ah! that 'ud be a horse of another colour. I be grateful for what you've a-done for me — don't you be mistakin' me on that point — but I can't afford to be givin' away gratis what ought to be good for golden sovereigns."

"How many do you want?" inquired Githa.

"I've no wish to seem graspin'," replied Bob virtuously. "No one can accuse me of tryin' to get more than my dues, but I'm not denyin' as five pounds would be a very handy little sum just at present, as circumstances is rather awkward."

"I have five pounds in the Savings Bank; you shall have it if you really have any information to give me."

"You shall be judge of that, and I reckon you'll be surprised when you hear what I've got to tell. Jane, is there anyone a-listenin' on the stairs?"

"Not a soul, and the door's locked," said Mrs. Gartley, who stood by, consumed with curiosity, and almost more eager than the girls for the coming revelations.

"That be all right, then. I don't hold with eavesdroppin'. I were always taught as it were mean and underhand. It was five quid as we mentioned, wasn't it? Thanks. There ain't nothing like bein' sure of one's ground. Well, as you're really anxious to know what I knows, I'll tell you. It were three years ago come last March, and I happened to be out one night after a little bit of business of my own which took me round by the Grange. It were quite late, maybe between twelve and one o'clock, and I were in a hurry to get back to my family, so I makes a short cut through the garden. All the house were shut up and dark, and it were plain as everyone was in bed, so

I says to myself. When I comes round the corner, though, if I don't see a light in one of the lower windows. As I goes past, I noticed that though the blind were down, it weren't drawn full to the bottom, and there was a chink of about half an inch left. I'm a man as takes a kind of interest in my neighbours, so I puts my eye to it, curious-like, and I gets a very good view into the room. There was old Mr. Ledbury, standin' by the fireplace, and he were turnin' over some papers in his hand. I'd take my Bible oath they was bank-notes. He counted 'em, careful-like, and put 'em inside an envelope. Then what does he do but go across the room—me watching him all the time at my peep-hole—and he twists a knob round, and opens one of the panels in the wall. He looks at it as if he was goin' to put the papers in there; then he seems to change his mind, he shakes his head and shuts it up again, and goes over to t'other side of the room, where there was a little oak cupboard. I could see him as plain as I sees you now. There was small drawers in that cupboard, and an empty space in the middle of 'em. He slides a piece of wood aside there, and takes a key from his pocket, and unlocks a little door at the back among the drawers, and he puts the envelope in there, and locks it up again. Then he goes back to his arm-chair by the fireside. 'Bob Gartley,' I says to myself, 'maybe you've found out something to-night, and maybe you haven't, but you'd best keep a still tongue in your head.' So I never tells no one, not even my missis here."

"That you didn't!" agreed Mrs. Gartley. "I'd be the last you'd tell. I can't make out what you're drivin' at."

"You wait and see, and you'll find out fast enough. That night as I looked through the window was the very one afore old Mr. Ledbury was took bad and died. When it came to readin' his will, there was a lot of talk in the village, and folks said as a big sum of money were missing, and couldn't be traced nohow, and he must have gambled it away. I'd my own ideas on the subject."

"But didn't you tell anybody?" gasped Githa.

"Not I! It weren't none of my business. I'd enough trouble on my own account just then, for me to want to be mixed up in anyone else's affairs."

"I remember!" exclaimed Mrs. Gartley. "You was doin' time. You got three months hard for puttin' a bullet through the keeper's hat."

"It don't matter what I were doin'," said Bob sulkily. "At any rate, I'd an engagement wot kept me from puttin' myself in a public position. When I gets back to Heathwell, do you think I were anxious to go and interview Mr. Wilfred Ledbury just then, and tell him my views? No, I'd had enough of lawyers for the present. They was inclined to doubt my word, somehow, and it hurts an honest man's feelin's to be told as he's a liar. I thought I'd keep my eye, though, on that little cupboard, but I found there'd been an auction, and it were sold. I couldn't get on the track of it, do what I would, or hear who'd a-got it, and I gives it up as a bad job. Then one day that young lady comes into the house paintin' our Hugh. There were an oak cupboard in her picture, and I knows it again in a minute."

"You don't mean to say — —" cried Gwethyn, springing to her feet.

"Aye, but I do! That be the very one as I sees old Mr. Ledbury put the envelope inside!"

Gwethyn and Githa left the cottage in a state of the wildest excitement. They went straight back to school, and ran upstairs to the studio. Fortunately no one was in the room, so they were able at once to begin investigations on the little oak cupboard. They pulled out all the small drawers, and poked and pushed in every possible direction, but not a sign of a secret hiding-place could they find. The wood at the back of the recess in the middle seemed perfectly solid, and could not be made to budge by the fraction of an inch. They were very baffled and crest-fallen. After their success in finding the moving panel at the Grange, it was the more particularly disappointing.

"I suppose Bob Gartley really did see what he says he saw?" ventured Githa rather doubtfully. "I wonder he never mentioned it before."

"Reading between the lines, I should say he had two good reasons for his silence," replied Gwethyn. "He was probably at the Grange that night on a dishonest errand, and didn't want the matter investigated, and also perhaps he thought he might find a chance some time to appropriate the notes. He spoke very regretfully about them."

"Do you think it could have been he who tried to break into Aireyholme?"

"I haven't the least doubt of it. That scare happened soon after Katrine had painted her picture of the cupboard. It never struck anybody to connect the two."

"He must have intended to get in through the dining-room window, go upstairs to the studio, and hunt about for himself."

"He might have managed it, if we hadn't had Tony that night. The darling roused us with his growling."

What was to be done next? That was the important question. If Bob Gartley's account were true, and a secret place really existed, probably the only way to find it would be to have a joiner up, and get him to take the spice cupboard entirely to pieces. But it was Katrine's property, and this could not be done without her permission. She was out sketching this afternoon with Miss Aubrey. Gwethyn promised to broach the matter to her when she returned.

"Don't tell anybody else, please," said Githa. "I'd rather this wasn't talked about in the school. If there really are bank-notes inside this cupboard, they won't be mine. I suppose they'll be Uncle Wilfred's, the same as all the rest of everything."

"Unless there were a will."

"No such luck! Ceddie and I weren't born under fortunate stars. I must be going home now, it's most fearfully late."

"Don't forget it's the Sports to-morrow!"

"Rather not!"

CHAPTER XXI

The Sports

THE Summer Term at Aireyholme always wound up with the Sports. They were as much of an institution as the dramatic performance given shortly before Christmas. The girls stuck to them with conservative zeal. Several times Mrs. Franklin had suggested some other kind of fête to celebrate the close of the school year, but concerts, tennis tournaments, or pastoral plays were alike rejected in favour of athletics. For the last week the Committee had been at work arranging the events and making copies of the programme. The prizes were on view in the studio, and were inspected with deep interest on the morning of the great day.

"I can't think why you should make such a fuss about sports!" said Katrine, who was touching up some sketches, and found her painting operations decidedly hindered by the crowd clustering round the table. "If you'd had an art competition, now, it would have been far nicer. Why didn't you?"

"Because we've got to think of something to suit the whole school, and not just a few hobbyists," returned Viola rather touchily. "You're absolutely obsessed with painting. We monitresses take an all-round view, and consider the general good."

"Isn't it for the general good to elevate public taste?" asked Katrine, who never missed an opportunity of arguing with Viola.

"Certainly; but it's not fair on an occasion like this to have a competition for which only an elect number are eligible. Sports are democratic things. Every one has the same chance."

"Now there I don't agree with you. Some girls are better at running and jumping, just as others are cleverer at music or painting. Sports aren't a scrap more democratic, really; they only offer a different field of battle. Your artistic genius may be a duffer at a sack race, and your crack pianist a butter-fingers with a ball. You must admit that!"

"I shan't admit anything of the sort. It's well known in every school that athletics are the fairest things going. That's why they're so popular."

"But from your own reasoning — —"

"Oh, I say, stop—for the sake of peace!" interrupted Diana. "We're going to have the Sports, so what's the good of barging about them? If you'd write a few extra programmes, Katrine Marsden, instead of giving your opinions, there'd be some sense in it."

"I thought you had enough."

"We could do with half a dozen more. It's horrid to be short; and extra visitors sometimes turn up."

It was the tradition of the school that the summer fête should be held on the last Saturday in July. Though not the actual breaking-up day, in the estimation of the girls it was almost as good. After Friday's classes there were no more lessons; Monday would be devoted to packing, and on Tuesday all would be speeding away by train to different points of the compass. It was a kind of "do-as-you-please" day; rules were relaxed, and everybody made the most of the holiday. A band of helpers, under the superintendence of the Games Committee, spent the greater part of the morning preparing the playing-field, forms were carried out to accommodate the spectators, hurdles and other obstacles were arranged, and the ground for the long jump freshly raked.

"It's frightfully rough on Coralie that she mayn't compete this year!" said Hilda Smart. "She's something wrong with her heart, I believe; anyhow, the doctor has absolutely forbidden it. Poor old Corrie! She's so disappointed! She was ever so keen on winning a medal. She'll just have to sit and watch, like a visitor."

"And Tita has blistered her foot, and can't run, so two of us are off," commented Diana. "It's hard luck on the Sixth!"

"Never mind; we've got Gladwin and Ellaline! They'll have to brace up for the credit of the form."

"Trust them! But some of the Fifth are A1, and may steal a march on us."

"Not while Dorrie Vernon's alive! I'd back her against anybody."

"Has Katrine Marsden put her name down for anything?"

"Only for the bicycle race. She thinks the other competitions hoydenish!"

"If you'd called them Olympic contests, and required candidates to come attired in ancient Greek costumes, she'd have been madly enthusiastic!" grinned Diana.

"Much jumping one would do in classic draperies!" sniffed Hilda scornfully. "What does that kid want hallooing at us over there?"

Novie Bates was running down the field yelling at the pitch of her voice for Diana.

"You're to come—at once!" she shouted. "Mrs. Franklin wants you. I saw the telegraph boy coming up the drive."

Diana promptly dropped her rake, and fled towards the house, followed by Hilda and the rest. On this most propitious day the results of the Matriculation Examination might be expected to be published, and the three candidates were on the qui vive for news. Mrs. Franklin was standing by the front door, with the yellow envelope in her hand, but she did not divulge its contents until Dorrie and Viola also came hurrying up.

"All passed. Viola first division, Diana and Dorrie in the second."

The welcome information was handed on from girl to girl, till in a few minutes everybody in the school knew of it, and ran to offer congratulations to the heroines of the hour. The Principal, who had always considered Diana's mathematics shaky, was looking immensely relieved. It was a triumph that all were through, and a very happy finish for the term. Last year two out of the five candidates had failed, a deep humiliation to Mrs. Franklin; but this success restored the credit of Aireyholme. It put everybody in a good temper, and made quite a gala atmosphere in the establishment. The monitresses took their laurels with an air of dignified humility. They were gratified, but left the rejoicing to their friends.

"Of course, when you've worked for a thing, it's a comfort to pass," admitted Viola, with would-be nonchalance.

"If I'd got a First Div. I'd be too proud to know what to do with myself!" declared Laura Browne ecstatically.

"Will your names be put in the newspapers?" asked Yvonne with awed admiration.

"We ought to run up a special flag!" suggested Jill Barton.

"There! That's enough cock-a-doodling on our behalf!" said Viola. "Some of the rest of you must do credit to the school this afternoon. I hope you're all in good form. Don't go tearing about the place, and getting yourselves too hot beforehand. It's a waste of superfluous energy!"

The Sports were to begin at half-past two, and by that hour the competitors and the greater number of the spectators were in their places. Invitations had been sent to residents in the neighbourhood, and though the visitors were not so many as on Waterloo Day, there were quite enough to fill the seats which had been carried out for their accommodation.

Githa arrived rather late. It had been intended that she should motor over with her uncle and aunt, but at the last moment Mr. and Mrs. Ledbury were delayed by a telegram, the contents of which they did not disclose to her, and she had set off on her bicycle. By quick scorching she managed to join the ranks of the school just in the nick of time. She waved to Gwethyn, but there was no opportunity of speaking, for the girls were ranged according to their forms. Miss Andrews and Miss Spencer were respectively to be starter and time-keeper, and Mr. Boswell and the Vicar would act as judges. The prizes, arranged on a small table, would be distributed by Mrs. Boswell. The Patriotic League had been anxious to forgo prizes altogether, and offer bouquets of flowers or crowns of laurel to the victors; but this decision was overruled by Mrs. Franklin, who thought the school honour demanded at least a few inexpensive medals to grace the occasion.

"I shall not get silver ones this year," she had decreed; "but as we have the die, the cost of metal ones will be comparatively trifling. Mrs. Boswell is very kindly giving the form trophy, and Mrs. Gordon the prize for the bicycle race. Miss Aubrey, the mistresses, and myself wish to pay for the medals amongst us, and the shillings which you girls usually subscribe can be sent either to the National Relief Fund or to the Belgian Fund, whichever you choose."

This arrangement satisfied even the most patriotic conscience. All had felt that the Sports would not be complete without medals, though they were heroically prepared to make the sacrifice. The Athletic Prize badges were coveted distinctions at Aireyholme, and were treasured by their winners almost above the books generally awarded for successes in form examinations. This summer the medals would be specially attractive, for they would seem almost like military decorations. Each girl was wearing her form rosette—the Sixth pink, the Fifth green, and the Fourth blue; the monitresses in addition had white favours, and the members of the Games Committee, whose duty it was to keep order and marshal the competitors, wore a "C" embroidered on a mauve ribbon.

The first event was the junior plain race. The fifteen members of Form IV started with great enthusiasm, and tore over the ground as rapidly as their respective running powers permitted. Big Hebe Bennett, Bertha Grant—also fat and scant of breath—and Myrtle Goodwin were soon distanced by their more agile companions. Yvonne and Mélanie made a gallant struggle, but fell behind, and after an exciting heat between Garnet Adams and Gwendolen Jackson, ended by Nora Parnell making a sudden spurt and beating them both.

In the higher forms Megan Owen and Ellaline Dickens proved the Atalantas. Megan, though short and stoutly built, was remarkably swift-footed, and Ellaline, tall and willowy, covered the ground at a swinging pace that distanced even Dorrie Vernon, the crack champion of the Sixth. Dorrie redeemed her character, however, in the next event; her record in the long jump was the highest ever known at Aireyholme, it evoked loud cheers, and she retired with the satisfaction of knowing that her feat would be duly entered in the athletic minutes of the school. The high jump came next on the programme; juniors led the way and showed much agility. For several rounds ten of them cleared the bar; but the next trial proved fatal to seven, leaving only Novie, Myrtle, and Githa on the field. It was a hard contest between these three. They were very evenly matched; Novie was the tallest, but Githa had the best springing power, and came off victor in the end.

"Glad the poor old Toadstool's scored," commented Dona Matthews to Gwethyn. "It's a tremendous feather in her cap, because she hasn't been able to practise as much as the rest of her form. Those kids have been at it half the evening, all through this week. Our turn next! Hope you're feeling fit?"

"I'll do my best, but I always find the feminine petticoat an encumbrance — even a gymnasium skirt is apt to catch. Boys have that immense advantage at athletics."

"Well, it's the same for us all, so we must take the petticoat as a handicap."

Gwethyn was fairly good at jumping, and held her own well in the form. She kept up pluckily when Beatrix, Susie, and even Dona had fallen out. A large coco-nut mat had been placed for the girls to jump on to, but the grass was very dry, and just where the spring must be taken it had become slippery. Gwethyn, so near to victory, slid, alas! as on ice, and came a heavy cropper. She got up ruefully rubbing her leg, not seriously injured, but too temporarily lame to make another trial, and the triumph was scored by Rose Randall; not even the Sixth, who followed, being able to break her record.

The sack race for juniors was attended with much merriment. The fifteen members of the Fourth, fastened up securely to the neck in clean sacks, were laid on their backs in a giggling row. At the word of command from the starter they struggled somehow to their feet, and began to make whatshuffling progress they might. It was a case of most haste least speed, for over-zealous hurry only resulted in a fall, and often five or six girls would be squirming like caterpillars on the ground. Hopping, stumbling, tripping, anything but running, the competitors made their slow way, till Jess Howard, the foremost, literally tumbled across the ribbon, lying mirthful and speechless till she was raised and released from her impediment by the stewards.

The bicycle race was less of an open competition, for only those could enter who possessed machines. There were ten candidates altogether, Katrine, Gwethyn, and Githa being among the number. It was the sole event in the Sports for which Katrine would compete; she affected to consider running and jumping only fit for juniors, and stood aloof from such "childish recreations" (as she termed them), greatly to the indignation and scorn of the monitresses, who held a brief for athletics. The race was by no means plain riding. Two long rows of flowerpots had been placed, with due intervals between them, and in and out among these the competitors must guide their machines in a tortuous twist. It was a matter of balance and careful steering, and Katrine, who was perhaps a little too airily confident, came to grief over the ninth pot, rather — I am afraid — to the satisfaction of some of the members of the Sixth, who chuckled together at her want of prowess. Katrine, however, had the virtue of being able to take defeat in a sporting manner. She wheeled her bicycle away, and watched the finish from a quite disinterested point of view. Gwethyn did well, but she was still a little stiff with her fall on the grass, and she lacked practice. Githa, whose daily cycling to and from school made her absolutely at home on her machine, had a decided pull over the others, and won by several points. It was her second victory that afternoon, and the school applauded loudly. Her pale cheeks flushed with pleasure at the sound of the clapping. It was sweet for once to be appreciated — she, who was generally such an outsider among the boarders.

"Good old girl! You outshone yourself!" cried Gwethyn with an admiring slap on the back. "You wound about like a boa constrictor!"

"Thanks for the comparison—I'd rather be a toadstool than a snake!" laughed Githa.

The stewards were collecting and rearranging the flowerpots, and a team of juniors came forward for the tortoise race. A difficult competition this, for each candidate had to conduct marching operations mounted on two flowerpots, and was required to balance herself on one leg on one pot, while she cautiously and skilfully moved the other pot forwards. Putting a foot to the ground necessitated returning to the starting-point, and several times the foremost competitors, in their anxiety to hurry along, let zeal exceed caution and lost their balance. True to the title of tortoise, the slow and steady made the surest progress, and Bertha Grant, the hindmost in the opening running, scored at this event. On the whole the girls voted the obstacle race the best fun. Every competitor rapidly worked a sum, submitted it to Miss Andrews, and if correct tore away to scramble through some hurdles and run over a raised plank. She was then required to open a parcel, take out a long skirt and put it on, continuing her course, much encumbered by its flapping, to climb more hurdles as a finish. Lena Dawson, Dona Matthews, and Dorrie Vernon won credit for their respective forms, the latter particularly distinguishing herself, as she arrived at the goal without having torn her long skirt, an achievement not accomplished by Lena or Dona.

The last event, the North Pole race, was confined to juniors. The girls were first blindfolded with handkerchiefs, then paper-bags were tied over their heads, and thus incapacitated from seeing, they were turned loose to grope for the "North Pole", a stick placed in the centre of the field. Attendant scouts kept them on the course, gently turning them towards the goal when they strayed to other points of the compass; but in spite of this help they would often pass groping hands within a few inches of the stick and fail to grasp it. After much fun and excellent "collie work" on the part of the scouts, Meta Powers tumbled quite by accident over the winning-post, bearing it with her to the ground as she shouted a stifled "Hurrah!" from within her paper-bag.

CHAPTER XXII

The Old Oak Cupboard

THERE yet remained the form trophy to be competed for, winners only in the previous events being eligible as candidates. To ensure equal chances for all, the test was to be a handicap race, age and height being taken into consideration. The judges carefully placed the competitors, tall Rose Randall getting little advantage over Dorrie Vernon, though she was two years younger, and Jess Howard being in a line with Dona Matthews. Githa had been given her starting-point, and was standing in readiness for the signal, when she noticed her uncle and aunt arriving upon the scene. How late they were! They had missed almost the entire programme. Who was that stranger in khaki whom they had brought with them? They were introducing him to Mrs. Franklin, who was shaking hands, and finding seats for all three. Some friend of Uncle Wilfred's, she supposed — but here her reflections were brought to an abrupt close, for Miss Andrews gave the signal, and the race began. Owing to the handicaps it was a closely matched affair; all were on their mettle, and exerted themselves to the uttermost. At first Dona seemed to be making the best progress, but Dorrie and Ellaline were coming up fast from behind, and passed her. Githa ran steadily until the two Sixth Form girls were in a line with her; then with a sudden spurt, of which she had hardly believed herself capable, she sprang forward, kept her advantage, and a whole yard in front of them touched the ribbon. The Fourth rent the air with their cheers. The trophy was by far the most important event of the afternoon, and the girl who had secured it for her form was the heroine of the moment. Too much out of breath for speech, but conscious of her honours, Githa walked back to receive the congratulations of her comrades. Two medals and the trophy! She could scarcely believe her good fortune.

Mrs. Boswell, with smiling face, had turned to the prize-table, and Miss Andrews was marshalling the winners in the order of their events.

"The poor old Toadstool looks quite pretty for once," said Jill Barton, as Githa, with shining eyes, and cheeks flushed with unwonted colour, received her two medals and the charming little clock which would henceforth adorn the mantelpiece of the Fourth Form room.

"When she's through her ugly duckling stage, I believe she'll turn out rather handsome," agreed Ivy Parkins. "I always said she had good features, only she looked so drab and depressed. Her expression has changed lately, and it makes an immense difference. She doesn't scowl like she used to do."

It was indeed such a bright, beaming, animated girl who expressed her thanks to Mrs. Boswell, the donor of the clock, that Mrs. Ledbury looked quite amazed. She beckoned her niece to her side.

"Come here, Githa! I'm glad to see you do so well. I want you to speak to this gentleman" (indicating the khaki-clad officer). "Do you know who he is? I thought not! Well, it's a surprise for us all."

But as Githa looked up into the kindly face turned smilingly down to greet her, old wellnigh forgotten scenes of early childhood came rushing back, and with a swift flash, half of intuition, half of memory, she divined the truth.

"You're my Uncle Frank!" she exclaimed.

Later on in the afternoon, when tea was over, and the visitors were dispersed about the garden, Githa took her new uncle for a walk in the orchard. She did not feel in the least shy with him, and clung to his arm, stroking the khaki sleeve—a caress she would never have dreamed of venturing with Mr. Wilfred Ledbury.

"I got your letter all right—that's what brought me," confided Uncle Frank. "I never meant to show my face in Heathwell again, but if you children want me, that's a different matter. So you think you'd like to live with me, you young witch? Well, wait till the war's over, and we'll see what can be managed. Your brother tried to run away, did he? The rascal! I'm glad he's

213

ready to serve his country—the navy will be the making of him. I must have a look at the Grange, for old sake's sake. Now tell me about your little self and your doings."

Then somehow Githa began pouring out the whole story of the last few weeks' happenings, including the finding of the movable panel at theGrange, and ending with Bob Gartley's confession on the preceding afternoon. Her uncle listened attentively.

"I should like to see this oak cupboard," he remarked. "You say it belongs to your friend Katrine, the sister of Marsden whom I met in hospital? Would she show it to us now?"

"I'm sure she would. I'll go and fetch her. Please wait for me here."

Githa returned in a few minutes with both Katrine and Gwethyn. They were anxious to make Captain Ledbury's acquaintance and to ask for news of their brother Hereward. The account of his progress was satisfactory.

"He'll have joined his regiment again by now, I expect, lucky chap! He wasn't on the 'serious' list, so had no need to be invalided home. Oh, he's in the best of spirits! He kept us all alive in the ward with his jokes. Never met such a fellow for making puns!"

"Just like Hereward!" exclaimed the sisters proudly.

Katrine led the way to the studio, and did the honours of the little spice cupboard.

"I didn't know when I bought it that it came originally from the Grange," she explained. "It had changed hands twice before I got possession of it."

"Githa and I spent half an hour or more over it yesterday, but we couldn't find any secret place," added Gwethyn.

Captain Ledbury had stooped down, and was making a careful examination. He pulled out all the small drawers, and felt carefully behind them.

"I dare say it's twenty years or more since my father showed me how this works. I've almost forgotten the trick. Which side was it, now? Right or left? Why, of course, I remember! You push both together. It's rather stiff. Right-o! It's moving. Oh, good biz!"

A thin panel of wood forming the back of the recess had slid aside, revealing a small door with a keyhole. It refused to open, and was evidently securely locked.

"With your permission, Miss Marsden, we shall have to do a little burgling," remarked Captain Ledbury. "Perhaps my penknife will serve as a 'jemmy'."

"Oh no, Uncle Frank!" cried Githa. "Don't force it! Wait half a moment. I've got it here in my pocket. Look! Try this—the key that I found inside the panel at the Grange. I've kept it most carefully, in case I should ever find what it belonged to."

"I believe you've solved the problem!" murmured her uncle.

All watched eagerly as Captain Ledbury made trial of the little key. It fitted exactly. The rusty lock creaked as it turned, and the door flew open.

The space revealed was very narrow; there was only just room for a fat envelope that was wedged inside. Uncle Frank tore the letter open with impatient fingers. It contained a pile of bank-notes and a sheet of writing-paper. He studied the latter attentively for a moment or two. Then he turned to his niece.

"This concerns us very much, Githa. It's your grandfather's last will, duly witnessed, and apparently in good order. You and Cedric and myself benefit considerably. It's a lucky day for the three of us. I shall keep this packet, and place it at once in the hands of the solicitor who is named as executor."

"So Grandfather hadn't forgotten us, after all!"

215

"Not a bit of it. You'll come in for a very nice little fortune some day, young lady! This is better than winning clocks and medals!"

"I never won anything in my life before. The key has proved my mascot this afternoon."

"When one's luck turns, it often comes with a rush," chuckled Uncle Frank.

"Bob Gartley really told the truth for once in his life. He'll deserve the five pounds I promised him."

"He shall have it, though I'm afraid the scoundrel will only squander it at the 'Dragon'. Perhaps we can think of some way of helping the wife and children. I wish I could persuade him to enlist — the discipline of the army is just what he needs. I remember him very well when he was a lad, and he had the elements of good stuff in him then. Pity it's all run to waste. One never knows; after this illness a completely fresh start in life might make a new man of him. It's wonderful what serving their country has done for some of our fellows; in their case the war has been a blessing in disguise."

"Oh, it would be glorious if he'd go for a soldier!" agreed Githa. "Perhaps he will if you talk to him, and tell him about what's going on at the front."

"What a good thing it is to be extravagant sometimes!" exclaimed Katrine. "I'm so glad I bought that cupboard from Mrs. Stubbs. If she'd sold it to a dealer in London, the secret might never have been discovered."

"It's certainly the best bargain you could have made," agreed Captain Ledbury.

Monday morning saw the bringing out of thirty-six travelling trunks, and a corresponding number of damsels busy with the joyful employment of packing to go home. Rules had vanished to the four winds, and the girls flitted in and out of one another's dormitories, and talked to their hearts' content.

"Father and Mother will be home in ten days!" proclaimed Gwethyn jubilantly, sitting on Rose Randall's bed amidst a litter of underlinen.

"We're to go and stay with Aunt Norah until they come. Mother won't bring me the cockatoo — she says they're so noisy, and such a nuisance on board ship; but she's got another surprise for me, only it's not alive. Well, never mind! Perhaps Tony wouldn't have liked a cockatoo. He'd be frightfully jealous if I set up another pet, the poor darling!"

"We're going to Windermere for our holidays," said Rose, wrapping up boots and stowing them inside her box. "We're to stay at a house close to the lake, and I mean to learn to row."

"We shall be off to our country cottage in North Wales," announced Beatrix Bates.

"And Bert and I have an invitation to Scotland," exulted Dona Matthews.

"Girls!" cried Jill Barton, bursting suddenly into the room; "I've a piece of news to tell you. Oh, such news! You'd never guess!"

"Well, fire away!"

"Someone's engaged!"

"Engaged for what?"

"Engaged to be married, of course! What sillies you are! Can't you guess? Well, it's Miss Aubrey!"

"Never!"

"'To-who? To-who?' cried the owl!"

"To Mr. Freeman."

"Oh, I say! Hold me up!"

"Not really?"

"Mr. Freeman! Why, he's ever so old!"

"Not so very," interrupted Gwethyn, taking up the cudgels for her artist friend. "He's only rather grey, and, of course, Miss Aubrey isn't very young herself — though she's a dear. I'm immensely glad!"

"Why, so are we all! I hope she'll have the wedding during term-time, so that we can go and see her married. Wouldn't we cheer her, and throw rice and old slippers, just?"

"I don't fancy anything's fixed yet; the engagement is only just announced."

"It will be Mrs. Franklin's turn next, perhaps!"

"No, no! Surely Ermengarde wouldn't permit it!"

"Besides, what would become of the school?"

"Joking apart, we shall miss Miss Aubrey dreadfully."

Gwethyn, who rushed to impart the interesting news to her sister, found Katrine kneeling on the floor of their bedroom, packing canvases.

"It will be our gain," was the latter's comment, "because I suppose Miss Aubrey will come to live at Hartfield when she's married to Mr. Freeman. How lovely to have her so near! I shall often run in and have talks with her. It's something to look forward to. Gwethyn, I've decided to give my picture of the old spice cupboard as a good-bye present to Githa. I believe she'd like to have it."

Katrine looked with a sigh at her portraits of Granny Blundell and little Hugh Gartley. The ambitious hope which she had cherished in connection with them had fallen to the ground. She had shown the painting to Mr. Freeman, but he had not encouraged her to submit it to the hanging committee of any Art Gallery.

"Your work is still too crude and immature for exhibition, child," he had said, kindly but truthfully. "You need to go and study, and learn many things. Persevere, and keep pegging away, and you'll do well in course of time, I dare say. Art needs an apprenticeship as much as anything else. The old masters themselves began as pupils in the workshops of others."

Leaving her would-be masterpiece out of the question, Katrine had quite a nice little collection of sketches to take home with her. She had made distinct progress during her stay at Aireyholme, and she knew that her father and mother would be pleased with the result of her work. She looked forward also to showing one or two of her best landscapes to the head master of the Hartfield School of Art when she should begin her autumn course there.

"I'm sure I've really finished with ordinary school for good now," she soliloquized, taking the box of hairpins (which she had brought from home) out of the dressing-table drawer, and trying the effect of coiling up her long pigtail. "I've grown half an inch since I came to Aireyholme, so if I'm not grown up now, I ought to be."

"Well, you can't have a coming-out dance till the war's over, for there'd be no partners," laughed Gwethyn. "You must possess your soul in patience, and wait till Hereward and his friends come back."

"May that be soon!"

"It's been a ripping three months," continued Gwethyn. "I've enjoyed myself immensely here. I never dreamt I should, and yet it's really almost been the time of my life. I don't want to go back to Hartfield High School. I'm going to ask Mother to let me stay on at Aireyholme instead."

"Yes," agreed Katrine slowly. "It's been better than I expected—the lovely country, the village, the sketching, Miss Aubrey, the Grange, the discovery inside the old oak cupboard, all have combined together to make it—what shall I call it?"

"THE JOLLIEST TERM ON RECORD!" pronounced Gwethyn emphatically.

Milton Keynes UK
Ingram Content Group UK Ltd.
UKHW010704260923
429409UK00004B/344

9 791041 951826